Text Classics

JAMES ALDRIDGE is the author of more than thirty books for adults and young adults, including novels, short stories, plays and non-fiction, as well as television scripts and journalism. His work has been published internationally in forty languages.

He was born Harold Edward James Aldridge, in 1918 in White Hills, a suburb of Bendigo in Victoria, and he grew up in the town of Swan Hill on the Murray River. As a young man he worked in Melbourne as a copyboy, and then in the picture library, at the *Sun* newspaper.

In 1938 he moved to London where he worked on the newspaper the *Daily Sketch* for a time before becoming a war correspondent in the Middle East and Europe during World War II. His first novel, *Signed with Their Honour*, was based on that experience. It was published in 1942, in both Britain and the USA, and it quickly became a bestseller.

In the mid-1960s Aldridge began to write for a younger audience, setting his novels in the fictional town of St Helen, which was closely based on his childhood home of Swan Hill. *The True Story of Spit MacPhee* was published in 1986 and won the *Guardian* Children's Fiction Prize and the New South Wales Premier's Ethel Turner Prize. The novel was made into a television mini-series in 1988.

Aldridge won a Lenin Peace Prize in 1972 for 'his outstanding struggle for the preservation of peace'. That year he also won the Gold Medal for Journalism from the Organisation for International Journalists. And he has won the World Peace Council Gold Medal.

James Aldridge married Dina Mitchnik in 1942, and they had two sons. He now lives in London.

PHILLIP GWYNNE was born in Melbourne in 1958 and spent part of his childhood in Waikerie in the Riverland district of South Australia. He has written more than twenty books for young adults and children, including his debut novel *Deadly, Unna?* which won the 1998 Children's Book Council of Australia's book of the year and sold more than 250,000 copies. Phillip lives in Bali.

ALSO BY JAMES ALDRIDGE

Signed with Their Honour
The Sea Eagle
Of Many Men
The Diplomat
The Hunter
Heroes of the Empty View
Undersea Hunting for Inexperienced Englishmen
I Wish He Would Not Die
The Last Exile
A Captive in the Land
My Brother Tom
The Statesman's Game
The Flying 19
Cairo: Biography of a City
A Sporting Proposition (Ride a Wild Pony)
The Untouchable Juli
Mockery in Arms
The Marvellous Mongolian
One Last Glimpse
Goodbye Un-America
The Broken Saddle
The True Story of Lilli Stubeck
The True Story of Spit MacPhee
The True Story of Lola MacKellar
The Girl from the Sea
The Wings of Kitty St Clair

The True Story of Spit MacPhee
James Aldridge

Text Publishing Melbourne Australia

textclassics.com.au
textpublishing.com.au
The Text Publishing Company
Swann House
22 William Street
Melbourne Victoria 3000
Australia

First published by Penguin Books Australia, Melbourne, 1986
This edition published by The Text Publishing Company, 2015

Cover art & design by W. H. Chong
Page design by Text
Typeset by Midland Typesetting
Printed and bound in Australia by Griffin Press, an Accredited ISO AS/NZS 14001:2004 Environmental Management System Printer

National Library of Australia Cataloguing-in-Publication

Author: Aldridge, James, 1918– , author.

Title: The true story of Spit MacPhee / by James Aldridge; introduced by Phillip Gwynne.

ISBN: 9781922182074 (paperback)

ISBN: 9781925095074 (ebook)

Series: Text classics.

Subjects: Grandparent and child—Australia—Juvenile fiction.

Orphans—Australia—Juvenile fiction.

Adoption—Australia—Juvenile fiction.

Australia—Social life and customs—Juvenile fiction.

Other Authors/Contributors: Gwynne, Phillip, 1958– writer of added commentary.

Dewey Number: A823.3

CONTENTS

A Boy Living on a Marvellous River
by Phillip Gwynne

JAMES Aldridge was born in Bendigo in 1918, and he spent his childhood in the Victorian country town of Swan Hill. He wrote in 1977 that it was 'a Tom Sawyerian sort of boyhood on our lazy Murray River which had steamboats, floods, good fishing and hunting and the sort of river adventure that lasted as a faint and unbelievable nostalgia for the rest of my life'.

Aldridge left Australia for good when he was twenty, becoming a distinguished war correspondent. It was his experiences in World War II and then the Cold War that he drew on for his early fiction. In the 1960s, however, Aldridge returned to that 'faint and unbelievable nostalgia' of his childhood town for inspiration.

The town, the townsfolk and the 'lazy River Murray' proved to be a rich lode of material. Aldridge wrote a series of eight books set during the Depression in St Helen, his fictionalised version of Swan Hill, starting with *My Brother Tom* in 1966. *The True Story of Spit MacPhee*, published in 1986, was the sixth.

Though published as young-adult literature in Australia, Aldridge never thought of these books as that: 'All my stories have been written about children, not as children's stories,' he said in an interview in 1987. In fact, the St Helen books were published as adult fiction in many countries.

The Murray River, with its 'complex twists and turns in the currents and eddies' courses through *The True Story of Spit MacPhee*, in much the same way as the Mississippi River does through the *Adventures of Tom Sawyer* and *The Adventures of Huckleberry Finn*. (One wonders if Australia's mightiest river had a similarly poetic name—perhaps the Aboriginal Tongala—whether it would figure more predominately in our literature!)

Spit's character is defined by the river. With his overloud voice and habit of spitting, he is an awkward presence in town; nobody seems quite sure what to do with 'this wild, barefoot and growing boy (he was almost eleven)'. On the river, however, he comes into his own. He knows all the Murray's moods—from high and fast in winter to low and clear in summer. He fishes the river, he swims in the river, and he spends 'a lot of his time studying and trying to puzzle out the course of every curve and current'. In his author's note, Aldridge tells us that he 'borrowed a useful nickname from an old friend'. Spit is the perfectly aquatic name for the book's central character. Spit MacPhee, like Huck Finn, has river water in his blood.

If water is the vital force of this book, then that other elemental force, fire, is the destroyer. It is fire that kills Spit's father, that 'burned his lungs to shreds', and the same fire that disfigures his mother and leads to her premature death. And a fire in the renovated boiler, in which Spit lives with his grandfather, ultimately causes the death of his guardian, and renders Spit an orphan.

Despite these tragedies, this book is remarkably free of sentimentality—the death of Crispie, Spit's best friend, is dealt with in a only few lines:

> One day Crispie didn't come to school. He didn't come the next day, and on the fourth day Mrs Masters told the class that Crispie had been bitten by a tiger snake in one of the canals near his house and he had never recovered.

It is almost inconceivable that a modern YA novel—including my own—would let such an event go without at least a few paragraphs of hand-wringing and psychologising; Aldridge just gets on with the job.

Unlike many more recent works, this novel is not greatly interested in the interior lives of its characters; we actually spend little time inside the head of Spit MacPhee. He is essentially a man, or a boy, of action, not contemplation. Perhaps this is due to Aldridge's training as a war correspondent, or his life long identification as a Marxist, but it is the larger forces at play—the big universal themes that have engaged writers since Homer and Plato—that he is concerned with, namely: what is an individual's duty to society, and what is society's duty to its individuals? Once he has fire take away Spit's family, and a snake his best friend, once he has effectively cut Spit adrift, Aldridge is able to explore those questions: how will the citizens of St Helen treat one of its vulnerable members; what will become of this barefoot boy?

I, like Aldridge, grew up in a small country town. I, too, used that experience to write fiction, especially in my first books *Deadly, Unna?* and *Nukkin Ya*. Those books engage with many of the same contradictions of rural living as Aldridge's book, especially how country towns can be big hearted but also narrow-minded.

Whereas my books are predominately concerned with racism—the divide between the Indigenous and non-Indigenous populations—it is sectarianism that is Aldridge's preoccupation, in this case a tug-of-war, as both sides lay claim to Spit, a boy who has set foot in a church only 'a couple of times'. It is perhaps difficult for the modern teenage reader to understand the depth of the antipathy that once existed between Protestants and Catholics in a 'country as divided and passionate as Australia was by sect and prejudice'. However, there might be case for suggesting that this schism has been replaced in modern Australia by one between Christians and Muslims.

It's almost an axiom of current young-adult literature that the central character must undergo some sort of change—in fact, it's almost what defines the genre. And there are no shortage of people in this novel who want to change Spit MacPhee, from the hyper-Protestant Betty Arbuckle, who is determined in sending this 'African heathen' as she describes him to a Boy's Home in Bendigo, to the kindly Grace Tree, who wants to adopt him.

Spit resists change, however. Ironically, it's those who come into contact with him who are transformed in one way or another: Ben, Betty Arbuckle's beleaguered son, discovers a spark of rebellion, Sadie Tree overcomes her fear of the river and learns to swim, Grace Tree finds the gumption to stand up against her authoritarian husband, and the husband himself, Jack Tree, finds the compassion to accept this awkward boy.

It is up to the reader's imagination to keep the Murray flowing, to breathe further life into the characters, to decide what becomes of them. But my inkling is that Spit MacPhee will continue to be true to himself. Yes, he may very well wear shoes to school, but he will continue to be as Aldridge describes him:

> A natural boy in a natural landscape; a boy living on a marvellous river; a boy with unique talents; an Australian boy who asked absolutely nothing of anyone because he expected others to ask nothing of him.

The True Story of Spit MacPhee

Author's Note

Without giving too much away I should admit from the outset that I have stretched the 1928 Act which I mention here to its very limit, though not beyond its real terms. I have also borrowed a useful nickname from an old friend, who would forgive me if he were still alive. In any case it's not about him or his family, it's all fiction, but he would probably have enjoyed the use I have made of the name we so affectionately used on him.

1

Betty Arbuckle, a particularly good woman of St Helen, a natural beauty and a devoted evangelist, was trying once again to do something about Spit MacPhee. Betty was worried that, with no real parental care, this wild, barefoot and growing boy (he was almost eleven), needed more help now than he could get from a grandfather who was already half mad and becoming increasingly so. When old Fyfe MacPhee had first come to St Helen, in the State of Victoria, most people had thought him a bit odd, but in the last few years he was generally considered to be as mad as a hatter.

Spit himself would sometimes have to fight boys or girls or even adults when he heard them give that little laugh and tap their heads when old Fyfe walked by. Though not always. It depended on how Spit himself felt about his grandfather, or how angry they were with each other, because sometimes (though rarely) Spit didn't care what they or anyone else said about him. Yet at other times, with the same boy or man who laughed, Spit's fists would suddenly flash out, or his bare feet would kick hard at a man's shins with surprising force if he thought that there was a case to answer.

What worried the lovely Betty Arbuckle was the obvious fact that the old man's madness was becoming permanent rather than spasmodic, so that Spit himself was more often left to his own devices, living as they did in a world of their own down by the river. To Betty Arbuckle Spit was like a stray dog that either had to be put down or taken off gently to some home that could care for him properly. She had always been worried about the boy from the day of his arrival in the town, but now that he was already ten, almost eleven, he needed a safer haven than his half-mad grandfather could give him.

That was why Betty felt very strongly about it although she knew it was by no means the general opinion of the rest of the town. Whenever she had attempted to visit old Fyfe in his extraordinary little house, his quite crazy house by the river, she had been shouted at by both Spit and old Fyfe. She had been insulted in Scottish, even in Gaelic, and told to mind her own bloody business. She had been threatened with violence, and Spit himself had once emerged from the house and thrown a bucket of river water over her, drenching her from head to toe. A few hours later, still determined to do her best for the boy but refusing to be angry with him, she had returned with Sergeant Joe Collins, the policeman, insisting that he do something about the old man and his violent behaviour. 'If only for the sake of the boy,' she had said to Sergeant Collins.

Spit and his grandfather had seen Sergeant Collins coming. In fact Sergeant Collins had deliberately announced his noisy arrival in plenty of time for them to shut the front door on him. But he had called to them through the door that they ought to come out and apologise to Mrs Betty Arbuckle, or he would have to do something about it.

'Do what? Ye old fool,' Fyfe MacPhee shouted through the door. 'Get out of my garden, Collins, or ye'll get the same. And get ye away with that silly blasted woman. Get ye away with her ...' It was a cry of bitter pain from old Fyfe.

Sergeant Collins wanted nothing to do with Betty Arbuckle, or with Fyfe or Spit, but he shouted through the door, 'Mind your language, Fyfe, or I'll put you in charge.'

'What charge?' Fyfe shouted back, his fists hammering on the other side. 'Get out of here, ye old fool.'

A few more heated Scottish insults began to escalate the situation, and Sergeant Collins urged Mrs Betty Arbuckle out through the gate, ignoring her protests. Kicking disgustedly at a lump of hard mud, Sergeant Collins told Betty, 'There's nothing I can do, Mrs Arbuckle. They haven't broken any law, and though old Fyfe is as mad as a hatter, I can't do anything about it.'

'But that boy is growing up like an African heathen.'

'That's not my business. If you want to do something about that you'll have to go to the Shire Council or the magistrate or someone. Not me. And anyway you had no right to come down here telling the old man you want to inspect the house and take the boy away.'

'I didn't say that.'

'No, but that's what you want. And that's none of my business.'

'It's not right ...'

Betty Arbuckle's loveliness was always enhanced

by her religious passion, but in her own kind of abnegation of it she did her best to disperse her loveliness by a blunt cut to her hair and by wearing dull and dowdy clothes and buckled shoes with flat heels. But even this could not spoil her beauty. In fact the more she tried to disfigure it the more she seemed to enhance it. Her house, her husband (he was the Water Board inspector for the town) and her two children were also encouraged to be barren, and the sight of Fyfe MacPhee's wildly painted little house on the river bank and his habit of walking around the town shouting at people in the middle of the night had long ago convinced her that Fyfe MacPhee, sane or insane, was something of a devil in the flesh.

It was true that old Fyfe could look the part, and what hinted at some sort of hell in his background was that nobody in the town knew anything about him, even though he had now lived in it for more than ten years. His secrecy, his shouting hostility to any kind of questioning, his sudden fits of madness, and finally the arrival five years ago of Spit as a five-year-old boy, were all facts looking for trouble. And as Betty Arbuckle walked up the slope, across the railway line and away from the little house, she was still arguing with Sergeant Collins that she must do something about the boy. She must somehow get him away from that dangerous old man and find him a place in her evangelical sect's Boys Home in Bendigo.

'For his own sake,' Betty said unhappily.

2

Fyfe MacPhee had arrived in St Helen not long after the First World War, and even then he had looked like an old man because he was small and grey and grizzled, with hard, wild eyes, a harsh voice that shouted everything in a bri-braw Scottish accent, and a battered old hat pulled tight on his head. Nobody had even seen him without that tight little hat which sat there as if it were part of his scalp.

He had arrived in O. Gilpin's Rolls Royce, which was not a limousine but a van that furnished supplies to the O. Gilpin stores throughout the mallee towns: a dusty but familiar visitor. After a few weeks, when the town's curiosity had been aroused by old Fyfe's behaviour, all that anybody could discover was that he had come from Manangatang. He had paid O. Gilpin's driver five shillings for the lift and had walked the last mile into town because the driver didn't want the manager of the local store to know that he had given anyone a lift. A few people saw him arrive – walking along the main road carrying a small suitcase and a wooden box which, in the light of what followed, contained his tools as a clock and watch repairer and an expert tool setter.

Fyfe lived at first in a small room behind Charlie Kruger's garage where he began his work as a watch and clock repairer and tool setter by going from house to house asking the women, who were usually the only ones at home, if they had clocks or watches needing repair, or if their husbands' razors needed resetting, or their chisels, planes or anything else with a double-edge needed re-shaping. But these were a reluctant necessity to his clock and watch repairing.

If one of the ladies said, 'Will you sharpen my scissors for me?' Fyfe would shake his head and shout, 'I am not a scissors sharpener. If they need to be set I'll do it and sharpen them for ye, but I'm no scissors sharpener.' He would not sharpen any plane or chisel or any other tool unless it was double-edged and needed to be re-set, and if someone persisted he would shout angrily at them and leave. But as he began to do a fair business at back doors he was soon to be recognised not only as the kind of tool setter that even carpenters would take their tools to, but the best watch and clock repairer in town and the cheapest as well.

He was considered no more than a bit odd because he never spoke without shouting, as if he had no other way of talking, even though he talked sense. But one day he had walked around the streets shouting nonsense for no reason. Afterwards he had locked himself in his room and emerged two days later in his normal, grizzled form. It was obvious then that there was something awfully wrong with him, but because it had not happened again for some time, some people forgot it and simply thought of him as being a little crazy. Thereafter, he was tolerated as a bit of a joke, and eventually he had made casual friends whom he could talk to: Tom Smythe the blacksmith, the two Benson brothers who looked after the telegraph poles, and Tom Yard who was a carter with a fine team of horses. But he shouted at them all as he did with everybody else. What he said to them was considered friendly enough, but with them too his shouting could seem quarrelsome and aggressive.

What became his craziest venture was his shift to the river bank. Fyfe had discovered on one of the shady banks of the little Murray river an old square boiler that had been there for years. After some enquiries he found out that it was owned by Tom Smythe the blacksmith, and that the river bank where it lay was under the jurisdiction of the State Rivers and Water Supply Commission. Fyfe bought the boiler from Tom Smythe, and paid two pounds a year for the use of a patch of river bank big enough for the boiler and a small garden. Then, after cutting a couple of holes in one side of it with Tom Smythe's help, he had turned the old boiler into a curious little house. The boys who swam in the river further upstream believed that it had once been the boiler of an old river boat, the *Mundoo*, which had sunk thirty or forty years ago in a bend of the river. But it was too big for that. It was really the remnant of an old plan to build a big pumping system for a canal to be drawn from the little river, a plan that had been abandoned even before the big pumps had arrived.

Fyfe MacPhee had worked hard on the interior of the boiler, and eventually he had built a little extension to the side of it which had become his workshop. And though the extension was a visible part of Fyfe's house, nobody had ever seen inside the boiler or the extension. Outside, he painted the boiler bright red and green, with a blue wavy line all around the sides.

He completed the house with a picket fence and a sign on the front gate which said IN and OUT, which Fyfe adjusted every time he came and went. He planted a flower garden on the river side (the front), and a vegetable garden at the back; and under the big gum tree he kept chickens for eggs. The boiler itself was tucked into the shade of a big peppercorn tree and another tall, dry gum, and here old Fyfe settled down to live a strange and secret sort of life which meant keeping himself to himself.

He was, by now, nothing more than a town character who had unlucky moments of madness but was always harmless, although difficult to get on with because of his inability to talk in anything but an aggressive shout. Moreover he never seemed to listen, although somehow he did hear everything that was said to him. But there was one other aspect to his madness that encouraged the laughs at his expense. On occasions he would attack the outside of his boiler with a fourteen-pound hammer, hitting it all over its sides and top and bottom, knocking all its internal decoration to the floor, and shouting with each blow, 'Ye never had any steam in ye, no pipes, but I'll show ye ... I'll show ye ...' Smash would go the hammer, and after five minutes, when his fury was spent, Fyfe would become a broken old man, sitting on the step of the boiler holding his head, helpless now instead of the grizzly and bad-tempered and shouting old Scot the town was used to.

All this was before the appearance of Spit, who had arrived one day in early summer. The old man had disappeared for two weeks to return with a five-year-old boy whom the town discovered (by guesswork and a few captured hints) was his grandson, Angus MacPhee. Where the boy had come from, and what he was doing in St Helen with his grandfather, nobody knew. Most people thought the boy would stay a few days or weeks and then return to his mother, wherever she was. But he stayed on, and while he was there old Fyfe began to build another extension to his boiler. This time it was a proper little cabin, which he built solidly with timber and old windows and a serious door. He built it day and night, so that the people above the railway line would sometimes hear his hammer going at two o'clock in the morning. They knew better than to ask Fyfe why he was in such a hurry, but when he had finished it what the curious among the town's people saw was a tiny two-room house with a corrugated iron roof barely eight feet above the ground, but all neat and solid. As a final touch Fyfe painted it red and green, like the boiler, and painted the same wavy blue line all the way around it.

To many of the town's people it was worth a Sunday stroll down by the river to see it, providing they didn't stop to stare, or provoke Fyfe into showing his temper.

While this was happening, the town made its first contact with the five-year-old boy. He was taken by his grandfather wherever he went, and the boy copied his grandfather in all things. He shouted aggressively because the old man did, and he spat (or tried to) because old Fyfe, who smoked a short cubby pipe, spat noisily and frequently. Inevitably the boy was soon known to the town as Spit MacPhee, and it was a nickname he didn't mind, which was lucky because when he eventually went to school he didn't have to get into fights over it. But in the formation of his character, which was already like his grandfather's, he would spit drily and emptily and forcefully to state his position. By the end of that summer he was a brown, bare-legged, barefoot copy of the old man who never seemed to restrain him, even though he shouted at the boy the way he shouted at everybody else. By the end of that summer Spit was left free to wander where he liked in the town, or along the river, or even across it on Pental Island. He learned to swim in a few days, and thereafter the river became his natural home. He was afraid of nothing and nobody, and was soon so well-equipped to look after himself that it persuaded some of the worried women of St Helen, notably Betty Arbuckle, that in fact he was a little too good at looking after himself. Like eating people it was wrong for a six-year-old to be so recklessly free, and it was about this time that Betty Arbuckle first decided she would have to do something about the future of this boy who needed a proper home with proper care, which meant the Boys Home in Bendigo.

But then, one Monday morning, when Spit had been with old Fyfe for three months, the old man switched the sign on his gate to OUT, and taking Spit by the hand he caught the morning train to Bendigo – a large town one hundred miles away. Fyfe returned next day with Spit and a tall red-headed woman. It wasn't known at first sight who she was. All three were the last off the train because it was obvious that the lady did not want to be seen. But she was noticed anyway. Though it was the 1930s and the fashion then was short skirts, the lady wore a skirt to her ankles. Even more peculiar, she wore a brown veil that covered her face down to her neck so that only a few strands of her bright red hair were visible. She held Spit's hand in her own gloved hand, and Fyfe carried her suitcase as they walked straight to Tom Smythe's gig. It had been waiting for them, obviously pre-arranged by old Fyfe. The gig had a little oval step for mounting to the padded seat, but the veiled lady couldn't make it without Fyfe's help. Once up on the seat, still holding Spit's hand, Tom Smythe drove them to the little house by the river, and it was obvious then that she was Spit's mother and that Fyfe had built the little cabin expressly for her.

But once she was in it nobody thereafter caught more than a passing glimpse of her sitting in the back garden. She would sometimes sit there on a deck chair, holding a faded green parasol low over her head. Sometimes she was shelling peas or peeling potatoes or sewing, but more often than not she simply sat there as if that was all she could manage, never speaking to anyone, even when some of the ladies shouted a greeting to her. Sometimes Spit was seen spread across her knees, face down, kicking his legs, but nobody ever saw her face.

Eventually, a real explanation seeped through a report, in a Bendigo paper, that Mrs Mary MacPhee had been badly burned when her house in White Hills, near Bendigo, had caught fire. Mrs Joyce Andrews, coming from Bendigo to visit her sister in St Helen, had seen the case reported in the Bendigo *Advertiser*. The real tragedy was that Murdoch MacPhee, old Fyfe's son and Mary's husband, had managed to rescue the boy, but in returning for his wife and rescuing her from the back of the house, he had burned his lungs to shreds and was already dead on his way to hospital. Mary MacPhee had been badly burned on the face, legs and back, and she too had suffered some sort of lung injury from the heat and smoke. Only the boy had escaped untouched.

The town of St Helen was a normal town, and the sympathy for the MacPhees was natural and widespread. But unfortunately old Fyfe's shouted hostility to all questions or offers of help made any expression of sympathy difficult. It was particularly difficult for Betty Arbuckle, because now she had to think of the mother as well as the son. She too needed help and Betty was sure that personal salvation was the only way to rescue her. Never daunted by the devil in the flesh, or by setbacks, she had tried to call on Mary MacPhee only to meet old Fyfe, who happened to be digging in the garden. He threatened her with the spade and chased her off, shouting after her, 'Ye spying minnie. Y're after seeing her face, aren't ye, but if ye come down here again I'll throw you in the river.'

Spit was too young then to hurry her on her way with a bucket of river water, and Betty Arbuckle had not called on Sergeant Collins in those early days because she knew that Collins, like most people in the town, was on the side of the MacPhees. In fact, after some time, Betty had to admit that with his daughter-in-law there, old Fyfe began to control his temper a little, despite his threats to anyone who offered help. His sudden outbursts of wild shouting at anybody in the street and his mad attacks on the boiler stopped entirely. When it was time to start school, it was Fyfe himself who took Spit to be registered, and though Spit wore a clean, un-ironed smock, and clean pants, he still had no shoes. But at least he was off the streets, and because the river was rising he was not so much in it now but along its bank watching the currents. What did not change were the noisy exchanges, because Spit and his grandfather went on shouting at each other as if that was the only way they could talk to each other, and the people above the railway line would hear them exchanging early morning arguments at the tops of their voices every morning before school.

It remained like that – a rather neutral situation, until one cold, wet, winter's day in July, Mary MacPhee died. Initially only Dr Stevens and the Reverend Mackenzie of the Presbyterian church knew about it. Then, most people heard about it when they watched her funeral, attended only by Fyfe and Spit. It saddened many people in the town, and Betty Arbuckle wept for the woman whom nobody had actually seen in her terrible disfigurement, although it worried Betty that the boy might have seen his mother's badly burned face. That in itself was a frightful condemnation of what the boy had to suffer in those horrible conditions.

After the funeral old Fyfe and Spit had locked themselves up for two days and nobody had heard them shouting at each other. But it was only a matter of time before Spit was back at school and roaming freely again. Once more they shouted at each other, and once more Fyfe appeared from time to time on the streets, denouncing nobody in particular but simply walking around in a state of fierce invective. Spit was seven when his mother died. Now he was ten ('almost eleven' he would say when he was asked his age), and it was the accumulation of those three years of the boy's motherless condition that had persuaded Betty Arbuckle to try once more (the sixth time in three years) to do something about the boy, and it had brought her back that day to the little red and green boiler house on the river bank.

Something had to be done. The boy was now so fearless, so bold, so outspoken, and so equal to anyone, adult or child, so dirty (she was sure), so neglected by the old man and so lacking in any moral and spiritual guidance (he had never been seen in the Presbyterian church, or at Sunday school) that somehow he had to be saved from what was clearly and obviously an unChristian future. It wasn't fair to the boy to leave him like that. The beautiful Betty Arbuckle, with close haircut and buckled shoes, was more determined than ever not to be defeated by the swearing and insults of a mad old man. Soaking wet from Spit's bucket of water, she went home singing her favourite hymn:

> Praise my soul the King of Heaven
> To His feet thy tribute bring.
> Ransomed, healed, restored, forgiven,
> Who like thee His praise should sing.
> Praise Him, praise Him,
> Praise Him, praise Him,
> Praise the Everlasting King.

Then her two favourite lines: 'Slow to chide and swift to bless. Praise Him, praise Him ...' And finally her private addition to it: 'Give me strength, his soul to save.' Because salvation to Betty was God's pity, and she was sure that sooner or later she was going to save Spit from that Godless little house.

3

But though Spit seemed to be a leaf caught in something of a mortal storm, almost every boy in town liked him and admired him; and in return Spit himself was friendly to anybody who would accept him for what he was and could tolerate his habit of shouting rather than talking, and his routine gesture of dry spitting with his tongue. Spit's personal toleration of all and sundry was more like an equaliser between friends rather than the kind of mateship that Australians loved so much.

Girls were inclined to keep well clear of Spit, avoiding him as a barefoot ruffian. In response, Spit ignored the lot of them (though later there would be one exception to this). When he did get into a fight with boys his own age it was usually over a point of honour rather than a contest for some sort of superiority. If he was beaten by a bigger boy he never admitted defeat and would only accept his punishment on the understanding that there would be a return bout another day, which sometimes he forgot. In this regard he never bore a grudge, although he had his likes and dislikes. Among his very few dislikes were the son and daughter of Betty Arbuckle and her husband, Frank, who read the water meters and checked the town's water supply. He was also responsible for keeping the water mains in good condition.

Like Betty, Frank Arbuckle had been saved in his youth because (like Betty) his parents had also been saved. But whereas Betty was sustained in her salvation, Frank was overwhelmed and beaten by it, exhausted and helpless in it. Betty got life and vigour from her faith, whereas Frank followed silently behind – easily frightened, worn out, and only able to do the best he could. Like his ten-year-old son Ben, Frank was an easy victim for Spit's retaliations whenever Betty Arbuckle attempted to get into old Fyfe's house. Spit's usual response was to choose a moment in the night, find some remote corner of the town, and lift one of the small water mains' inspection covers. Then he would jam a piece of wood into the ball-cock that was used as a valve when sometimes the mains had to be tapped. The flood that followed was not easy to stem but needed quick attention, and Frank Arbuckle always knew who had done it. To all Frank's complaints Sergeant Collins always gave the same reply: 'You catch him at it, Frank, and I'll see he gets punished.'

'The little devil is too cunning for that,' Frank Arbuckle said. 'But I'll get him someday, Joe.'

But Sergeant Collins knew that Frank Arbuckle was as much afraid of Spit as he was of his wife, and of old Fyfe, and of his own twelve-year-old daughter, Joannie. So he would do almost anything to avoid Spit under any circumstances.

Spit, for his part, didn't spare the Arbuckle children: Ben his own age, and Joannie who was older. He terrorised Ben simply by waiting from time to time until Ben happened to be fifty yards in front of him in the street. Then Spit would shout, 'Look out, Ben, I'm after you.' And setting out on his fast bare feet after the fleeing Ben he would roar his threats, never trying to catch him and never intending to harm him, but out simply to remove him from consideration.

But one day, instead of fleeing at full speed, Ben ran a little way in his heavy, black boots and then suddenly stopped and turned around to face Spit, who was amazed. Spit got ready for a fight, but instead of offering resistance, Ben was in tears.

'Why don't you leave me alone, Spit,' he said. 'It's not me, it's my mother. So leave me alone ...'

This so startled Spit who, recognising a *cri de coeur* despite himself, didn't know what to do except to shout in reply, 'Well I'm after her, Ben, so you'd better tell her to look out.'

'I know, Spit, but I can't help it.'

Ben's tear-stained face was already too much for Spit, and the best he could manage in retreat was, 'What does she think she's doing?'

Thereafter he left Ben Arbuckle alone. Joannie, though, was another problem. Spit could not threaten her with violence, and Joannie would stand up to him and accuse him of being dirty, smelly and mad like his grandfather. Spit's reply was usually a shouted insult about her mother being a crank, which didn't frighten Joannie so that Spit had to resort to one or two 'bloodies' or something worse. Joannie could stand almost anything except bad language, and as a rule she covered her ears and ran away. Joannie was even prettier than her mother, but she didn't have her mother's resolute innocence. She always wore a pinny, her hair was tied in two curious little horns above her ears, and like her mother she wore buckle shoes and thick stockings. But like her mother she couldn't dim her own prettiness, and like her mother she firmly believed that the Lord Jesus needed everyone to turn a shamed and obedient face to the world and acknowledge their sins in order to be saved.

'You were born wicked, Spit MacPhee,' she would cry out as she fled.

But apart from the Arbuckles and a few other people who tried to interfere, Spit made a point of never threatening anyone without cause. If the men, women, boys and girls of St Helen left him alone, he would leave them alone, and in those sort of live-and-let-live conditions he was given a fair amount of good-natured respect, even from adults. What helped him was his dour self-confidence, because he was always rather serious for a boy. When he stood at the back door to face Mrs Evans (or Mrs Jackson or Mrs Ellison) to say to her, 'Do you want to buy a fish, Mrs Evans?' he was making an offer that had to be accepted or rejected without any nonsense. If Mrs Evans asked him how much he wanted for the Murray cod he would give his price. But if she made a mistake and asked him, 'Is it fresh, Spit?' he would shout, 'What do you think it is, Mrs Evans? I just caught it.' If he chose to take offence he would take his fish and walk away.

In this particular case Mrs Evans mentioned it to

her husband and said, 'He really is a bit mad, Bert. Just like the old man.'

'I don't know, Dot,' Bert said. 'If you start doubting Spit's word you know what to expect – a blast from the furnace.'

'Well, I wish he wouldn't shout the way he does.'

'That's the old man in him,' Bert said. 'The kid's never known anything else. You can hear them shouting at each other any day of the week when you walk along the railway line. Day or night.'

Bert and Dot Evans were among the people in town who liked both Fyfe and Spit, despite the fact that Spit teased their dog, Patchy, which put Spit and Patchy into a curious relationship. Patchy would always bark fiercely and instantly whenever Spit came or went up the slope to and from the boiler house. It was enough for Patchy to hear Spit's raised voice, even in the distance, and a fit of barking would follow. But if Spit went through the Evans' front gate to offer a fish for sale Patchy was all over him with eager paws and licking tongue. Dot and Bert even took a quiet delight (being childless) in knowing when Spit came and went because of Patchy's bark, and they were among those in town who thought that Betty Arbuckle had no right to march down to the boiler house to make trouble for them.

'Betty's been after young Spit ever since his mother died,' Dot said.

'So what the devil does she think she's going to do with him, if she gets him?' Bert asked her.

'Send him off to that Boys Home in Bendigo she's always talking about,' Dot replied. 'The trouble is that old Fyfe is getting madder and madder every day, and some day he's going to go right off his head. The other day he tore up all the flowers in his garden and threw them into the river, and he and Spit were at each other for hours afterwards.'

'It's the kid who is looking after the old man these days,' Bert said. 'But I wonder, Dot, if they even know what they're doing. They don't seem to know what else they can do but live that half-mad life down there.'

That was where Bert and Dot left the problem, as most of the townspeople did whenever they gave a passing thought to the old man and the barefoot boy living in their red and green house on the river bank. That is, all except Betty Arbuckle.

4

The town knew almost everything visible about Spit and old Fyfe except what went on behind the front door of the little red and green boiler house. Spit now slept by himself in the boiler, and Fyfe had moved into the little cabin extension he had built for his daughter-in-law. To some people in town it was considered shameful that such a bright and active boy had to live in such a place, but others said it was nothing more than a sort of gypsy caravan made of riveted steel plates. Every boy in town envied Spit, but he had to defend his boiler against his grandfather's need to attack it from time to time with a fourteen-pound hammer. He would wrestle with old Fyfe, get a grip on his arm and simply hang on, wrapping his bare legs around his grandfather's spindly knees, shouting, 'No you don't, grandfather. Leave off ... Take it away.' It worked if Spit was there, but sometimes he would come home from school and find that his grandfather had been at work with his hammer, and everything inside the boiler was in shambles.

Spit's life was divided into various separate parts. Living on the river became for him the source of life itself. He fished in it and swam in it. He set crayfish nets in it, long lines and shrimp tins. And he spent a lot of his time studying and trying to puzzle out the course of every curve and current in the little Murray, the depth of every hole, and where there could be perch or bream; or most important the tasty Murray cod. Whenever he caught a cod, even at night, he would try to take it alive and kicking to houses along the railway line. As late as nine o'clock there could be a knock at any one of the back doors along the line and Spit would be offering his catch hanging on a tether. He knew all the Catholic families along the line so he would try to offer them a fish on Thursday night or Friday morning early.

What he had become a specialist in was the big crayfish that lived in the little Murray. He knew better than anybody else in town where to lay the crayfish drums made of old bicycle wheels and chicken wire. He used a sheep's head from the butcher's for bait, and when he had caught two or three he would take them to one of the two hotels in town and demand five shillings each for them and get it. That became his own money, and he saved it in a tin which he hid in a curious little locker in the underside of the boiler where his grandfather couldn't find it in one of his fits of unpredictable destruction.

Inside the house or the boiler he had his duties, some given him by his grandfather, others taken on unplanned simply because they were necessary. Old Fyfe was calmest and quietest when he was bent over his bench, magnifying glass pushed into his fire-rimmed eye, and the fine tools of his craft gripped delicately in his short, square, quivering fingers. Almost from the first day that he had brought Spit with him from Bendigo he had allowed the boy to peer through the eye-piece at watches and clocks, whole or in pieces, and eventually he had given Spit an old clock and a set of clockmaker's screwdrivers and a pair of fine pliers and let him do what he liked. Spit had little difficulty taking the old Westclox Big Ben apart, but in the more complicated business of putting it together again he and his grandfather had shouted at each other, and only by trial and error had Spit put it all back, aged eight, with deft fingers. He could now assemble simple escapements in pocket-watches, and often did so for his grandfather; but he was not allowed to touch wrist-watches or old time-pieces.

When someone from the town brought a watch to old Fyfe for repair Spit would often receive it and write out the little tag in his heavy large left-handed writing. He would take money, and sometimes give an approximate date for completion, and would often have to shout at his grandfather to get it done in time. On occasions the old man would abandon his bench for days on end, and that was usually when he wandered into the town, talking to himself, shouting at anybody who took his fancy, gesticulating and making incomprehensible demands on unlucky neighbours in such braw Scots that they couldn't understand him and sent him packing with a laugh or a joke. Though violent in speech, old Fyfe was never physically violent except when Jack Taylor and Peter Mayfair, both in their early teens, had tried to snatch off his hat. At first Fyfe had brushed them off like bothersome flies, but when he realised what they were after he had ripped a paling from Mrs Burns' picket fence and lashed out at both boys and chased them down the street shouting, 'Ye think I'm mad, ye naughty dogs, ye carnal little beasties. But I'll show ye.'

Next day Spit had confronted Jack Taylor, who was twice his size, and warned him to leave his grand-father alone. 'And don't touch his hat. You leave that alone, Jack.'

'Okay, Spit,' Jack said. 'We didn't mean your old man any harm.'

'Well you'd better watch out,' Spit warned. 'He'll make mincemeat of you if you go after his hat.'

'Okay, okay …' Jack said, taking it too as a warning from Spit himself.

In fact only Spit knew the agony and pain his grand-father suffered after one of these bouts of madness. The worst of them was not those he suffered in the street, but inside the house when he would suddenly crouch on the floor with his head between his knees, groaning and hitting the top of his head with his fists, while Spit looked on, helpless, aware that he must not say or do anything until the agony had passed. If it happened at the wrong time Spit would have to prepare the lunch or the dinner, or water the garden with buckets from the river, or light the oil lamps which he kept filled with kerosene, or put people off if they came for their watches or their re-set tools.

After one of these bouts Fyfe MacPhee would usually say in a drenched voice to Spit, 'How long did me noise last this time?'

'A couple of hours, grandfather,' Spit would reply. 'You got up twice, and then you were on the floor again. You couldn't get up.'

'You didn't leave me did ye?' the old man would shout anxiously.

'Not me,' Spit would reply at the top of his voice.

'Are you sure?'

'I tell you I was cleaning the wicks, and filling the lamps.'

'I saw ye …' the old man would roar.

'Well, that's what I was doing, wasn't I?'

'I know what you were doing.'

Thus they would return to their usual behaviour, to their endless giving and taking in response to each other.

What they had to share they shared without decision. Every Saturday morning at dawn Spit would light a fire under the copper near the big peppercorn tree and fill it with water from the river. Then Fyfe would throw in all the clothes that needed washing, the sheets and shirts and shorts and anything else handy. After twenty minutes boiling he would lift the washing out piece by piece with a wooden stick, wring it out, and hang it all on the line between the trees. Spit also had to light the kitchen fire every morning and prepare the porridge at night in a black iron pot. Fyfe had once kept half a dozen hens and a few pullets for the eggs, but he had cut off their heads in one of his fits and thrown the headless bodies, still wriggling, into the river. It was one of the few times when Spit was in tears. He had come home to find the devastation, and because he had known every hen and pullet by name, and was used to them eating out of his hand, he had considered them his pets. But he said nothing to his grandfather and the old man was surprised the next day when he went out to get the eggs and realised what had happened to the hens.

Sometimes old Fyfe would bake bread – hard, dry, bannocky bread, but Spit preferred white bread, and he would insist on bringing it home after school from the baker's, or he would catch one of the delivery vans on the other side of the railway line in the early morning.

But buying and selling were part of the second category of his life. This was Spit in town. He did most of the shopping for butter and jam and meat, and he would collect the four-gallon tins of kerosene for the lamps in a little cart he had made from a fruit box and a pair of old pram wheels. He would also use the cart to bring home horse manure from Mr Walker's stables for his grandfather's garden. But most of his carrying was done in an old leather hunting bag he had found under the boiler, and he carried it over one shoulder, so that it reached almost to his ankles. He wouldn't carry fish in it but he used it for anything else he sold in season: potatoes or tomatoes or beans from Fyfe's garden, and because they were usually perfect vegetables there were always women at their back doors who would buy them because Spit always chose households near the centre of the town which didn't have their own vegetable gardens.

He sometimes had problems with the vegetables when Mrs Andrews, for instance, always asked, 'What have you got today Spit?' and when he said, 'Peas,' she would say, 'Let me see them.' Normally this could have produced a vigorous response from Spit: what did she want to see them for? But Mrs Andrews had always said to him, 'And how is your grandfather, Spit?' which was enough to remove her from one of his sharp rejections.

Spit had his other friends in town. He would some-times turn the blower on the forge for Tom Smythe the blacksmith, and he would hitch a ride with Bob Taylor the baker in his horse-drawn cart, or a dink home on Jack Burrow's bike as he delivered the meat. But though he kept his stocky, barefoot distance with most people, he had no real enemies. Even Mrs Betty Arbuckle was not so much an enemy as a crank, and when his mate, Crispie Cornforth, told him that Betty Arbuckle was after him again, and was determined to get him to the Boys Home in Bendigo, Spit shrugged it off and said, 'She doesn't know what she's doing. My grandfather'll make mincemeat of her. And anyway how does she think she's going to get me off to an orphanage in Bendigo when I am not an orphan?'

'That's what she's after though,' Crispie said.

But to Spit Mrs Betty Arbuckle wasn't really a menace, she was simply a permanent troublemaker who made his grandfather angrier than usual. Once out of the way she was out of mind, except when he decided on the spur of the moment to pick on Joannie or Ben.

There were two more categories to Spit's life in St Helen which, when his real troubles began, were an established part of his special environment. One was his life at school, and the other was his friendship with Sadie Tree.

School to Spit was a winter period when the river was swollen and he couldn't fish effectively or lay his crayfish drums or swim across to Pental Island. He didn't mind school, he could even like it, and he could always sit still long enough to tolerate lessons because he had always been used to sitting still with his grandfather on the step by the river, or in the house, or on the seat in the vegetable garden or even at the work-bench. The only real trouble he gave Miss Masters, his teacher, was the boom of his voice and the size of his writing. Spit always writ everything large – big bold letters which too soon filled a line and a page. No discipline that Miss Masters put on him could reduce the size of his letters, and being left-handed he held his exercise book sideways to write towards him. Though Miss Masters never tried to make him write with his right hand, she had tried consistently to correct his letters by insisting that he keep the book straight.

'That way,' she told him, 'you can see what you're doing.'

'Yes Miss,' Spit said, 'but then I can't do what I'm seeing.'

'You're too stubborn,' Miss Masters would say in despair.

'Yes Miss ...' Spit would boom.

Miss Masters had long ago given up trying to soften his voice although sometimes it was unbearable, but she did her best with Spit. She always knew when old Fyfe was going through a quiet period because Spit's primitive homework was then reasonably disciplined. But during the bad patches Spit would ignore all home-work and take his punishment without resentment or concern. Next year Spit would pass into the first grade of the secondary school, and Miss Masters, a grey-haired professional who always kept two pencils stuck into her thick grey hair like antennae, was concerned for him because he was the only boy in her class who still did not wear shoes or socks; and that would not do at the higher school. But she knew there was little that she could do about it because she couldn't talk to old Fyfe. Nobody could. She could only hope that they would solve the problem between them in their own way.

'You're always a problem, Spit,' she would sigh, but not without affection.

'Yes Miss,' Spit would boom back.

Out of the classroom and out of school Spit was a come-and-go friend to most of the other boys, but when he played cricket or football with them he gave the game everything he had. This was often effective, though not always so, particularly at cricket when he wanted to hit every ball for six. If he connected it worked. If he missed the ball everybody nearby ducked in case the bat left his hand in its wild swing. If he was bowled out he always spat dispassionately at the wicket and handed the bat over to the next man.

His closest friend, Crispie Cornforth, was a country boy who rode to school on a bike from a poor and salty farm five miles up the little Murray. Spit would get a dink home on Crispie's bike but they would always part at the railway line, and if he met Crispie out of school on a Saturday it was usually on Pental Island, not at the farm. Their friendship depended on no surroundings, and they knew it.

But Crispie was the only person in town who had ever questioned, indeed dared question Spit about his grandfather.

'What does he do it for, Spit?' Crispie asked him one summer's day when they were lying on the hard cracked mud of the big river, out of sight and sound of town and people, fishing and making the best of a hot day on the big river. 'I mean why does he go around shouting at everybody?'

'He's got something wrong with his head,' Spit replied.

'Everybody in town thinks he's crazy.'

'That's what they think,' Spit said. 'They don't know anything about it.'

'My old man says he ought to be locked up.'

'Well ...' And, with his usual habit of defending his grandfather, Spit turned his head and spat at a passing bee. 'If they lock him up I'll go and burn the place down. They don't know anything about it, Crisp, that's all I'm saying.'

'Well, I always say, "Hello Mr MacPhee," and you know what he says back to me?'

'No,' Spit said. 'But I'll bet he lets you have it.'

'He always says, "You've got big ears, Willy Wastle."'

'He likes you,' Spit said.

'Why does he call me Willy Wastle?'

'That'll be his name for you, Crisp. He does that all the time. Sometimes he calls me Tam Glen or Davie Bluster,' Spit said, and they both laughed at the old man's wild sport with their proper names.

They were good friends – planned to be for life, but one day Crispie didn't come to school. He didn't come the next day, and on the fourth day Miss Masters told the class that Crispie had been bitten by a tiger snake in one of the canals near his house, and he had never recovered. He was being buried that day, and Spit decided on the spot that he would never forget Crispie and would never have another friend as long as he lived.

It was early summer. Spit was still 'not quite eleven', and now that his real trouble was about to begin he had no Crispie to support him. In the end it would be Sadie Tree who would become the other part of him – like Crisp, only being a girl Sadie was different.

5

Sadie Tree lived in a house downstream, where the little Murray and the big Murray joined. Her father, Jack, owned a Dodge tourer and he was the Pastoral and Livestock Inspector for the district: a strict, soldierly man who, as an Anzac at Gallipoli, had discovered something good in the best moments of soldiering. In the attack on Suvla Bay he had taken charge of a machine-gun position when all the officers and sergeants had been killed, and he had done it well enough and bravely enough for a General to raise him from Private to Officer in the field. Since then he had kept his faith in soldiering and in old soldiers as the best thing in his life. He was the Secretary of the St Helen's branch of the Returned

Soldiers League, and his first loyalty in the town (apart from his family) was to any man who had been a soldier. Old Anzacs always knew that he would help them if he could, they could count on him, but this belief in the comradeship and pride of arms made something of a disciplinarian of him at home, although for his luck he had married a silent and obedient and gentle wife, Grace, and now had a silent and obedient and gentle daughter, Sadie, both of whom accepted his discipline, and respected and loved him nonetheless. In the end, Spit's predicament would make a change in this mix of modesty and discipline, but that was to be the end, not the beginning.

Sadie was a quiet girl and a clever girl who watched everything, saw everything, and said so little that she was hardly noticed even by girls her own age. Nobody resented her and nobody bothered her, and those who did notice her said that she got her silence from her father, the strong silent Jack. But if Sadie had inherited his silence (it was really her mother's) she did not have his strength, because Jack was used to having his own way so that Sadie and her mother always gave into him, as if it was the normal and the right thing to do. There was never any conflict in the Tree family.

Spit liked Mrs Tree because she was always silently there. She was often alone with Sadie when her husband was away on one of his inspections, and she would sometimes walk by herself, or with Sadie, along the river bank and stop to admire old Fyfe's garden. But neither she nor Sadie would ever say anything at all to old Fyfe. They left him alone if they passed by when he was in the garden. When Spit, in turn, offered Mrs Tree a fresh cod at her back door on a Friday (they were Catholics) and wriggled it fiercely under her nose, she would smile, almost laugh, and wait without saying anything for Spit to name his price. She would always accept it, pay it, and take the fish without saying a word except to say, 'Thanks Spit'. If Sadie was around when this was happening Spit hardly noticed her, although he was often faintly aware that she was always inspecting him as she did everybody else. But she would say, 'Goodbye Spit,' as he left, and that always startled him because he would shift a little on his bare feet and shout back, 'G'day, Sade,' and then forget her a few moments later.

It was the river that eventually made them friends. Spit's passion for watching the currents and sending small, flat, pointed 'boats' along the river carrying messages to unknown destinations, took him often along the bank downstream to pass by the Trees' house, which was not right on the river but a little way back from it nearer the railway line. Spit would write his left-handed messages on old newspaper saying, 'Help. I'm shipwrecked. 20 *longtude, 62 latude*. Come quick.' His grandfather had once given him a hard and shortened version of *Kidnapped*. Tying the message around the mast of his little flat boat he would swim out to the middle of the river, launch it, and then walk along the bank to follow it through the swirls and eddies until it either lost its message, got stuck on the opposite bank where it was too far away to swim to, or finally disappear for ever into the faster mainstream of the big river.

He loved to guess or calculate the complex twists and turns in the currents and eddies, or puzzle over the reasons for their endless variety, and he was absorbed one day in one of his little boats when a voice behind him said, 'They always end up under that big tree, near the bridge.'

Spit, surprised by the sudden and very quiet arrival of someone behind him, swung around and found Sadie Tree standing with her hands behind her back watching him.

'How do you know?' Spit said.

'Sometimes I follow them when they're in the big river.'

'Tell us another one,' he said disbelievingly. He knew that once they were in the big river they either got swamped by the fast current or were lost to view. 'You can't see them in the middle.'

'Yes, you can,' Sadie said. 'They always come in on the other side near our place. Then they go around and around where the posts are, then they cross to the other side again and come back near the bridge.'

'You can't see them across the other side,' Spit insisted.

'Yes you can, with my father's field glasses.'

'What do you mean?'

'You can see for miles through them.'

'Tell us another one,' Spit said.

'Honest, Spit. Wait here and I'll show you.'

When she came back with the field glasses – a worn but good pair of military 8 x 30s – she showed Spit how to focus them, and then handed them over.

'You're right,' Spit said generously. 'You can see everything.'

Sadie blushed and put out her hand for the field glasses. But Spit wasn't going to part with them so quickly. They were hanging around his neck and he meant them to stay there for a while.

'If we run for it we'll find the one I just put in,' he said and set off along the river bank without waiting to see if Sadie was following.

She followed, and in thus proving the accuracy of

46

her observations, she and Spit established their mutual fascination for the weird behaviour of the river. But it was a private discovery and it became at first a secret friendship. Sadie knew that her father would object because he thought Spit wild, and in need of discipline. So rather than create a situation which would end in a downright denunciation of it, Sadie kept it to herself. That is, she told only her mother.

Mrs Tree thought about it for a moment and then said, 'Don't tell your father. He'll only tell you to keep away from Spit.'

Implied in this response was Mrs Tree's permission for Sadie to talk to Spit if she wanted to, because Mrs Tree liked him and trusted him. And, in allowing it, there was also a silent contract between them which left Jack out of it, even though he liked to rule the house even in his absence. But it was not a serious conspiracy. Grace Tree respected and admired her husband, and Sadie loved her father, but because neither one had any particular friend they depended on each other to keep for themselves some of the fragments of their own lives – the unimportant fragments which mother and daughter considered harmless and inoffensive to Jack. After all, Spit was only a small boy, and Grace Tree had always felt, like Betty Arbuckle, that some day Spit was going to need help, although she wasn't quite sure what sort of help it would be. Certainly not Betty Arbuckle's Boys Home, she knew that much.

It seemed natural thereafter for Spit to devise a system of sending messages downstream to Sadie, rather than addressing them to unknown and unlikely persons. At first it was a trial run of one little flat pine boat which they both followed, and the message on this one was written by Sadie and read, '*I am sick. Send me a doctor,*' which Spit had instantly rejected.

'If he's sick, all he has to do is walk up to the railway line and ask somebody in one of the houses to get Doctor Stevens. So what's the use of that?'

'What's the use of saying you're shipwrecked?' Sadie said. 'It's the same thing.'

'No it isn't. Nobody's around when you're shipwrecked, so you can't ask somebody up the railway line to help you.'

'You can't get shipwrecked in a river,' Sadie insisted.

'What do you mean? What about the old *Mundoo* where the boiler came from?'

'That was years ago. There aren't any river boats on the little Murray anymore, so nobody would believe you.'

Spit conceded the point because his private world

had finally been penetrated, and his imagination now had a companion.

They operated their message system successfully all summer, so that in the end Spit was writing genuine messages to Sadie. 'I am going swimming tonight.' Or 'I am up at the old Point. Home at six.' When Spit went swimming off the steps near the boiler (he never swam with the other boys higher up) Sadie would sit on the hard mud steps and watch him. She couldn't swim herself, and when he tried to persuade her she said, 'Not me, Spit. I'm afraid of the water.'

'But it's dangerous living by the river and not being able to swim. What if there's a flood?' he told her.

'My father doesn't want me to go in when he's away,' Sadie said. 'That's why I'm afraid, I think.'

'He won't know.'

'He'd find out.'

'What does your mother say?'

'I don't know, Spit. If you ask her she might let me.'

'Me? Why should I ask her?'

'She trusts you. Only don't tell anyone else.'

Spit as a plenipotentiary was blunt rather than diplomatic. 'It's no good if she can't swim, Mrs Tree,' he said, and this was his one-and-only argument.

In fact Mrs Tree agreed with him. 'But I'll have to

be there, Spit. At first anyway, and she's never to go in unless you're near her.'

'Okay, Mrs Tree,' Spit agreed.

With Mrs Tree sitting on the mud steps, and Sadie in a new bathing suit, he taught her to swim. His methods were not persuasive but impatient, as if it astounded him that she couldn't just walk straight in and do what he did.

'Just paddle your arms and legs,' he shouted at her.

Mrs Tree listened and watched and took the girl's punishment for her, but she said nothing. Sadie was twice in tears, shouting (for her) at Spit, 'I can't. I can't …' which Spit treated with anguish and contempt. 'Yes you can,' he said. 'You're not even trying, Sadie. Look.'

To demonstrate the ease of it, Spit was under and over the water and halfway across the river and back in a violent, skilful, splashing demonstration of how easy it was.

'I'll never get it,' Sadie said.

'Go on. You just have to do it.'

In the end she did it, so that in those first miraculous strokes of a dog-paddle Sadie accepted thereafter a lifelong debt to Spit. Her mother too was so pleased that she insisted on Spit (dripping wet) sitting in the kitchen and drinking a glass of raspberry vinegar. It was the first time that Spit had been invited to sit in anybody's kitchen, and though he was always bold in the grip of a new experience, he was about to leave quick. But then Mrs Tree offered him a second glass. Anything more than the essentials was manna to Spit. He would sometimes buy an icecream or an aniseed ball because he had a sweet tooth, or a snowball for a penny, but this was a different kind of indulgence so he said, 'Yes thanks,' and Mrs Tree gave him the second glass of the thick red cordial. Sadie had been watching him and smiling, still happy with her first few strokes in the water.

'Can we do it again tomorrow?' she asked him.

'All right,' Spit said. 'But you have to learn to put your head under. It's no use learning to swim unless you can put your head under.'

'All right, all right,' Sadie said. 'I'll give it a go.'

Mrs Tree watched them both, and in a moment's pause between Spit's long draughts of the red vinegar she said, 'How old are you, Spit?'

'Eleven,' he said, and then as if in this silent kitchen he had suddenly heard the violence of his own voice for the first time, he said it again a little quieter, and he retreated too. 'I'm eleven now, Mrs Tree,' he said, 'but I'll be twelve next birthday.'

'I thought so,' Mrs Tree said. 'You're the same

age as Sadie. She'll be eleven in January. When is your birthday?'

'Last week – the fourteenth,' he said.

It was, in its way, another tie, and instead of wanting to get out quick Spit looked around him at the kitchen and, seeing an old, marbled, mantle clock above the fireplace, he said, 'We can fix that if it stops.'

'I know,' Mrs Tree said. 'But it's still going strong. It belonged to my father.'

'It probably needs cleaning,' Spit said.

'No. I think it's all right,' Mrs Tree said.

'Well … if it stops,' Spit said threateningly at the clock.

'Don't worry,' Mrs Tree said. 'We'll have it around to your grandfather in a jiffy.'

Though Spit and his grandfather seemed only able to shout at each other, Spit was also used to long silences with old Fyfe, so it was easy for him to sit in this kitchen of silence with two people who said little or nothing at all. He had finished his raspberry vinegar and he was aware that Mrs Tree was looking at him the way nobody else in the town looked at him, although he didn't know what exactly it meant. Sadie seemed simply to be waiting for him to do something or to tell them something. When he finally decided it was necessary he said to her at the top of his voice,

'I'm going fishing tonight by the willows. Do you want to come?'

'In the dark?' she said.

'Of course. That's the best time, up by the willows.'

'What will your grandfather say?' Sadie asked him.

Spit looked surprised. 'Nothing,' he said. 'I'm always up there. Sometimes he comes with me.'

'Is he going with you tonight?' Sadie asked.

'No. He's …' Whatever Spit was about to say he changed his mind about it. 'Do you want to come?' he said to Sadie.

Sadie was readily frightened and yet she was also determined. 'Can I go?' she said to her mother. 'Just for a little while.'

'But it's so dark,' her mother said. 'You won't be able to see your way near the river.'

'That's nothing,' Spit said. 'I know the way blindfold.'

Mrs Tree looked worried, but she too had her own way of making a difficult decision. 'You'll have to hold her hand, Spit. I shan't let her go otherwise.'

'You mean just on the way up there?' Spit said.

'Yes. And when you're at the willows, Sadie has to sit right away from the river. No paddling or swimming. I want you to promise me that.'

'That's all right,' Spit said. 'It would frighten the fish anyway.'

Mrs Tree was still worried but she said to Sadie, 'Do you really want to go?'

Sadie pulled in her lips nervously and nodded.

Spit said he would come at seven o'clock, and he would give a special whistle, which he demonstrated piercingly. Then, saying in a business-like way, 'I have to go home now,' he was up and out in a few seconds, leaving Sadie and Mrs Tree feeling rather sorry in their quiet kitchen that they had suddenly lost a noise and a force and a small attack on their isolation, which left them feeling rather empty.

'It's such a pity,' Mrs Tree said to Sadie.

Sadie didn't ask what was the pity, but her silence and her slight frown asked the question anyway.

'He's a very nice boy, considering all the problems he and old Mr MacPhee have had to live with.'

'He doesn't seem to mind,' Sadie said.

'I don't think he really understands,' Grace Tree said but did not go any further. She shook her head a little and left it there.

At first nobody was aware of Spit and Sadie's friendship. It wasn't difficult to keep it modest enough to be unobtrusive, and it gave them a chance to enjoy themselves. Sadie was a good pupil, and it wasn't too long before she was swimming more than a few strokes and learning to dive and keep her head under water. Spit also taught her how to fish, how to bait with worm or mussels, and how to cast the line out. She knew where all his crayfish drums were, a secret that Spit normally kept to himself, because someone in town was sure to take a look at them and maybe steal the crayfish if they knew where they were. He couldn't get her across to Pental Island because that was going too far for Mrs Tree's comfort. But Mrs Tree no longer walked along the river bank at night waiting anxiously when Sadie went with Spit to the willows, or to inspect his crayfish drums. She had given Sadie an electric torch, but after trying it out one night when it was particularly dark, Sadie said to her mother, 'It's not much use, Mum, because when your eyes get used to the dark you can see a lot more than you can see with a torch. And Spit can see everything.'

What became a habit, too, was Spit's visits to the Trees' kitchen, although he would never accept their invitation to eat his six o'clock tea there. 'I have to eat with my grandfather,' he would say, and they didn't press him. But he knew, without being told, to keep away when Jack Tree was at home, although he was now curious about Mr Tree. Previously he had taken no more notice of Jack than he had of most of the adults in town who either greeted him, ignored him, or treated him and his grandfather as freaks. Occasionally Jack Tree – deciding to notice him – would say 'Goodday, Spit,' in his crisp, upright, disciplined way, and Spit would return the greeting equally at the top of his voice.

So, like everyone else in town, Spit kept his distance from the Tree household when he had to. But the day that he saw Mr Tree by the river looking carefully at the water's edge, Spit considered himself to be on equal ground. The river was his domain. He watched Mr Tree without greeting him, and when he was finally noticed Mr Tree said, 'Hello, Spit. It's still pretty low, isn't it? It isn't rising at all.'

'It hasn't started yet,' Spit said.

'It's been a long summer,' Jack Tree said.

To Spit the longer the summer lasted and the longer it took for the river to begin its autumn rise, the better. But for Jack Tree, and his district stock and pasture problems, it was a question of water in the Riverrain where the dairy herds were. Jack would always look back on these long dry summers as harbingers of drought, and if the weather didn't change soon there could be trouble.

'You haven't noticed any rise at all in the last week or so?' he said to Spit.

Spit always kept a willow sprig on the very edge

of the river at right-angles to see if it was rising or falling, and he could report to Mr Tree that the river had fallen another two inches in the last week. 'It's still going down,' he said.

'They're keeping the weir wide open too,' Mr Tree said thoughtfully. 'So we're going to be in trouble. How are the fish?' he asked Spit.

'All right,' Spit said. 'Do you want to buy a cod?'

'You shouldn't catch so many,' the soldier replied. 'You're depleting them.' And he was on his way up the slope to his house when Sadie came running along the river path from upstream calling, 'Spit, it's your grandfather. You'll have to come quick.' Then she saw her father and stopped where she stood.

Spit said, 'Goddamn,' and was off, running like a muscular, fleet-footed hare along the path, with Sadie and Mr Tree following him. They found old Fyfe lying twisted-up on the very edge of the river, his hands clamped tight over his ears, his face distorted as he groaned and swung his head from side to side, and his legs stiff and straight. He was shouting something that was too broken to understand.

'He's having a fit,' Mr Tree said, kneeling over him.

'No he isn't,' Spit shouted. 'It's not a fit. Don't touch him.'

'We'll have to get him inside,' Mr Tree said.

'That's no good,' Spit said. 'Just leave him alone. Don't touch him.' And Spit tried to push Jack Tree out of the way.

'He'll fall in the river if you don't move him,' Jack insisted as Spit kept pushing him off.

'No, he won't. Just leave him alone, and go away. Go away.' Sadie and Mr Tree stood for a moment, undecided, watching the old man's suffering. But then Sadie said, 'Come on, Dad,' and she pulled at his arm. 'Spit will do everything.'

'He needs some help.'

'No, he doesn't,' Sadie said, pulling at her father. 'You've got to leave them.'

Reluctantly, Mr Tree allowed himself to be led away by Sadie as Spit took one of the buckets of water, always waiting at the river bank for kitchen use, and threw it over his grandfather. Fyfe groaned a little and ground his teeth but then he subsided, and as Mr Tree followed the fleeing Sadie up the slope they heard Fyfe shouting, and Spit replying angrily, 'You're too near the river, Grandpa. You've got to get up.'

'Poor Mr MacPhee,' Sadie said miserably as they hurried around the big trees to their fenced-in house to get to the back door instead of the front.

'He's a tough old bird,' Mr Tree said. 'Although I've never seen him like that before.'

'Why is he like that?' Sadie asked her father. 'Is he really mad?'

'Not all the time,' her father said. 'But he's getting worse, and some day he's going to go clean off his head. No doubt about it.'

'What'll happen to Spit then?' Sadie asked. 'What'll he do?'

'Betty Arbuckle will probably get him,' Mr Tree said.

'But she'd send him away to the Boys Home in Bendigo, wouldn't she?'

'Probably.'

'That's not fair.'

Mr Tree was surprised to hear so much sudden conviction from his daughter. 'It doesn't have to be fair or unfair,' he told her severely. 'It's just the way it is. Spit needs some discipline, and that's the sort of place where he'd get it.'

Sadie didn't accept it, even though she knew she must accept it.

'You keep away from that old man,' Mr Tree told her. 'In case he gets dangerous.'

'Yes, Dad,' she said, and when they had joined Mrs Tree in the kitchen Sadie said nothing at all about

59

old Fyfe because if anything was to be said about it her father would do the saying.

That night, when Sadie had gone to bed, Jack Tree told his wife what had happened. 'The old man was lying there like a grizzly bear in agony,' he told her. 'His hat was off, but he had on a sort of felt skull cap which looked as if it was glued to his head.'

'Last week,' Grace Tree said, 'Mrs Evans told me he was seen walking around the town in the middle of the night, shouting at all the dogs and opening all the front gates, with Spit walking behind him closing the gates again.'

'You keep the back door locked,' Mr Tree told her.

'But he's harmless, Jack,' Mrs Tree said quietly. 'He could never hurt anybody.'

They were sitting in Mrs Tree's spotless, linoleum kitchen. While Mrs Tree labelled the glass jars of her preserved apricots, Mr Tree was saving electricity by working on his reports at the other end of the kitchen table – not only a soldierly man but a neat man with a neat moustache, organised papers, and a dry pipe in his mouth which he sucked but didn't smoke.

'You're not to take a chance,' he ordered his wife. 'The old boy could easily turn violent.'

Mrs Tree didn't argue, but she inspected her husband carefully for a moment before saying,

'We really ought to do something about that boy, Jack.'

'What do you mean – do something? Do what?'

'I don't know,' Mrs Tree said. 'But he and old Fyfe can't go on much longer the way they are. Spit is a nice boy, and someone should help him.'

'How?'

'I don't know how,' Mrs Tree said unhappily. 'But there must be some way.'

'Leave him to Betty Arbuckle. She'll do something. The best thing for him is probably that home in Bendigo.'

'That's not right Jack.'

'Well, right or wrong, there's nothing you can do about it, Grace, so leave him alone. He's a grubby little devil, and he's like the old man. He can look after himself.'

'He can't be grubby if he spends so much time in the river.'

'Keep him away, that's all I'm saying. Don't let him hang around.'

'He doesn't hang around.'

'Then what are we arguing about?'

Grace felt guilty now. She wanted to tell her husband more about Spit, but Jack had made his position too firm and clear to do it now. Nonetheless, when

61

he went off again on one of his inspection tours she allowed Sadie to go on swimming and fishing with Spit. The trouble was that other people had seen the children together, the Evanses, Mrs Andrews up the slope, the station master's wife, and Mr Moon the butcher. Sooner or later it would all leak out.

It was Sadie who told her more than anyone else could possibly know about Spit and his grandfather, because Sadie had been watching and listening and thinking about them, and she had reported everything she had seen and done to her mother. Sadie had not only seen inside the boiler, but she could now sit quietly in Mr MacPhee's workroom with Spit and watch them together. It had been quite simple. She had said to Spit after they had been swimming one day, 'Can I see inside your boiler house?'

Spit's first reluctant reply was, 'I dunno ...' But Sadie simply waited as if she knew he would change his mind, and he did so. 'All right,' he said. 'But no telling anybody.'

'No. I won't tell anybody.'

Spit took her through the front door of the house, through the workroom where old Fyfe was working on a clock, and into the extension which finally opened into the boiler itself.

What she saw amazed her, because there was

nothing else like it in the town of St Helen. The inside walls of the boiler were painted yellow, and though rust from the rivets had streaked the sides, the whole interior had its own painted designs – not the wavy line of the outside walls but a black fish, a lily-like flower with a green stem, something that looked like a firework bursting, and a red tomato. She had never seen anything like it. Spit's narrow, wooden bunk with an old quilt on it was at one end under a cut-out window, and at the other end she could see a table painted bright red, and on it a bundle of old books, mussel shells, lines, and the bits and pieces of clocks and watches. She could not take it all in at a glance, but afterwards she remembered a flower pot with a fern in it, an old acetylene bike lamp, and a painted kerosene tin which had been cut into curls and twists around the top. It was full of old wire and pieces of wood and horseshoes and dried crayfish claws.

'It's fantastic,' Sadie said. 'It's great, Spit. It's absolutely great.'

'Don't say anything about it,' he said. 'That's all.'

'No, I won't. I swear.'

It seemed quite simple thereafter for Sadie to sit in the extension, which was where Spit had his own bench and where she could watch him shape the little pine messenger boats, make sinkers for his fishing lines out of lead slugs, and (another of his secrets) fit spokes into a rusty bicycle wheel which he would eventually add to the rest of a half-built old bike which still needed a front wheel, handlebars, two pedals and a seat.

'But where did you get it from?' she asked him.

'I got this and that from the back of Sykes' bike shop, and some at the blacksmith's, and here and there and everywhere.'

Spit almost forgot her sometimes as she sat on a small three-legged stool; and when his grandfather shouted at him, 'Ye maun put the potatoes on, or ye won't be eating supper,' she moved with him into the small kitchen at the end of old Fyfe's workroom where she helped him peel the potatoes. Spit was a quick impatient peeler of potatoes, and he filled a cooking pot from a bucket of river water on the floor. He put it on the wood stove, which he poked fiercely, and then shouted at his grandfather, 'You didn't put any wood on the fire.'

'Well put it on now.'

'That's what I am doing.'

Sadie listened to them and whispered to Spit, 'Why are you always so angry with each other?'

Spit didn't lower his voice but said indignantly, 'We're not angry with each other.'

'But that's how it sounds, Spit. Everybody thinks ...'

'They don't know anything about it,' Spit said, and he was putting two mutton chops in a wire folder to grill them when he said, 'Do you want a chop?'

'No, thanks. I'll have to go home in a minute for tea.'

She left reluctantly, but thereafter she would come and go to the little house without any difficulty. Old Fyfe had looked quizzically at her once and said with a sort of grim laugh, 'How are ye dressed, Jean Armour, aye sae clean and neat.'

Sadie, in her own advice to herself, had always been frightened of old Fyfe, but in the little house with Spit she lost all her fear of him, and though she didn't understand what he said to her most of the time, she always smiled at him and one day said to him, 'Can I watch you mend the clocks?'

The old man's face, grey as it was and grizzled as it was, and so often pained, ground itself into a smile. He stared at her for a moment. 'Stand there,' he said.

'Give her the glass,' Spit said to his grandfather.

'You be quiet, ye cairn ...'

'I was only trying to help,' Spit shouted back.

Sadie listened and watched, unafraid, and the old man pointed to the clock he was working on and said, 'Ye don't need the glass. It's the clock of Mrs Andrews, and if ye look at the coggies there ye'll see all her powder, pink and dirty, and look at her grey hairs that she brushes into the clock. All in a bedroom, the clock stays, and it maun tick with its face down.' He showed Sadie the scratched glass of the clock. 'And all that grease on her face. She's winding it up wi' her fingers thick with that awfu' gruel.' Mrs Andrews' face-creamed finger marks were stained into the clock where she held it to wind it.

'I never thought ...' Sadie began in amazement.

But old Fyfe had lost interest in his demonstration, and Sadie stood still to watch his quivering hands working with the diminutive screwdrivers, holding them miraculously still long enough to undo the minute screws. The old man crouched over his bench, a tiny figure. It was neat and clean, and she could smell the fine oil he used on the clocks he was repairing. Sometimes it seemed to be a quiet, rumbling fury, and other times it was more like a Scottish bee buzzing. Noise, in fact, seemed to be his only relief, as if it were a desperate diversion from whatever was going on in his head.

Like that, Sadie learned to sit and watch not only old Fyfe's clock and watch repairing, but the way he re-set planes and razors on his oilstone and with the tiny grinder, using a strop to finish them with.

While she watched old Fyfe, Spit would sometimes behave like a housewife, sweeping the floor or cleaning the stove; or he would leave her when he watered the garden or chopped the wood for the stove, and she began to love the place. But she was surprised one day when, helping Spit with the spokes of the old bicycle wheel, she heard her mother calling her.

'Oh, my gosh,' she said, handing Spit the pliers with which she was holding the spokes in place for him. 'What time is it?'

'I dunno,' Spit said, 'but – maybe your father's come home.'

'Goodbye, Spit,' Sadie said as she rushed out. 'Goodbye, Mr MacPhee,' she shouted. And, calling over her shoulder, she said, 'Be back tomorrow.'

But in fact she would not be back on the morrow, because that night old Fyfe burned down the house, and Spit's days of security and safety were finally over.

6

Spit had awakened to hear his grandfather banging and opening and then banging and opening again and again the front door. At first Spit lay still and did nothing because it was not unusual for his grandfather to wander around in the middle of the night making a noise and shouting nonsense. Sooner or later it would stop and the old man would drop exhausted on his bed to sleep it off, groaning and twisting and covering his head but eventually subsiding. But this time it seemed different because Spit could see a reflection of a light through the boiler's window. Instead of simply shouting, his grandfather was also singing, which he sometimes did when he was working at his bench, but never in the middle of the night.

Spit got out of bed, and still wearing the old shirt he slept in and pulling on his trousers, he went through the house and found his grandfather holding the front door open and wrenching violently at it as if he wanted to tear it off its hinges.

'Grandpa,' Spit shouted at him. 'You've got to stop. You're making too much noise.'

But he knew his grandfather couldn't hear him. What puzzled Spit was the hurricane lamp which his grandfather had managed to light. It was on the path leading to the gate. Deciding quickly that it was the best thing to do, Spit picked it up but didn't blow it out. Old Fyfe was still singing, but sometimes he laughed the grim and curious and agonised laugh which was often a sort of punctuation to his shouting. When Spit tried to pull his arm he held the door tight and shouted, 'I'm awfu' cold … awfu' cold.'

'You can't be cold,' Spit told him.

'It's an auld auld killick,' Fyfe said in his agony. Then he left the door and walked down the path to the gate, which he also tried to pull off its hinges. It was too well made, and Fyfe suddenly crumpled to his knees and held his hands to his ears and began to moan.

'It maun kill me, cairgie … It's awfu' bad …'

'Come on, Grandpa. Come back inside,' Spit said anxiously, aware that though it looked like the old man's usual behaviour in such moments, this time there was something else that was different and disturbing. Spit held up the lamp and caught a glimpse of tears running down his grandfather's face. Then, in a quiet, almost normal but pained voice, his grandfather looked up at him and said, 'Go away, cairgie … run away, d'ye hear me. Run away from me. Go on … Go on, I tell ye.'

Spit had never before heard that sort of calm if desperate sense in his grandfather's voice, and he didn't know what to make of it. 'Go on w'ye,' Fyfe shouted as if he was trying desperately now to contain some terrible danger that could not be held off much longer. 'Run off, cairgie, and don't come back. Don't ye come back, do y'hear …'

Spit understood the words but he couldn't grasp the meaning or the reason. He shifted from one bare foot to the other, holding up the hurricane lamp so that he could see his grandfather's upturned face. What he saw was a subterranean terror in the old man's eyes, and it was the first time in his life that Spit felt frightened by his grandfather's behaviour.

'What's the matter, Grandpa?' he said. 'What's wrong?'

'Will ye go ...' the old man groaned.

Spit knew that he had to stay; above all he had to stay. 'I'm not going anywhere,' he said. 'You've got to get inside. It's no use shouting out here. You've got to go in.'

The old man's face made some final tortured gesture towards sanity, clawing at it, trying to convince the boy. Then it broke into madness as if everything he had been holding back had finally defeated him and had now overcome him. He no longer saw. He no longer recognised. He seemed no longer to have any link with anything except the awful torture in his own mind. And, seizing the lighted lamp from Spit, he walked slowly up the path and threw it through the open door of the house.

It was too unexpected for Spit to stop him doing it, and as the lamp glass smashed and the kerosene spilled and caught alight Spit ran straight into the flames. Without thinking about it he tried to damp them out with his bare feet. When he felt the burning pain of it he looked around for one of the buckets of water that were usually kept near the stove. One bucket was empty and the other one only half full, awaiting a fresh refill in the morning. He threw the half bucket of water over the flames which made no impression on them, so he rushed out and down to the river to fill one of the buckets on the banks. By the time he had struggled back to the house with it, the whole floor was alight and also the curtain that divided off his grandfather's bed. He threw the water over the floor but again it made no impression, and though his grandfather was standing in the doorway looking at the flames and shouting, Spit ignored him and ran back to the river once more for water. But this time he knew as he threw it on the flames that it was hopeless for him to go on alone.

'Grandpa, get out. Don't stand there,' he cried.

The old man didn't see or hear, and Spit pulled him out of the doorway. Then he set off down the river and up the slope to the house he knew best, Sadie Tree's. The back door was a wire screen door so there was no use hammering on it. Instead he shouted, 'Mr Tree. Mr Tree. Our house is on fire. Mr Tree ...'

It took a few minutes, but Jack Tree heard him and called out, 'Who is it?'

'It's Spit MacPhee. Our house is on fire. Will you come and help me?'

'Did you call the fire brigade?'

'No, I can't.'

'All right. I'll do it.' Mr Tree shouted from somewhere within. 'Go up to the Andrews on the other side, and Tim Evans. Get their help. I'll be down.'

Spit was off up the well-worn path to the railway line, and he repeated his cries at the back doors of the Andrews' house and the Evans'. Then he raced back to the house and found Jack Tree already there and the fire so fierce now that it was sending sparks high in the air and crackling fiercely. Mr Tree was running back and forth to the river carrying buckets of water which he threw over the flames, but now it was obviously out of control.

'Where is my grandfather?' Spit shouted.

'Down by the steps. Get some more buckets.'

'It's no use,' Spit cried. 'It's no use any more.'

'Do as you're told,' Mr Tree ordered. 'Get the buckets.'

They were joined by Mr Andrews and his son Jolly and then Mr and Mrs Evans and Joan Gillespie their neighbour. There were only enough buckets and kerosene tins with wire handles for six people, and though they all poured water onto the fire it was obvious that it couldn't be put out. By the time the volunteer fire brigade had reached the railway line, and were on the river bank with a hand pump, there was not enough left of the house to bother about. As the fire began to subside in the ashes, the only thing left standing was the charred boiler. By now, too, there was a little crowd of people from the houses along the railway line. They had all done their best, but it was Mrs Tree and Sadie who went looking for Spit and found him, dripping wet, fifty yards along the river bank holding his grandfather half in and half out of the water.

'Did he go under?' Mrs Tree said. 'Is he drowned?'

'No. He fell in,' Spit said. 'But I got him out.'

With Sadie's help from above, and Spit pushing from the water, Mrs Tree pulled old Fyfe up on the bank.

'He's sick,' Spit said. 'He fell in. He didn't know what he was doing.'

Old Fyfe was now lying so twisted and helpless that Mrs Tree said to Sadie, 'Go and get your father. Quick.'

As Sadie ran off, Spit said, 'He didn't know what he was doing. He just threw it in ...'

'Threw what in?' Mrs Tree said.

'The hurricane lamp. He just threw it in.'

'He needs a doctor now, Spit. He's unconscious. Are you sure he didn't go under?'

'No, he didn't. He'll be all right,' Spit insisted.

'But he looks bad, Spit. He needs help,' Grace told him.

'I tell you he'll be all right,' Spit insisted.

When Mr Tree arrived, black and wet, Mrs Tree simply pointed to old Fyfe and Mr Tree looked closely and nodded.

'We'll get him up to the house and I'll get Doctor Stevens,' he said. 'You stay here with him, Grace, and I'll get the others to help.' He dropped a hand on Spit then and said, 'Your house is gone, Spit. There's nothing left of it.'

'Oh no …' Mrs Tree said.

'It's all right,' Spit said, fighting back. 'My grand-father will build another one.'

'Maybe. Maybe,' Jack Tree said. 'But you wait here until I get back.'

Spit had to push away Jim Evans' dog, Patchy, who had escaped and was pawing and licking him as he stood guard over his grandfather. 'Get away, Patch,' he was saying as Jack Tree and Jim Evans and two others returned and lifted old Fyfe off the ground and set off up the slope with him.

But Spit was already ahead of them, trying to stop them. 'Where are you taking him?' he said, blocking their path.

'He needs a doctor,' Jack Tree told him. 'We'll take him up to our back verandah and get Doctor Stevens.'

'He can stay in the old boiler. It didn't burn down.'

'It's burned out, Spit. It was all that paint on it. And anyway it's half-full of water,' Mr Tree said. 'In fact you'd better come with us too. You can't stay down here.'

'Come on, Spit,' Mrs Tree said. 'We'll look after your grandfather.'

Spit, confused now, followed them up the slope, holding on to his grandfather's wet shirt. And Sadie, walking beside him, whispered, 'Maybe he was drowning and you saved him?'

'No, he wasn't. He just didn't know what he was doing.'

'How long was he in the water?'

'Only a little while. His head didn't even go under.'

'Did he jump in?' she asked softly. 'Is that what he did?'

Spit didn't deny it. 'But he didn't know what he was doing.'

Spit would never remember afterwards all the details of that night, but in its sequence he would remember the long wait in Mrs Tree's kitchen for Dr Stevens to come, and Mrs Tree and Sadie sitting silently beside him.

When Dr Stevens finally came and looked at old Fyfe, he told Spit that they would have to take his grandfather away to the hospital. This time Spit didn't protest because he knew that it was out of his hands now. What had changed his mind was the sight of his grandfather when they had laid him out on the floor of the Trees' verandah, and he had seen his grandfather under the electric light. Spit was still holding his grandfather's shirt in a tight grip, but he suddenly let it go when he saw his grandfather's face. It wasn't the grey, grizzled, fierce and combative Scot's face he had lived with for so much of his life; instead it was a white, shattered old man, helpless, almost lifeless, with the fire gone out of him so that his twitching mouth and staring eyes and his clawlike hands had invented a substitute who looked nothing like his grandfather. Spit knew that they had to take this one away, and when they had carried him out to Dr Stevens' car Spit didn't go with them, he waited at the door until he heard them drive away.

'You'll have to stay here the rest of the night,' Grace Tree told him. 'You can sleep on the old cane bed on the verandah.'

'I have to get back,' Spit said, opening the wire door to go.

She held him back. 'What for?' she said. 'There's nothing left, Spit. So wait until tomorrow.'

'I want to see if my bike's all right,' he said.

'Spit, you haven't got a bike.'

'He was building it himself,' Sadie said, 'from bits and pieces.'

'Well you can't do anything about it tonight,' Grace told him. 'There's nothing more you can do. So

77

wait here and I'll get some covers for you. And Sadie – you go off to bed now.'

Sadie glanced quickly at Spit but didn't say anything to him because he wasn't looking at her or listening, and as he sat down at the kitchen table Grace went out to get the covers for him.

When she came back Spit had his head in his arms on the table. She thought he was crying, but when she touched him on the shoulder she realised he was asleep. 'You'll have to sleep in this,' she said to him when he lifted his head. She gave him one of her husband's old shirts. 'Your clothes are still wet.'

'I'm all right,' Spit said, and when he lay down on the cane bed on the verandah, which she had padded with blankets for him, Grace didn't argue with him but let him be, and in a few moments he was asleep – so heavily asleep that Grace sat on the couch near him for a while looking at his face which, in sleep, had lost its self-sufficiency and its rather serious and confident air, and was now the face of an eleven-year-old boy who was finally vulnerable and exhausted.

'You're going to need all the care and attention you can get this time,' Grace said to the sleeping figure and, sighing as she left him, she added, 'But it shouldn't be from Betty Arbuckle.'

When Jack returned he found Grace asleep in a

chair near the kitchen stove, and when he told her the kettle was boiling dry she said, 'It's the second time. What happened? What about old Fyfe? Is he all right?'

Jack washed his hands and sat at the table and watched her making tea. 'When we got him to the hospital the old man sat up and began to fight and shout. He's completely round the bend this time. They had to hold him down.'

'What does Doctor Stevens say?'

'He doesn't think he's got much chance of coming through this one.'

Grace thought carefully for a moment before saying what she had to say. 'What about the boy?' she said. 'What will happen to him now?'

'I'll see Sergeant Joe Collins in the morning. The police will have to do something about him, or the council, or one of the churches.'

'Or Betty Arbuckle,' Grace said unhappily.

'I suppose so. He's a Protestant, so they'll have to look after him.'

Again Grace hesitated and then she said, 'Couldn't he stay here for a while, Jack, until they sort it out?'

'What are you talking about?' Jack Tree said. 'It's not our problem.'

'It wouldn't hurt for a day or two.'

'Not here,' Jack Tree said. 'How's the tea?'

'It's drawing,' she said and poured it. 'But he can't go back to that boiler any more, and Betty Arbuckle lives on the other side of town, miles from the river.'

'What's that got to do with it?'

'He's used to it down here. It's where he lives.'

'Yes, but not in this house. Have some sense, Grace.'

'I meant just for a few days, until they know what to do with him.'

'Joe Collins will find something.'

'But it's a shame, Jack, to just turn the boy like that over to the authorities or to Betty Arbuckle. Betty'll send him away to that Boys Home.'

'It'll have to be done sooner or later if the old man's locked up. So there's no use getting soft about it. He can't stay here, and that's all there is about it.'

Grace didn't argue because she couldn't argue. But she knew that her husband was right. If old Fyfe was finally and completely mad, then sooner or later Spit would have to be cared for by some sort of authority. A few days on the back verandah wouldn't be of much use to him.

'He really is a nice boy,' she said. 'That's the pity of it.'

'He's a tough little bushie,' Jack said, 'and he'll survive anything. So don't worry.'

'I'm not sure about that,' Grace said sadly. 'He's not as wild as you all seem to think he is.'

She washed the tea cups and listened to her husband cleaning himself in the bathroom. She took another look at the sleeping Spit, and it seemed to her that with the smell of smoke and fire and damp on him, Spit too had been burned to the ground. How, she wondered, would he emerge from the ashes this time?

7

When Spit woke up at dawn he knew instantly where he was, and without having to think about it he was out the back door and down to the river to see what was left of the house and the boiler. What he expected when he reached it was exactly what he saw – an ugly pile of charred wreckage, a chimney still standing, some smouldering timbers, sheets of twisted corrugated iron on the ground, and nothing left of the house or the extension except the boiler. Nonetheless, it was a shock to see it in broad daylight because when he stood and looked at it he knew that his home had gone.

He walked cautiously into the mess. The buckets which Jack Tree and the others had used to fight the fire with were lined up near the front gate, which still stood, although the fence and flower garden had been trampled down. The gate sign said OUT and Spit pushed it to IN as he passed through it, feeling the damp sharp ashes under his bare feet. He was afraid to continue because of the broken glass and the nails. Remnants of clothes and curtains, and his grandfather's stuffed chair, were still smouldering.

It was the boiler he wanted to get to, and by raking his way through the mess with a piece of wood he reached its gaping side. The extension had been burned to the ground, and now there was only an open hole leading into the boiler. When he put his head inside it he realised for the first time that the fire had ruined the inside of this too. His bed was burned, so were his table and the boxes. The walls were black and charred. The wooden floor had gone. Instead, there was a pool of black water in the iron bottom. The little windows at both ends had been smashed, and he had to avoid the broken glass underfoot. What he saw now was the boiler almost back to its natural state.

His original intention had been to cook himself some breakfast and afterwards to clean out the boiler. But there was nothing to cook. Although the stove was still there and the chimney still stood, the Coolgardie food safe was a twisted, empty wreck. Eggs and butter and jam and porridge and tea had all gone to the flames, and the kettle had lost its handle. He found a pair of old shoes his grandfather usually kept for working in the vegetable garden and, flopping about in them, he set about rescuing what he could of his grandfather's equipment, and whatever clocks or watches were left. He raked out his grandfather's tools from the mess of damp ash – the vice and clamps and the lathe and grinding wheel, and he put them into a box which he had found intact in the garden. But none of the clocks and watches in the process of repair were worth bothering about, although he found Mr Temple's razor. He then set about emptying the water from the boiler with a bucket, and he was still at it when Sadie walked down the slope.

'What on earth are you doing?' she said.

'Cleaning it out,' he told her. 'I can fix it up a bit if I can get rid of all this water.'

'Your breakfast is ready at our place,' she told him.

'I'm not hungry,' he said.

'But you can't fix the boiler now,' she insisted, 'so come on. My mother's waiting for you.'

'Is your father still there?'

'Yes, but he won't do anything to you.'

'Well ... I want to see my grandfather, and he'll probably try to stop me,' Spit said.

Sadie sighed. 'No, he won't, Spit. Anyway you have to have breakfast.'

It was sound logic, so Spit pulled his feet out of the old shoes and went up the path with Sadie. When he entered the kitchen, Jack Tree was at the table eating bacon and eggs. He looked up at Spit and said, 'You'll have to wash before you sit down at this table, Spit. You look like a blackfeller.'

'Sadie,' Grace said quietly. 'Give Spit the towel I left on the couch, and then both of you come and get your breakfast.'

Spit had never before washed under a running tap in a basin, and when he saw the colour of the water as it left his hands and face he tried to clean the basin too until Sadie said, 'Never mind that. Just wash your face and hands.'

Even so, the towel received a fair residue of the black and the grey from his face and hands. When he was seated at the kitchen table he looked boldly at Mr Tree and said, 'What did you do with my grand-father?'

'He's still in the hospital. Where did you think he was?' Jack said.

'I don't know. Are they going to let him out today?'

Mr Tree shook his head. 'Not today,' he said.

'What are they keeping him for?'

'He's too sick,' Jack Tree said.

'He'll get over it all right,' Spit insisted. 'He always gets over it.'

'This time it's not so good.'

'Am I allowed to go and see him?' Spit asked.

'You'd better talk to Dr Stevens about that,' Jack said. 'But your grandfather won't be able to do much for you now, Spit, so you might as well get used to the idea.'

'I don't want him to do anything for me,' Spit argued. 'I'm going to fix up the boiler myself, and we can live in that.'

Jack Tree – dressed for work in his collar and tie, and with his hair brushed and his face spruced – was in no mood for Spit's nonsense. 'You can't do a damn thing to that boiler,' he said to Spit, 'so don't even think of trying it.'

Spit's instinct to attack as the best means of defence sustained him. 'Anyway I'm going to fix it,' he repeated grimly. 'I don't care what anybody says.'

'You can't live down there any more,' Jack Tree told him, 'so you'll only be wasting your time. Joe Collins will fix up some place for you to live for the time being.'

Grace Tree knew she had to stop them, and she put a plate of bacon and eggs and a cup of tea in front of Spit and said, 'We'll see about that when you've had your breakfast.'

'We are not going to see about anything,' Jack told her. 'I'll take Spit around to Sergeant Collins, and Collins will fix him up with a place to sleep.'

'But Jack ...'

'No, Grace. Have you got any other clothes?' he asked Spit.

'No. But I'm not going to Sergeant Collins.'

'Somebody'll have to look after you.'

'I can look after myself,' Spit shouted angrily.

Jack Tree stood up. 'I'm not going to argue with you,' he told Spit. 'I'm taking you to Sergeant Collins.'

'Not me,' Spit said and he was off the chair and out the back door before Jack Tree could catch him.

'Oh Jack,' Mrs Tree said. 'Look what you've done.'

Jack Tree was so surprised to hear protest in his wife's voice that he lost his temper. 'Of all the crazy ideas you get sometimes. I'm only trying to do what's best for the kid and now, by God, I'm going up to get Joe Collins.'

Mrs Tree said nothing and Sadie finished her breakfast in silence. But when her father had driven off in the Dodge she slipped out quietly and went down to the river to see if she could find Spit. She thought he would be hiding somewhere, but he was emptying the boiler again, and when she warned him that her father had gone to get Sergeant Collins, Spit said, 'Don't worry. He's not going to catch me.'

'But what are you going to do, Spit? Even if you can fix the boiler how are you going to cook your food? And where will you get your money from?'

'I've got some money. I'll be all right, as long as your father doesn't try to catch me.'

'But I think he's really trying to help you, Spit.'

'Well if he comes down here with Sergeant Collins, I'm off.'

'I suppose you're right,' Sadie said. 'Give me a pail and I'll help you.'

'I've cleaned up the glass, but if you come in here you'll only get dirty.'

'I don't care,' Sadie said, and taking off her sandals and tying her plaits across the top of her head she followed Spit's method of scooping up the water with an old enamel jug and throwing it through the smashed window. She was hurling a half-full jug of water out of the boiler, almost the last of it, when she saw her father and Sergeant Collins coming down the path under the big trees.

'It's them,' she called to Spit. 'They've come.'

Spit was at the other end of the boiler, his shirt was off and he was now barefoot like Sadie. He dropped the jug he was using and, saying 'I'm off, Sade,' he ran out through the ashes and down to the river where he dived in. By the time Jack Tree and Sergeant Collins reached the bank he was halfway across the river, and because there was a current he was carried downstream.

'Come back, you little dingo,' Sergeant Collins shouted.

But Spit was well on his way to Pental Island, and when he scrambled up the bank on the other side he stood there for a moment to get his breath.

'What do you think you're doing?' Sergeant Collins called out to him.

'You're not going to get me,' Spit shouted back.

'Listen, Spit. If you want to see your grandfather you'd better swim back here. You're not going to see him if you don't come back right now.'

'That's not fair,' Spit said.

'That's the way it is, so get back here.'

'Are you going to lock me up afterwards?'

'What would I do that for? I'm not going to hurt you, so come back here and I'll take you up to the hospital to see your grandfather.'

'Don't do it, Spit. They're tricking you,' Sadie called out.

'Sadie!' Mr Tree said, and for the first time in his

life he smacked his only daughter across the legs. 'Put your shoes on and get back home,' he told her. 'What are you doing down here anyway?'

'I was helping Spit,' Sadie said defiantly and ran off to collect her sandals and retreat up the slope.

'Come on, Spit,' Sergeant Collins called again. 'Your grandfather wants to see you.'

Spit hesitated, then he began to walk upstream. 'All right,' he said boldly. 'But that's all I'm going to do. I'm going up to see my grandfather. That's all I'm doing.'

'Then come on, I haven't got all day.'

Spit chose his spot and plunged into the river, and when he reached the near bank he was exactly at the steps.

'Have you got another pair of pants?' Sergeant Collins said.

'No. Everything was burnt.'

'He's got a shirt somewhere,' Mr Tree said, 'so put it on and let's go.'

Spit picked up his shirt from the gate and walked up the slope between Mr Tree and Sergeant Collins, who kept a vigilant eye on him because he expected Spit to run off again at any moment.

'We'll have to do something about you, Spit,' Sergeant Collins said to him. 'You're becoming a bit of a stray.'

'Leave it till later, Joe,' Mr Tree said quickly.

'But I've got that damned Betty Arbuckle on my back already,' Sergeant Collins said under his breath to Jack Tree.

Spit was put in the back seat of Jack Tree's Dodge tourer (though only after Jack had covered it with a piece of canvas from under the front seat) and he watched the town pass by, crouched forward and gripping the side support of the hood. He knew that he was more or less a captive now, and that what happened next would depend on his grandfather. He knew, too, that there was no point asking either one of these men how his grandfather was, because nobody would ever know that except Spit himself. They were always wrong about his grandfather.

When they reached the low, cottage hospital and were walking up the path under the shady trellis of sultana grapevines, Sergeant Collins said, 'Now behave in there, Spit, and for heaven's sake talk quietly. Don't do any of your shouting. It's a hospital.'

'I know,' Spit said. 'I know what to do.'

In the dark, aseptic place Spit rubbed one foot on the other while he waited for Sergeant Collins and Mr Tree to come back. They had been taken away by Sister Campbell with whispers and quick, sharp looks at Spit. In fact Spit had the impression that Sister

Campbell was annoyed with Jack Tree. She said to him, 'Not the boy, surely.' And Jack had said something in reply that Spit didn't hear. In a few moments she came back and told him to 'come along'.

'You're all wet,' she said to him, looking at his trousers.

'I was in the river,' he said.

'Haven't you got another pair?'

'They were all burnt,' Spit said.

'It just isn't right,' Sister Campbell muttered, not at Spit but at the world that surrounded him. 'I'm sure we've got some trousers here that will fit you.'

'I'll be all right,' Spit said, and when Sister Campbell opened the door of a rather cool, dark room with wooden Venetian blinds, he couldn't see anything for a moment. Then he saw dimly his grandfather, lying on a bed.

'Open the blinds,' Jack Tree said to the sister.

'It's not right, Mr Tree,' Sister Campbell said.

'Yes it is. He's got to see his grandfather sooner or later.'

Sister Campbell pulled a cord and the slats of the green Venetian blinds opened. In the light of day Spit saw what was left of his grandfather. He had almost forgotten his last view of him on the Trees' verandah. Now, in a confirmation he didn't want of his grandfather's disintegration, Spit saw that he was strapped by the wrists to the iron bedstead. And though the wild look in his eyes had returned, the rest of his face no longer had anything alive in it. It was worn out, wasted, gone. Even when his grandfather had suffered one of his attacks before, when he couldn't see or hear anything and would finally collapse in agony, Spit had always seen a man alive under the agonised and troubled shell. But looking at his grandfather now, he knew that in this dislocated and distorted face, and in the violent, uncontrollable jerks and twists of his body and the tortured mouth, there was nothing that he could depend on to rescue him.

'You said he wanted to see me,' Spit shouted accusingly to Sergeant Collins. 'He can't talk when he's like this.'

'He kept talking about his cairgie. That's you isn't it?'

'He didn't want to see me at all,' Spit said. 'He never does like this. What did you do with his cap?'

Spit had never seen his grandfather without his skull cap, and now that his head was bare he saw why that cap had always been in place. Instead of hair, Fyfe MacPhee had a dark raw stain on his crown and two deep scars in a simple cross – from the top of his scalp almost to the neck, and the other way almost from ear to ear. It was another destructive dimension to his grandfather that left Spit with very little hope for either his grandfather or himself.

'You just tricked me,' he shouted at Sergeant Collins.

'Listen, Spit. It was the only way.'

'We wanted you to see him, for your own sake,' Jack Tree told him. 'And here's Dr Stevens. He'll tell you what's up with him.'

Dr Stevens dropped a hand on Spit's shoulder and said to Jack Tree, 'I'm not sure if it's right to tell him, Jack.'

'We won't be able to do anything with him, or for him, if you don't tell him the truth,' Jack Tree replied.

'All right,' Dr Stevens said reluctantly, and told Spit to come with him.

Spit had to run to keep up with Dr Stevens who was six feet four inches, and when they reached the little surgery of the hospital Dr Stevens closed the door and told Spit to sit down.

'No thanks. I'll stand up,' Spit said.

'I know how you feel, son, but everybody's trying to do their best for you.'

'I don't want them to do anything,' Spit said.

'I'm sure you don't. But you're going to need help now.'

'No, I'm not. I can look after myself.'

'All right. All right. But I've got to tell you about your grandfather. Do you know what he's got under those scars?'

'No. He always keeps his cap on.'

'He didn't tell you how he got them?'

'No. He never told me anything about it. Not about things like that.'

'Well, we don't know either. But under those scars he's got a silver plate in his head. Sometime or other he was badly hurt, and they put in the silver plate to protect his ... his ... his brain box, if that makes it simpler for you. Do you understand me?'

'Yes ...'

'But as he got older, and his skin and muscles and nerve structure shrank a little, or lost their tension, that silver plate has been pressing harder and harder on the soft stuff in his head, where all his sense and his feeling comes from. It must have been hell for him, and he must have known he could do nothing about it. In fact it was so painful that I wonder he managed to survive this long.'

'Can't you fix it?' Spit asked.

Dr Stevens hesitated, wondering what to say, how much to tell the boy. He was a kind man who was always hurt by this aspect of his profession. 'I'm afraid not,' he said slowly. 'It's done real damage this time, and all we can do is see that he doesn't suffer any more excruciating pain. Although even that is doubtful. He's in terrible pain now.'

Spit's voice rose. 'Why did you tie his hands to the bed. What did you do a thing like that for?'

'Because he can't control himself and he could hurt himself.'

'Can't he come home? Can't I look after him?'

Again Dr Stevens hesitated. 'Not this time,' he said, reluctant, and saying what he had to say word by word. 'I'm afraid, Spit, that he'll never come home again. That's what I've got to tell you, old son. He's not mad, you and I know that. But his brain now is being destroyed, and he will never be normal again, not even for five minutes. They wanted me to tell you this so that they can fix you up with a place to live, and someone to look after you.'

'You mean they all want me to leave the boiler?'

'That's right. There's nothing left of it anyway, is there?'

'You're not going to let me see my grandfather any more?' Spit said.

'You can see him any time you like. But we'll have to do something about him, Spit. We can't keep him here.'

'But he's all right,' Spit insisted again. 'And he won't hurt you.'

'He's too sick,' Dr Stevens said with a shake of his head.

Spit was sure now that they were aiming him away from his grandfather. 'You want to take him away,' he said. 'Don't you?'

'We'll have to, Spit. He needs a different kind of hospital now. They can look after him better in Melbourne than we can here.'

'Melbourne ...'

'That seems to be the only way,' Dr Stevens said with a sigh. 'In the meantime you'll have to move in with someone.'

'They can't make me, can they?' Spit said, and this time he was appealing to Dr Stevens to join his resistance movement and confirm his right to be left alone.

'I'm afraid they can,' Dr Stevens said. 'That's the trouble, old son.'

Dr Stevens was known in St Helen not only for his long-legged lankiness but for his belief in raw foods and for his refusal to eat fish or meat or even eggs. Which explained his slow and careful way of speaking and his well-known patience with dogs and children and sick women and with his Nash motor car. 'I'm sorry for you, Spit,' he went on, 'but we can't let you run around loose.'

'Who's going to run around loose? I can fix up the boiler.'

Dr Stevens smiled. He was a mildly sad man, so that what he said was mostly in sorrow rather than a threat. 'They just won't let you do that, so come on and we'll see what Sergeant Collins and Jack Tree plan to do with you.'

When they went outside Sergeant Collins and Jack Tree were waiting under the vines in the shade, and Spit knew that these two men had already decided what to do with him.

'We're taking you over to Mrs Arbuckle,' Sergeant Collins told Spit. 'She'll be able to look after you for the time being.'

'I'm not going to Mrs Arbuckle's,' Spit said.

'Oh, yes you are,' Sergeant Collins told him. 'If you don't do as you're told, young feller, I'll lock you up.'

'You can lock me up any day,' Spit said.

'Mrs Arbuckle's all right, Spit,' Mr Tree said. 'She's a bit of a crank, but she'll be as good as a mother to you.'

'Not me,' Spit said firmly. 'I'm not going to stay there.'

98

'Listen, son, you don't want to end up tomorrow in that home in Bendigo do you?' Mr Tree said to him. 'Because that's what'll happen if you don't do as you're told. You don't want to be taken away, do you?'

Spit was biting his top lip, knowing that he had no way out.

'Why don't you make the best of it,' Mr Tree told him. 'It's the only way.'

'I'll only do it,' Spit said, loud and desperate, 'if you don't take my grandfather away.'

They all looked at Dr Stevens. He hesitated, as he almost always did. 'All right, Spit. We won't take him away. We'll do what we can for him – for a little while anyway.'

'What if you trick me again?' Spit said.

'Nobody's going to trick you again, Spit,' Dr Stevens said. 'I can promise you that.'

There was nothing more to say because the adults were now embarrassed, and Spit was trying to hold himself together. They were halfway to the gate, Spit and Jack Tree and Sergeant Collins, when Sister Campbell ran out of the hospital and called after Spit and told him to come back.

'What for?' he said.

'I found a pair of trousers for you,' she told him.

'Mine are all right now,' he said, staying where he was.

Sister Campbell joined them and she felt his pants. They were still damp but dry in places. 'You don't want them?' she said, holding up a pair of very short pants.

Spit shook his head but Sister Campbell rolled them up and gave them to him anyway. 'You might need them when school starts,' she said.

Spit was not in a thanking mood, but he put the trousers under his arm and climbed into the back seat of the Dodge.

He was still holding himself together when they left him at Mrs Betty Arbuckle's clean, bare and untainted house, with a final word from Sergeant Collins to behave himself. 'And remember,' the Sergeant said, 'if you try to run away, or refuse to do as Betty tells you, we'll pack you off to Bendigo on the next train. It's for your own good, Spit, so for God's sake do as she tells you, otherwise I can't help you any more.'

Betty Arbuckle greeted him at the door as if she had been expecting him, as if the anticipation of years had finally been justified and rewarded.

'What's your real name, Spit dear?' she said to him.

'Angus,' Spit said. 'Why?'

'Because you have to have a proper name now.'

Instinctively, Spit saw this sudden need for a proper name as a threat to what he had always had been in St Helen – no more nor less than Spit MacPhee. He knew he was staring a Boys Home in the face.

'You call me Spit,' he said threateningly at Betty Arbuckle. 'That's my name.'

Betty, surprised at the vehemence, said, 'All right, dear, if you want me to.'

Somehow, still intact, he followed Betty Arbuckle through the wire door and along a corridor to the back verandah. Spit had left the short pants Sister Campbell had given him in the Dodge, and what broke him now was the pair of Ben Arbuckle's old short pants that Betty had ready for him on the bed in the wide verandah where, she said, he would be sleeping. There was also a pair of boots on the floor and a pair of darned grey socks on the bed, and when Betty told him to put on the nice pair of clean, dry pants, and the socks and boots, Spit tried grimly but could not prevent the tears that slipped out of his squinted-up eyes and ran down his cheeks. They surprised him and angered him, because he could not remember having cried before. He knew it was a stupid and traitorous mistake for his eyes to do that to him, and in defying

101

them he knew he was never going to put on a pair of Ben Arbuckle's old pants or boots. He wasn't going to do it.

Seeing his tears, Betty said, 'Oh dear,' but didn't press him. She was about to suggest a moment's prayer but she changed her mind about that and said, 'You don't have to worry, Spit. You can stay here as long as your grandfather is in hospital. And if he joins the Lord Jesus we'll make sure you get a proper home. You don't ever have to worry about that again.'

Knowing that he couldn't make a run for it, Spit stood silently and defiantly still; but he couldn't contain himself for long and he said, 'I'm not putting on any of those pants or boots of Ben's.'

'We can think about that tomorrow,' Betty said firmly.

Spit didn't argue, but began instead to edge his way out.

'Now Spit,' she said to him. 'Where do you think you're off to?'

'I'm going down to the boiler to get my grand-father's tools. Somebody'll take them if I leave them there in my cart.'

'You're not to go back to that boiler,' she said to him. 'And I don't want you to go anywhere near that river. You won't need those things of your grandfather's, so you can leave them there. I want you to promise me not to go near the river ever again.'

Since Spit's entire recollected life had been spent on what was to him the lifeline and sanctuary of the river, Betty was threatening his heart, his soul, his life and his liberty. Her house was a mile inland from the river, surrounded by other dry houses and other dry streets, and whenever he had been in this part of town his only desire had been to get back to the banks of the Murray as soon as possible.

'What's the matter with the river?' he said to her.

'It's best that you begin to forget all about that place where you lived down there. It only made you wild and Godless, like an African heathen. You've got to start afresh now, Spit, because soon you'll be coming to Jesus, and you won't need to go down to the river again. You can't live like that any more, and I know you *will* come to Jesus if you don't ever go anywhere near that place again.'

'Jesus has got nothing to do with it,' Spit said indignantly.

Betty Arbuckle had a temper, but because her voice was always soft, the best she could manage in anger was a hurt forbearance. 'That's a terrible thing to say,' she said. 'Everybody needs Jesus.'

Spit had no argument to that, and she went on,

'Now go and find Ben. He's gone to the Co-op to bring home a fourteen-pound bag of potatoes, so you can help him carry them. But don't you dare go near the river.'

Spit, still mesmerised by Betty Arbuckle's force and persuasion, walked out of the house on his bare feet and pointed himself aimlessly at the Co-op because he didn't know what else he could do. He knew he was now living under a threat, because Betty's plans for his future were so strong that she, more than anyone else, had convinced him that maybe his grandfather would never recover, even though she had not mentioned his grandfather. Moreover, he was very frightened of her forgiveness, because she bore him no grudge for the bucket of water he had thrown over her. And, without knowing why, she made him feel that he had now done something even worse, and ought to be punished for it.

'She's a cootie, a damn black cootie,' he was muttering when he saw Ben Arbuckle coming down the street.

Ben in his boots was hopelessly entangled with the fourteen-pound bag of potatoes. Seeing Spit he dropped them and was ready to make a run for it. But he recovered and stood his ground and tried to look defiant.

'What are you going to do?' he said nervously to Spit.

'Nothing, Ben. Your mother told me to help you carry the potatoes.'

Ben, still suspicious and ready to run, said, 'She did?'

'Yes. I'm going to stay at your place. Just until my grandfather gets better.'

'I know.'

Spit, without plotting it, knew that he needed an ally in Ben because he was about to defy Betty Arbuckle and go down to the river. 'Why don't you make yourself a cart to carry things like that?' he said to Ben, kicking the thick brown paper bag of potatoes.

Ben, hot and sweating, sat on his haunches. 'You've got to have wheels for a cart and I haven't got any,' he said.

'Why don't you go around the town and ask people if they've got any old prams they don't want,' Spit said.

'Ask who?'

'Anybody. All you do is knock at any old back door and say have you got some old pram wheels.'

'What's the use, Spit? I haven't got any tools anyway, and my father won't let me touch his.'

'I've got some of my grandfather's tools down at the old boiler, and if I go and get them I'll show you how to make a cart.'

Ben, still wary of Spit, while at the same time

begging in his boots and smock for toleration and friendship, couldn't quite believe what he was being offered.

'Do you mean you'll help me?' Ben said.

'What do you think I mean? I'll go and get the tools now if you like. D'you want to come?'

Ben now kicked the potatoes. 'I've got to get these home,' he said, 'and anyway I'm not allowed to go down to the river, particularly down to your place.'

'She won't know. You can give her the potatoes and then duck out quick.'

'Somebody'll see us and tell her,' Ben said.

'Well, we can say we just happened to be down that way. And I'll bring up my cart and you can use it any time you like.'

Friendship, co-operation and co-existence – Ben now had the choice of all that, even if it meant dire consequences at home. It was the biggest offer – the best ever made to him in his Sabbatarian life, and he took a quick and desperate hold of it before he could change his mind. 'All right,' he said. 'Only you'd better keep out of the way so she doesn't see us together.'

'I'll carry the potatoes, if you like,' Spit said, and with his stocky, muscular arms and his practised body he lifted the awkward, bulky bag to his shoulder and said to Ben, 'Is there anywhere I can hide my grand-father's things?'

'You mean at home?'

'Yes. In your back yard somewhere.'

'Under the house,' Ben said. 'Nobody goes there except me, although I'm not supposed to crawl under there because my father's afraid of fire.'

'Nobody'll hear us,' Spit assured him.

'All right,' Ben said with far more courage than he thought he had.

It worked well enough. Spit hovered a few houses away while Ben took over the potatoes, hurried up the path through Betty Arbuckle's neatly clipped runway of burning bush and, calling out to his mother, 'Here are the potatoes,' he dropped them on the two little steps at the back door and joined Spit, who was already on the run when he saw Ben clumping out of the gate in his heavy black boots.

Spit would have kept it up all the way to the river, but Ben was neither a fast nor a willing runner, so they had to walk by the post office, Ben nervously watching everybody in sight and trying to keep a little behind Spit, whispering to him, 'Watch out, Spit, there's Mr Thompson.' Or, 'There's Mr Andrews. He's seen us.'

'Come on,' Spit said impatiently, and when they had crossed the railway line and could see the boiler he was surprised to see fragments of burned wood being flung through the broken window.

'Somebody's there,' Ben said.

Spit was already ahead and when he reached the boiler he was not surprised to see Sadie Tree inside it.

'What do you think you're doing?' he said to her.

'Don't you want to clean it up?' she said.

'Yes, but Sergeant Collins says I'm not allowed to now.'

'That's what my father says,' Sadie told him. 'But I knew you'd be back.'

'They're going to lock me up in Ben's place,' Spit said, aware that he was exaggerating, though not by much.

'What's *he* doing?' Sadie said in surprise, pointing to Ben with a fragment of burned-out bed. 'Won't he tell his mother?'

'No, he's not supposed to be here either. I just came down to get my grandfather's things. They won't let me see him if I don't do what they want. If I don't stay at the Arbuckles they'll take him away. So it's no use cleaning out the boiler, Sadie.'

'Are they going to send you away to Bendigo?' Sadie asked.

'That's what they keep saying,' Spit said. 'But I'm not going down there. I'm not leaving my grandfather.'

'I found a lot of other things in the ashes,' Sadie said, 'and I put them in the buckets.'

'Can I see inside your boiler?' Ben asked, waiting outside.

'You might as well,' Spit said with a shrug. 'There's nothing left anyway.'

Ben, like the others, had always envied Spit his life in the boiler, and now that he was suddenly standing inside it, even in its burned-out condition, he knew that he was enjoying a privilege that Spit would not share with everyone. In fact he was surprised to see Sadie Tree here – and so friendly with Spit. But he didn't say anything about it. He simply stood and wondered at the difference, at the life that Spit must have lived here and, as a gesture to it, he longed to take his boots off but did not dare do it.

'We'd better hurry, Spit,' he said, 'or we'll be late for dinner.'

'Won't you be coming down here any more?' Sadie said.

'I don't know. Mrs Arbuckle says I'm not allowed to, but I don't know, Sadie. Does your mother know you're here?'

'Yes, but my father's gone to Nooah.'

'If I can't get down here will you look after everything for me?' Spit asked her.

'I'll come down every day,' Sadie said.

Together they packed Spit's cart with the box of Fyfe's tools and what Sadie had found and saved – a silver picture frame, pots, knives and forks, enamel mugs and basins, and a little silver parrot that old Fyfe had kept on his workbench.

'And this too,' Sadie said. 'Look.' Sadie took from her pinafore pocket a little enamelled and lined box with scissors, a nail file, needle and a thimble in it.

Spit looked at it for a while, never having seen it before. He gave it back to Sadie and said, 'It must have been my mother's.'

'What'll I do with it?'

'You'd better keep it for me,' Spit said.

'I might lose it.'

'No you won't,' Spit said, and he told Ben to go ahead with the cart. When Ben was on the way up the hill Spit told Sadie about the hiding place under the boiler where he kept his own money.

'All you have to do is push the side of this piece of metal under the boiler and it drops down,' he said, demonstrating it for her. It was obviously part of a system that had once had some use in the boiler's original purpose, but now it was a rare hiding place which the fire had spared. Spit took a little cocoa tin out of the hole and showed Sadie his money, all in coins. 'Two pounds four and six,' he said. 'I was going to buy tyres and a seat with some of it for the bike, but I'll leave it here now because I don't know where I can hide it in Ben's place. But don't tell anyone … I mean your father.'

'Don't worry,' she said as Ben called out to him: 'Come on, Spit, or we'll get into trouble.'

'See you later, Sadie,' Spit said as he slammed the little door shut and raced up the slope to help Ben with the cart.

They were more than an hour late for dinner which surprised them both. Frank Arbuckle was at the gate; he had been working in the garden, watching the street. He took out his pocket-watch and said, 'Where have you been, Ben, and what's all that?' He ignored Spit as if he still didn't know how to deal with him. 'You're not bringing that stuff in here,' he said to Ben.

'It's my grandfather's things,' Spit said boldly. 'Somebody would have pinched them if I'd left them down there.'

'All right. But get inside, both of you,' Frank Arbuckle said. 'You're in trouble. You were told not to go down to the river and you took Ben.'

'He had to help me,' Spit said.

'We didn't do anything wrong,' Ben said to his father.

'Your mother will decide that,' Frank said sadly. 'But you're both in trouble.'

They went inside to the back verandah where the Arbuckles ate their meals, and Ben stood wide-eyed and expectant before his mother while Spit, an alien here, didn't know what to anticipate.

'So you went down to the river,' Mrs Arbuckle said, upset for their wrongdoing rather than their lateness for dinner.

'I had to get my grandfather's things,' Spit said again.

'And you of all people went with him,' she said unhappily to Ben.

Ben said nothing, and Spit knew that Ben was almost in tears, though not quite.

'You're wicked, both of you. You've been tempted. Disobedience is like telling a lie, which is a sin in the eyes of the Lord and you know that, Ben, even if Spit doesn't.'

Ben said nothing, his wickedness inescapable, his joy in a rare and surprising friendship gone to ruin.

'And you're dirty, Ben. Look at you.'

Ben was smeared with black ash, his smock stained, his boots blotted; whereas Spit, used to handling dirt, was clean.

'You have to be punished, the pair of you, so you

can either do without your dinner now, or Frank will give you both a good hiding. Take your pick please.'

Spit had to think about it for a moment. Apart from an occasional strap at school he had never been beaten or slapped by an adult. His grandfather had never touched him because that was not the way they had lived. Though they had always shouted at each other, there had never been any question of obedience or disobedience needing punishment, so there was something here that Spit didn't like and didn't want and resented. On the other hand he was very hungry and he said, 'If he wants to give me a hiding, he can do it any time he likes.' He looked across at Ben, hoping for some support.

Ben had been so rarely disobedient that this was a new experience for him too. He had lived his life unable and unwanting to escape obedience, or the moral guidance of his forceful mother. Moreover he was afraid of all violence, so that in character he should have missed his meal rather than taken a hiding. But Spit's offhand acceptance of a hiding, together with a new hope in a friendship restored, gave Ben enough courage to say, 'I'd sooner the hiding than miss my lunch.'

Betty Arbuckle, in her Australian way, was not without a sense of humour, and she also knew her son. 'Are you sure you want to be brave?' she said to him.

Ben kept his eyes down, knowing that if he looked up at his mother he would collapse.

'You're a very bad influence, Spit,' Betty said calmly, 'and you won't like it,' she said to her son. She called Frank and told him to get the strap.

'I thought they were going to do without their dinner,' Frank said to her.

'They decided to take a hiding, so we'll have to make it clear to Ben that he must not be led astray. And we have to show Spit that he can't lead others into temptation. You've got to learn not to be wicked,' she said to Spit.

'What's wicked about it?' Spit protested. 'I was just ...'

'Please don't answer back,' Betty Arbuckle told him in her troubled voice. 'And don't shout at me like a navvy. You'll have to change your awful ways, Spit, and I'm only thankful that Joannie's not here to see what you've done to Ben.'

Frank Arbuckle had his razor strop in hand, a long double layer of leather with a metal hook at one end and a thickened handle of leather at the other. It was gashed with the cuts of a mishandled razor, and oily with lubricants like old Fyfe's own strop. Spit looked at it, judged its effectiveness, looked closely too at Frank Arbuckle who seemed unhappy and nervous, and decided that it was bolder to bend over willingly and submit rather than struggle and make it difficult.

'Bend over the chair, Spit,' Frank said.

Spit did so without hesitation, but Frank's first blow surprised him with the force because he had forgotten that Frank Arbuckle had a lot to remember him by. Spit had made too much trouble for him with the water mains to be easily forgiven, and Frank was not going to let this opportunity pass. In Frank Arbuckle's delayed punishment Spit felt the strop scour his flesh: *one, two, three, four …*

'How many, Bet?' Frank Arbuckle said. 'Is that enough?'

'I don't know, Frank. Give him at least half a dozen, so that he learns his lesson.' Betty was firm, but she wouldn't watch.

Spit flinched each time but he bore the half dozen successfully, though he knew that one or two more could have wrecked his determination not to cry out. As he straightened up he caught sight of Ben's face, and though he said loudly, 'You didn't hurt me,' Ben was unconvinced, and after two blows from his father he was in tears.

'I told you, Ben,' Betty Arbuckle said, almost in tears herself. 'I *told* you. And it's for your own good because you must not be tempted.'

Spit watched the blows, and though they were serious enough they were not as forceful as the ones he had taken on his own backside. But since it was simply a matter of an eye for an eye now, Spit didn't mind Ben's milder punishment because he knew that at the first opportunity he would block a water valve again.

What puzzled Spit was Betty Arbuckle's concern over dinner that he should get enough to eat. She offered him more potatoes and peas, and encouraged him to eat. She was a good cook, better than Spit's grandfather, and better than Spit himself who knew how to roast a leg of lamb. She was lavish with the bread and butter pudding, which normally Spit would not have looked at. He did not like milk. But he had to admit that Betty Arbuckle had made a delicious pudding of it. A cup of hot, sweet tea and Spit was satisfied, waiting now for Ben who was a slow and careful eater.

When Ben had finished, Betty Arbuckle gave them both a small square of torn white cloth, part of an old sheet, and she told Spit to wipe his hands and his mouth clean before she thanked the Lord for what they had received.

Spit followed Ben's example, and though he knew that grace was usually said before a meal rather than after it he listened as Betty Arbuckle thanked the Lord Jesus for His benefice, for His grace abounding and for His harvest of good for their bodies' health. He didn't bend his head or close his eyes, like Ben, but he watched Betty Arbuckle, fingers tightly laced together, her head held high in some secret esteem, her eyes closed, and Spit saw a beautiful woman in a moment of ecstasy. He could remember his mother, but only in confusion – his mother with an unblemished face and then his mother with the disfigured face which she had tried to hide from him, although he had seen it enough to remember it. After her death his only contact with women had been his business affairs at back doors, or an exchange of greetings, or lately his friendship with Sadie and her mother. But it was this woman whom he had insulted and punished, and who had punished him in return and threatened him, and who now had a veto on everything he did – it was this one who puzzled him with her conventions for sin and her begging appeals to the Lord to save her from wickedness. She fascinated him and frightened him, and he wished his grandfather would get better, even if he couldn't re-build the boiler. He wished above all that he could run away, because he knew for sure now that Betty Arbuckle's determination to do what was best for him would sooner or later end in the Boys Home in Bendigo, and he didn't know how he was going to escape that.

8

He decided in self-defence and as a temporary measure to do as he was told. He managed to get through the rest of the day helping Ben in the garden, mowing the lawn and trimming the already trimmed hedges. The interior walls of Betty Arbuckle's small house were bare of anything from floor to ceiling, because to Betty a picture on a wall was a wicked indulgence. Yet her garden plot was a gem, as if in suppressing her own temporal beauty she had to protect its equal in nature with roses, violets, pansies, zinnias, lilies, dahlias, little vines, passionfruit, and a neat lawn. It was one of the loveliest gardens in St Helen, and Spit liked it.

At night, sitting next to Ben's sister, Joannie, who

moved a few inches away from him because she whispered to him, 'You smell,' he had to repeat the words of the grace after the meal, and before Betty Arbuckle put him down in the hard but comfortable little bed made of an old door with a mattress on fruit boxes, she insisted that he say, as a fledgling in prayer, that now he lay himself down to sleep he must pray the Lord his soul to keep, and if he should die before he was awake, he pray the Lord his soul to take.

He could accept that, but what was still difficult for him were clothes and the socks and the boots he would have to put on in the morning if he was going to be allowed to see his grandfather.

'We have to begin right, Spit,' Betty Arbuckle said in a kindly way. 'So, starting today, you won't be running around like an African heathen any more.'

Spit had never worn boots and grey woollen socks in his life and he felt like a stranger to himself as he set out for the hospital next morning, his borrowed boots hitting the dirt pavement like horses' hoofs. He didn't mind the pants and the smock now, but the boots did something to him because he felt that as long as he wore them he was being tricked and betrayed.

'They're after you, Spit,' he muttered to himself as he clumped noisily into the hospital, almost into the arms of Sister Campbell.

'Good heavens, Spit. What have you got on your feet?' she said.

'Ben Arbuckle's old boots,' he said.

'Well take them off. It's too hot to walk around in boots. Did Betty Arbuckle tell you to wear them?'

Spit nodded.

'Oh heavens,' she said. 'Then leave them on, but she ought to have known better. Come on. We've put your grandfather in the little room outside in the garden which we usually have for fever patients.'

She led Spit through the hospital, out through the shaded verandah which was covered in bougainvillea and where there were three patients who said, 'Hello, Spit.' He went on through the back garden of fruit trees and vines to where there was a neat, green, wooden shed with a corrugated iron roof sheltered by two big gums.

At the door Sister Campbell, who was efficient and crisp because nurses were supposed to be efficient and crisp, stopped Spit before going in.

'Don't look too long at your grandfather,' she told him. 'It's better not to remember him this way. He won't know you, so it's no use trying to get a reply from him. Just don't expect … don't expect too much, will you?'

'No,' Spit said boldly, 'I'm not going to ask him anything.'

'Still …'

Sister Campbell opened the door, and inside it was dark, but she didn't open the blinds. By the light from the door Spit could see the bed, and his grandfather's face on a pillow.

'We've given him something,' Sister Campbell said, 'so he isn't strapped down any more.'

As his eyes became accustomed to the dim, almost dusty light Spit saw that his grandfather seemed to be in a very deep sleep. His tension was gone, and though his face now was grey and unshaven, it seemed finally freed from the pain of his life.

'Is he better?' Spit said in a whisper.

Sister Campbell shook her head. 'No. But at least he's not suffering any more.'

'When will he wake up?'

'Not today, maybe not tomorrow.'

'How is he going to eat?' Spit whispered again.

'Don't worry about that,' Sister Campbell said.

Spit watched his grandfather breathing. It was thin, light, fragile and transparent breathing, simply in-and-out, in-and-out, and he knew that it was the most his grandfather could manage. There was nothing else left of him.

'I suppose he's going to die, isn't he?' Spit said simply, although he looked up at Sister Campbell wanting a denial.

'Let's go outside,' Sister Campbell said, and she took him out into the sunlight. 'You know more than anybody how much your grandfather has suffered, Spit.'

'I know all that,' he said aggressively.

'You know that he really couldn't stand it much longer.'

'Dr Stevens told me all that.'

'Yes, but now we've given him something to stop the pain, Spit. It'll help, but he may never wake up again. He has suffered too much, more than a human being can stand, so now it's better that he doesn't have to suffer all that pain any more. He's an old man and it's time he was spared any more pain.'

'He's not so old,' Spit protested.

'Then he's lived a long, hard life, if you like. But it's over now, Spit, and there's nothing we can do about it. We just want him to quietly go to sleep.'

'You mean he'll never wake up at all?'

'No. He'll never wake up again.'

'Why? Can't you do something?'

Sister Campbell shook her head and Spit shooed away a fly that was bothering him.

'I didn't want you to know any of this, Spit, but since they did it to you anyway it's best you know now that he's going to slip away from us very peacefully.'

'Can I come back this afternoon?' Spit asked.

'Of course. But for heaven's sake take those boots off and I'll tell Betty Arbuckle to let you go around barefoot.'

'It's all right,' Spit said and this time he walked right around the hospital garden to get out. Once on the street he clip-clopped in his boots through the town and down the slope to the river, where he sat on the mud steps near the boiler, dangling his feet in the water which he sometimes did for relief. This time he remembered too late that he still had Ben's boots and woollen socks on. He was like that when Sadie Tree found him.

'What on earth are you doing?' Sadie said to him.

'Nothing,' Spit replied.

'You've got those awful boots all wet,' she pointed out.

'I know that,' he said. 'I forgot.'

'Did you get into trouble yesterday?'

'Yes, we both got a hiding.'

'She'll give you another one when she sees those boots,' Sadie said.

'No she won't. They'll be dry by then,' he said.

'Have you seen your grandfather?' Sadie asked, squatting down near him.

Spit dabbled his feet and nodded.

'Is he all right? Is he better?'

Spit didn't say anything but lay back with the sun on his face.

'Is he getting better?' she said again.

'They gave him something,' Spit said, and for a while they were silent. 'He's asleep.'

'What are you going to do now?' Sadie asked then.

'I don't know,' Spit said. 'I suppose I'll have to go back to Ben's place.'

'I wish you could stay with us,' Sadie said.

Spit got up and stamped his squelching boots. 'Listen to them,' he said, and Sadie laughed as the water squirted through the lace holes. 'I'm going to look at my crayfish drums,' he told her. 'Do you want to come?'

Sadie followed him, and when Spit pulled out the first drum and found a large crayfish in it he didn't know what to do with it. 'You can have it if you like,' Spit told her.

'I can't carry it, it'll nip me.'

They were standing under a willow tree that drooped over the river, and Spit pulled off a long, thin, supple branch of the weeping limbs and tied it gingerly around the crayfish's big claws. Then, wrapping it tight in a bundle of more willow and leaves, he went on to the next drum and the next, until it was time for Sadie to go home for lunch.

'Aren't you going up to Ben's place for your dinner?' Sadie said.

Spit was hungry but he knew that he couldn't face Betty Arbuckle or Ben or Joannie or Frank Arbuckle, even to satisfy his hunger. They were too much of a confirmation in the flesh that he would soon be on his own, and he didn't want that confirmed now. In fact he wanted it denied, and the only denial he had was here, where his life had been and where he wanted it to go on.

'I'm not going back there till tonight,' Spit said.

'What about your dinner?'

'I'll get some of the tomatoes left in the garden.'

'I'll bring you back some bread and butter,' Sadie said as she took the wrapped-up crayfish from Spit and walked up the slope. But when she came back after lunch with two jam sandwiches Spit had gone. She guessed that he was somewhere up river, so she walked around the Point, along the edge of the Italian pea farm and found Spit sitting under Mr Walker's mulberry tree on the river bank, eating mulberries and cutting out one of his little sailing boats.

'I've got six ready,' he said, 'so we can put them in here and see where they are by tonight.'

'The river's beginning to rise fast,' Sadie told him.

'Yes, I know.'

'It won't be long now before summer is really over,' Sadie said.

Spit didn't seem to be listening any more, and when he suddenly got up to go the last thing he said to Sadie before he set off into town to see his grandfather was, 'You chuck the boats in. Sade.' He pushed the pile of little boats into her hands and cut across the Walkers' lucerne paddock to take the short cut into the town and to the hospital.

He had been so quick about it that Sadie was left alone with her jam sandwiches, which she decided to keep for him in case he needed them later. After putting the little boats in the water and watching them for a while, she soon gave up because it was not much fun without Spit there to follow them with her.

9

It was Dr Stevens, not Sister Campbell, who took Spit
to the fever house and told him that he had to be a
brave boy.

'Why?' Spit asked, trying to keep up with Dr
Stevens' long legs.

'Well, Spit, you can take a look and that's all.'

Spit didn't understand, but when Dr Stevens
opened the green door and stepped in ahead he said,
'Now take a look, but don't be upset. He's gone and
there's no more pain now.'

Spit understood the words less than the sight of
his grandfather, who was hardly recognisable: a tiny,
shriven, hundred-year-old ghost, who nonetheless was

so peaceful and relaxed that Spit was frightened and wanted only to get out. He knew it was the end of his grandfather, and that this was finally what it all meant as he ran away from the fever house.

By the time Dr Stevens had caught up with him Spit had already removed from his thoughts the image of that figure on the bed. Instead, he had fixed permanently in his mind the memory of a grandfather bent over his work bench, muttering or shouting, his skull cap tight over his head as he filled in their lives with noise and abrasion, and then got them through each day as if each day had to be fought for.

'Are you all right, son?' Dr Stevens said to him.

'Yes, I'm all right,' Spit said.

'Don't worry, you'll be looked after,' Dr Stevens told him. 'They'll find you a home.'

Spit's only clear intention was to get as far away from the place as quickly as possible, and as he started off around the hospital rather than through it, Dr Stevens said, 'Come through this way. I want to talk to you.'

'I'm going around here,' Spit told him, and wriggling out of Dr Stevens' friendly grip on his shoulder he was too quick for the doctor to stop him as he ran around the garden and out the main gate.

Spit would never know why he decided to go back

to Betty Arbuckle's. There seemed nowhere else for him to go, except back to the boiler, and he knew now that his life in the boiler was over forever. He thought of going to Sadie Tree's place, but maybe Mr Tree would be there and anyway there was nothing they could do for him any more. Moreover he didn't even know what he wanted of anybody. The powerful certitudes of Betty Arbuckle seemed to be the only certainties there were now, and as he stood on the back step of the house, reluctant to go in, he shouted: 'Are you there, Ben?'

Ben wasn't there but Mrs Arbuckle was, and she opened the wire screen door and said, 'So there you are, dear. We were worried about you.'

'I got Ben's boots all dirty,' he announced aggressively.

Betty Arbuckle pushed him gently inside. 'You've been to the hospital, haven't you?'

'Yes.'

'I know what's happened, Spit,' she told him. 'Dr Stevens telephoned me. You'll have to be a brave boy now and put all your trust in Jesus. He's always there, and you'll know how good the Lord can be. Sit down and I'll give you a cup of tea.'

'No thanks,' Spit said, and he was surprised to see tears in Betty Arbuckle's glittering and almost happy eyes.

'Your grandfather has gone to join his one and only friend,' she said to him. 'Poor Spit. But it's a happier, happier place he'll find with Jesus, and I'm so glad for him, Spit, so you musn't cry.'

'I'm not crying,' Spit said, fascinated by the way she was trying to get a grip on him with her joy and her sorrow, which trapped him for a moment in the way she wanted it to.

'Now you'll have a proper place to live,' she told him cheerfully. 'I have written to the Boys Home in Bendigo and I know there is a place for you there, so try and be a good boy until they let me know when they can take you. It shouldn't be more than a week at the most, so I'll look after you until then, and I'll try to help you come to Jesus because you'll never be alone as long as you come to Him. Do you understand me?'

'Yes,' Spit said. 'You're going to send me to the Boys Home in Bendigo.'

'That's right, and there'll be lots of other boys there like you, so you'll be very happy there.'

Betty Arbuckle had such a tight grip on his arm that he wondered if she was going to lock him up until she could send him off to Bendigo in the train.

'Go and clean off your boots,' she told him in a hopeful, encouraging way. 'The brushes are in the box under Ben's bed.'

130

Spit knew then what he had to do. He went through the kitchen to the verandah and sat on the floor. He took off Ben's boots, the socks, and the smock, and he put them neatly on the bed he had been sleeping in. Then, waiting until he heard Betty Arbuckle busy and singing in the kitchen, he walked quietly through the back door, closing it carefully after him. He crawled under the house to take from his grandfather's things a frying pan, a billy, a plate, and a knife and fork. He bundled them into a sugar bag and, still being very cautious, he walked his quiet way out into the street. Once there he used his liberated bare feet to run all the way to the boiler.

He took some money out of the box under the boiler, flung his bag over his shoulder and went back up the slope to the shops. He bought two loaves of bread, potatoes, eggs, jam, tea, matches and sugar. He was so intent over his purchases that when Tim Evans in the grocer shop asked him where he was going with this stuff, he said, 'It's not for me, Tim,' and got out quick. At the boiler he packed his fishing lines into the bag with the food, rolled the lot up into two half-burned and badly holed blankets, which were covered in ash but dry now, and tying them up he hid them under one of the gum trees and went along the river and up the slope again to Sadie Tree's house.

131

'Sadie ...' he called softly at the back door.

But softly to Spit was loud enough to be a shout. He could hear Sadie practising the piano, and he waited a moment and called again.

Mrs Tree came out the back and said, 'Hello Spit. What's up?'

'I just wanted to talk to Sadie,' he said. 'I want to tell her something.'

'She's practising.'

'All right,' he said, turning to go.

'How's your grandfather?' Mrs Tree asked him.

'He's dead,' Spit said.

'Oh Spit. That's awful ... Come in and sit down.'

Spit stayed where he was. 'I just want to tell Sadie something,' he said. 'Can't I see her?'

He had no other way of talking but boldly, and Sadie, hearing his voice, had abandoned the piano. She joined her mother at the back door.

'Spit's grandfather just died,' her mother told her.

Sadie looked at Spit and didn't say anything and she watched him shifting nervously from one bare foot to the other.

'Can I tell you something?' he said to her.

'All right.' Sadie didn't ask her mother but simply followed him through the garden and down to the boiler.

'I'm going across the little river to Pental Island,' he told her. 'I'm not going back to Betty Arbuckle's because she wants to send me away to that Boys Home in Bendigo. So I'm getting out. They're not going to get me.'

'But how will you live over there? There's nothing there, Spit.'

'I'll be all right. But if I need something will you get it for me with the money left in my box?'

'Yes, but how will I know?'

'I don't know, but if I need something I'll try to sneak across first thing in the morning. Or I'll put a message on one of the boats so you can look out for it when it ends up near your place.'

'But they're sure to be looking for you, Spit.'

'I know. That's why I'm going across the river to the bush. They won't get me over there. Only don't tell your father.'

'I won't. But they'll be looking everywhere for you and sooner or later they'll guess you're over there on the island somewhere.'

'Even if they get me I'll run away again,' Spit said. 'I'm not going to that Boys Home in Bendigo, that's all I'm saying.'

'I'm sorry about your grandfather, Spit.'

'Well … he didn't know he was going to die so it's not his fault.'

'I know it isn't, and I'm going to ask my father if you can live with us.'

'He'll only be after me, like the others. Don't tell him anything. Don't tell anybody.'

'I wish I could swim well enough,' Sadie said, 'then I could bring things across the river to you.'

'Don't even try, the way you swim. It's too dangerous, and the river is really rising now. Anyway I'd better get going before they come down here looking for me.'

'How will you get all these things across?' Sadie asked as Spit picked up one of the two blanket rolls.

'I'll go across on my back holding one of them up. Then I'll come back for the other one. It's easy.'

But as Sadie watched Spit walk up river and then jump in with the roll he held over his head she knew it wasn't easy at all, and as he kicked himself across on his back she saw the roll dip in the water when he couldn't hold it high enough. She watched him struggle on the other side as he threw the roll on to the bank. He came back and landed twenty yards downstream. But he walked up river again and jumped in with the second bundle, and halfway across he shouted, 'I'm all right now, Sadie.'

'But it'll be dark over there in the bush,' she called to him.

'That won't hurt,' he called back, and when he had landed the second bundle she watched him climb up on the bank, pick up the two rolls, and start walking to the big clump of trees across the island and along the big river.

10

It took the town a little while to realise that Spit MacPhee had disappeared. By the time everybody in St Helen knew about it there were rumours that he had drowned himself or hidden in one of the trains going to Melbourne. He had been seen from one end of town to the other, but nobody could offer any real facts to Sergeant Collins whose duty it was to find him. The river was a logical place to look for Spit, but where exactly?

The first news of his absence had come from Betty Arbuckle who had waited for him at six o'clock tea time, and after questioning Ben and ringing the hospital she realised by eight o'clock, when it was fully dark, that Spit was being wicked again. But it was ten o'clock before she told her husband Frank to go down to the boiler to see if he was there.

'He won't be there, Bet,' Frank said. 'He'd know that I'd come and get him by the scruff of the neck if he was there.'

'He may be hiding there, just crying,' Betty said.

'He won't cry,' Ben told his mother.

'You get back to bed,' Betty told Ben, who had heard the fuss and was in the kitchen to see what it was about.

'I'll go down to the boiler,' Ben volunteered.

'No you won't. You get back to bed,' his father said sharply.

'Well ... I'll bet he's not there anyway,' Ben said boldly.

'You don't bet in this house,' Betty told him, and took him firmly on his way to the verandah.

'I won't sleep,' Ben told his mother defiantly as he got into bed. 'Not until Spit comes back.'

Betty Arbuckle was not in a mood to deal with her son's new rebelliousness, so she tucked him up and returned to the kitchen to tell her husband to go on. 'You'll have to look somewhere,' she said.

Frank Arbuckle put his boots on and walked through the dark streets to the railway line, then along the line to the path leading down to the river and the trees and the boiler. It was a dark night and he stumbled once or twice, but he found the boiler among its ashes, looked inside it, called, 'Spit where are you?' once or twice, and then went back home to tell Betty, 'He's not there. He's up and gone, Bet.'

'But he must be somewhere,' Betty said unhappily. 'He can't just sleep in the street.'

'Spit can sleep anywhere.' It was Ben again.

This time he got a quick and surprising slap across the backside which brought tears to his eyes and quick obedience, but he was mumbling in protest as he went back to bed, 'I told you so. I told you, didn't I?'

It was almost eleven o'clock and by now Betty Arbuckle was sure that Spit was not coming back at all. 'I'll ring Sergeant Collins,' she said. 'He'll have to do something.'

'What can he do?' Frank said. 'If Spit has disappeared it'll take more than Sergeant Collins to find him at this time of the night.'

'He might have fallen in the river,' Betty said.

'In that case he's well on his way to Adelaide by now, swimming like a fish.'

'That's enough, Frank,' Betty said. 'You ought not to be heartless about it. I'm going to ring Sergeant Collins.'

That was the first step in the town's discovery that Spit had run away. And, as the first man to hear about it, Sergeant Collins' attitude was predictable.

'That damned little dingo,' he said. 'Why can't he stay put somewhere. I don't even know where to look for him at this hour of the night, Mrs Arbuckle. But you can bet that he's safe and secure somewhere. He knows how to look after himself, so don't worry. He'll turn up all right.'

'But I have to worry, and you ought to do something.'

'Well you tell me where I can find him and I'll go and get him. Leave it until morning and I'll be after him first thing.'

'You ought to be able to do better than that,' Betty Arbuckle said angrily.

'Tomorrow morning,' Sergeant Collins told her and hung up.

'He's right,' Frank Arbuckle said, and in an unusual act of defiance took off his boots and told Betty, 'I'm going to bed.'

Betty Arbuckle, determined in her conscience to do something, walked to the front gate, looked under the house hopefully, turned her eyes to the clear and starlit sky above and asked the Lord Jesus to protect the wandering boy. Then she went to bed.

It was another two days before all the town became involved in Spit's disappearance, but not everybody in St Helen recognised Spit's problem. Those who were curious but not particularly concerned assumed that with his grandfather's death he would end up in an orphanage anyway, which meant Bendigo or even Melbourne itself. That should be the end of it. But there were plenty of others who realised that Spit had disappeared because he didn't want to be taken off to an orphanage, and though his disappearance seemed like a hopeless gesture of defiance, there was plenty of sympathy and support for him. Also enough confidence in Spit's character to believe that he could look after himself.

But where was he?

Sergeant Collins spent a wasted day looking into all the turns and twists of the river bank upstream and downstream, and into the two deserted houses and the old lean-to that Spit had used sometimes to store his crayfish drum in during the winter. He asked the Italians who ran the pea farm if they had seen Spit; then the Walkers, and at the other dairy farms that bordered the little river. The one person he didn't ask was Sadie Tree who was the only person in town who knew where Spit was. But when he asked the boys and girls who normally used the Point for a swimming hole

140

if they had seen Spit (he never swam there anyway) they all told the Sergeant, 'He's over on Pental Island, somewhere on the big river.' In fact they didn't know for sure where Spit was, but they knew that the island and the big river were Spit's territory, so where else would he be?

It was something that Sergeant Collins also knew but was reluctant to accept because it meant rowing a boat across to the island and searching the strip of bush – the tall old eucalypts – that bordered the big river. Even then, unless Spit could be surprised in his sleep, the chances were that he would hear or see anybody looking for him, and could easily hide somewhere if he was determined enough. He knew every inch of the bush along the big river.

'That little wombat is so bloody determined, God knows where he is,' Sergeant Collins told his wife as he sat down to tea after his wasted day.

The next morning, when Sergeant Collins crossed the river in the boat he had borrowed from the power station, Spit was fishing from a fallen tree on the big river where he could see all that was happening. He saw Sergeant Collins rowing across the river, and rolling up his lines he buried them with his bed rolls under a pile of leaves and ran along the edge of the bank as fast as he could go.

Spit felt safe enough as he picked his way along the river bank, but he was always alert for any one of the three threats to his bare feet which, though hardened and almost always suffering a missing toe nail or a bloody big toe, could be attacked on the ground. He was afraid of the poisonous black or brown or tiger snakes that lived in the grass or under the trees or on the river bank, and were often difficult to see until you almost stepped on them. He could not forget what had happened to his friend Crispie. He was also afraid of the big goannas which were like prehistoric monsters and were often aggressive and could run as fast as he could if they wanted to. But the nuisance which always made him yelp or swear were the hard little seeds – three-pointed spikes called bindi-eyes which lay on the ground almost anywhere in the open, and jabbed deep into his flesh if he stood on them. He had to hop several times to extract a bindi-eye as he ran, but he knew he was safe because he could move faster than Sergeant Collins, and could hide in dozens of places among the trees or on the river bank.

When he had plenty of distance between him and Sergeant Collins, he heard the Sergeant calling out to him, swearing sometimes and adding the threat: 'You'd better come out now, Spit, because we'll catch up with you sooner or later, and then I'll lock you up, you little devil, for wasting my bloody time.'

And finally, but more effectively: 'Your grandfather's going to be buried tomorrow, so you ought to be there, Spit. You can't miss the old man's funeral.'

Spit could still see Sergeant Collins who was dabbing his face with his wet handkerchief. It was a hot day, the Sergeant's jacket was undone and his cap was on the back of his head. He looked around from river to bush as if he knew that Spit was not far away.

'Come on Spit, be a sport. Nobody's going to hurt you,' he was shouting.

Emboldened by the Sergeant's obvious disarray, Spit shouted back, 'It's just another trick, and I'm not coming back.'

He turned then and ran as fast as he could through the tall gums to the river bank where he could still watch almost everything that Sergeant Collins did. As the Sergeant retreated to the little river Spit followed him all the way until the Sergeant was back in the boat and rowing across the little river to St Helen.

Spit returned then to his fishing because he had discovered that he was going to be short of food sooner than he had expected. He was forever hungry, he had finished the bread and all but two eggs, and because it was late in the season the fish were not always biting, so he had only caught one Murray cod and a couple of small perch. But now he made his fire on the river bank where it was safe and couldn't be seen from any distance. He had made, in his life, many fires, and cooked many a fish and boiled many a billy. It was easy and routine now. But he had to be careful. He climbed to the top of the bank from time to time to see if Sergeant Collins or anyone else was on the way back. Finally, when he had eaten the last of the cod and the last hard end of his white bread, he sat on top of the bank sipping hot sweet tea and thinking of his grandfather, wishing without any admission of his final and ghostly loss that his grandfather would be waiting for him in the boiler house again, and that their life there would go on forever.

But he knew he had to fight for himself now, and he cursed (in his best all-round selection) Sergeant Collins not for being the local policeman or a particular enemy but because he was the agent of everybody else who was out to get him. Finishing his tea he stood up, took the last dregs of sugar out of the enamel mug with his finger and said aloud, 'They're never going to get me.'

He washed out the mug and the billy and the plate in the river, covered the ashes of his fire, and began to dig with his feet in the soft sand and mud, looking for the big river mussels which were the best bait for Murray cod.

Now that he was discovered, and having carelessly revealed himself to Sergeant Collins, he decided to move further up the big river. Packing his two blanket rolls he slung them over his shoulder and made his camp in another clump of gums where he could still see anybody crossing the little river, although it was much farther away now. Since there was nothing to do but fish, he fished, and sometimes he sang one of the Scottish songs his grandfather had taught him, although he didn't understand the words because they were too Scottish to make any sense of. When it became dark, which always settled quickly now that summer was almost over, he made his way back to the little river, smacking the path in front of him with a stick so that he didn't step on a coiled up and sleeping snake. He swam the little river, climbed out cautiously, found a fragment of wood among the ashes of the boiler, cut a little boat from it, found also a fragment of brown paper, wrote '2 *bread and some eggs*' on it with a blackened splinter of burnt wood, made it into a sail, and set the boat on its way down to Pental Island by the time Mr Evans' dog, Patchy, put his visit on record, although nobody paid that much attention to connections like that except Sadie.

He knew that he had to be particularly careful with his camp at night, in case Sergeant Collins or someone else decided to sneak up on him in darkness. He made his fire under an overhang on the bank and he doused it when he had cooked his last perch and boiled his billy. He slept in his blankets, hidden under a fallen gum near the overhang, although he knew that snakes often lay along that particular tree when they sunned themselves.

He slept nervously alert, and spent the next day avoiding not only Sergeant Collins but Jack Tree and Frank Arbuckle and Tim Evans who had organised themselves into a posse to search out the bush along the banks of the big river. Seeing all three hunting him like a bushranger it became a challenge to Spit, and though he found little difficulty in avoiding them (sometimes he got around behind them and simply followed them) he was worried at the end of the day when he heard Sergeant Collins say to Mr Tree, 'We're in for some rain, Jack, and the poor little beggar will probably come in, once it starts to pour.'

'I'm not so sure,' Jack Tree said. 'He's a barefoot barnacle and he's not likely to be afraid of a little rain.'

'It's going to get awfully muddy, and if we get a bit of wind it's also going to be pretty miserable. In any case we'll bring Doug Stewart and half a dozen others tomorrow and we ought to get him somewhere sooner or later.'

'Maybe … maybe …' Jack Tree said doubtfully. 'In any case doing it this way is a dead loss. He's probably watching us right now, and laughing up his bare sleeve.'

'Maybe he'll get hungry,' Frank Arbuckle said, 'and that'll bring him in. Don't you think?' he appealed, knowing he would have to face Betty on his return without Spit.

'I don't know about that either, Frank,' Jack Tree said. 'He's better at catching fish in this river than anyone else in town. Anyway, let's go. We're just wasting our time doing it this way.'

Spit had heard enough and he did a wide circle around his pursuers to pick up his blanket rolls and then head for one of the thickest clumps of gums where he could shelter best from the rain when it came. He had not noticed the sky to the north-west because the timber and his concentration on his pursuers had obscured it. Now that he took a good look at the sky, he saw in the shadow of the setting sun a silhouette of thick black clouds etching a flat line along the distant horizon, and he knew it was going to be a bad night.

Rain, when it came to St Helen, was always a visible aggressor behind a waning in the sky, and its first splashing gum-drops were usually sudden and heavy once the thick clouds were overhead, particularly in late summer. He knew that this time it would probably arrive in the middle of the night, and he wished that he had brought his little tomahawk that he normally used to cut kindling with. It was still there in the garden shed. Now, when he reached the triangle of thick gums where there was some overhead protection, he tried to construct a lean-to with dead limbs and thick grass against one of the trees. But he knew it was hopeless so he returned to the river bank, found a sandy edge with an overhang under some exposed roots, and decided to sleep out any storm here if he had to.

But first he must cross the little river again to get the bread and eggs he had asked Sadie for. It took time to cover the longer distance to the little river, but he swam as quietly as he could, aware now of the faster currents of the rising river. He waited at the mud steps in the darkness for a moment before running quickly to the shelf under the boiler.

'Good old Sadie,' he said softly as he felt the bread and eggs and something else – a tin of sardines. They were all together in a sugar bag and there was a note tied with string around the sardine tin which he couldn't read in the darkness. He heard Tim Evans' dog bark, and somewhere above the railway line he heard a motor bike. It was enough to hurry him on his way, and he set out higher than usual to allow for the faster current and swam on his back, holding the sugar bag as high as he could. But again it got wet and he swore at Sergeant Collins for trying to trap him. At this moment he wasn't thinking of Betty Arbuckle and the Boys Home, he was far more concerned with the men at his heels.

He beat his way back under the threatening sky to his shelter beneath the roots of the big gum tree, and it began to rain as he tucked himself into his blankets. He heard the storm slowly rumbling overhead and he looked up at the big tree which, he knew, could topple over at any time once the winds began.

'But not tonight,' he begged the tree. 'Any old time, but not tonight.'

11

What Spit didn't know, after a night of thunder and lightning and heavy, windy rain, was that in the dull muddy morning there was a large following of his unseen and unknown friends behind the cortege of his grandfather's funeral. They had to bury him without Spit, even as ten men of St Helen went across the river in a phalanx to track him down. They were going to catch him this time, even if they had to hunt for him all day and all night. But thirty people of the town followed the funeral, and though some said it was really a gesture to the defiant Spit, hiding in the bush, for those who were there it was more a gesture to the strange and tortured old man who had done his best for his grandson, even as he tried painfully and often hopelessly to keep some remnants of his sanity intact.

Betty Arbuckle was on foot, and though she was here to bury the old man, she was more concerned about Spit's future than she was about Fyfe MacPhee's shadowy death. Nonetheless she was overcome; she was in tears, her lovely face always beautiful in its passion as she declared in her heart that she was deputising for Spit in the eyes of the Lord who would forgive his absence.

On the other hand Grace Tree, holding Sadie by the hand, walked self-consciously but determinedly at the very end of the little procession feeling out of place. She too was trying to formulate her own concern for this serious and wild little boy who had disturbed her own family. At the cemetery gate she sent Sadie home. Thereafter she stood at the back of the gathering to listen to the Reverend Mackenzie, the Presbyterian Minister, make his fiery appeals to the Lord to take up the departing soul of Fyfe MacPhee and make the best use He could with it.

Being a Catholic she was not at ease with the Reverend Mackenzie's Calvinist appeals to the Lord, although she considered him a fine man with nothing but good in his heart. But she was glad that she was here for Spit's sake, and looking across the open sandy grave at the tear-stained face of Betty Arbuckle, she too knew that it was Spit's life that was now the problem. Like Betty she was thinking more about Spit than the old man who was being returned to earth.

Grace left the ceremony before the others. Walking back to town, avoiding the fresh puddles along the muddy road, she was thinking about Spit. She had always known where he was hiding without having to think about it. The reason for his sudden flight seemed so obvious that she was surprised that the whole town didn't somehow organise itself to save Spit from being sent away to a Boys Home that was miles away in Bendigo. Now she was worried about him fending for himself on Pental Island, particularly at night. Like everybody else in town she knew about the snakes, but she had enough confidence in him to decide that he was safe enough for a few days at least, barring accidents.

She had also guessed that Sadie was helping him, and she didn't question her daughter or try to interfere. But when her husband had returned yesterday with Sergeant Collins from the first fruitless search of the bush along the river, she had said to him when he began to complain about the little devil wasting everybody's time: 'He shouldn't go to an orphanage, Jack. That's what is causing the trouble.'

'Well what else is there for him?' Jack Tree had said.

'I don't know,' she replied. 'But surely something can be done for him.'

'Maybe Betty Arbuckle will take him over,' Jack Tree said as they listened to a mosquito searching them out in the darkness as they lay in bed.

'But it's Betty Arbuckle he's running away from.'

'I don't know why,' Jack Tree said. 'If she decided to take him over it would be a pretty good thing for him. She's a kind woman underneath all that evangelical soap.'

'I know she's kind, but kindness is not enough. He deserves more than that, Jack. Even when he was with her for a few days Betty Arbuckle was trying to turn him into a copy of her own Ben, and that just won't work with Spit. Anyway if you do catch him and take him back to her he'll only run away again.'

'That's why he's better off in a proper place in Bendigo where it is a damned sight more difficult to run away. No bush down there.'

'It's wrong,' Grace insisted. 'It's terribly wrong.'

'I don't know why you're so worked up about this boy,' her husband said. 'For heaven's sake stop thinking about him. It'll turn out all right, so stop it.'

'I can't,' Grace Tree said in her firm, quiet way and

her surprised husband wondered again at her stubborness, although he decided not to pursue it in case her defiance persisted.

That had been yesterday. Today, as she walked away from the funeral, she hoped that even ten men wouldn't be able to catch Spit, even though she had listened to the storm last night and pictured Spit huddled somewhere on the island, wet and afraid, and feeling friendless and miserably alone. She was sure that in his heart her husband had been as worried in the night as she was, but his solution was not hers. She was determined not to accept the easy and obvious way out of the problem for Spit. 'It's wrong,' she told herself once more as she saw Sadie running up the slope to meet her.

'They caught Spit,' Sadie said breathlessly, 'but he got away and tried to swim across the big river to New South Wales. Dad and Mr Arbuckle are taking the boat down to the big river so they can get across to New South Wales and catch him if he does get across.'

'Poor Spit,' Mrs Tree said bitterly. 'I wonder what on earth he thinks of us all, chasing him like an animal.'

Spit, at the time, was not thinking of the population of St Helen at all but of the big river that was in full steam ahead of him – too full and too fast and too wide.

He had come through the wet storm last night rather well. His little caved-in bank under the gum tree roots had been fairly dry, and the thunder and lightning had not bothered him too much. There was a strong local theory that in a bad storm snakes, seeking protection, would crawl into the blankets of anyone exposed enough like Spit to the elements, so he periodically had to shake his blankets out to make sure that no snake tried to get in with him. When the wind had broken off a small dead limb from the gum tree and dropped it on his blanket he had leapt up in a moment of terror, swinging the blankets across his feet in a panic until he had seen the broken limb. He could swear effectively and fluently for the fear in his heart, and after telling weather, sky and tree what he thought of them, he flung the broken limb into the river, rolled himself up in his blanket and again went to sleep.

He was in a fairly good position in the morning to make his fire, and though everything was damp and dripping, the sky was blue again and he found enough dry sticks and leaves to get the fire going. He boiled his billy and toasted the bread. He missed butter, but when he opened the sardines he said, 'Good old Sade,' and read her note. It said: '*Tomorrow I leave you eggs and butter. Do you want some chump chops?*' He took a blackened stick and wrote '*Yes*' on the same

155

paper and put it in his trouser pocket to be delivered that night.

He stored his goods and chattels neatly under the roots and took his lines with him down river to a deep hole which he had not yet fished. He spent most of the morning failing to catch any fish, while keeping his eye on the little river crossing. But when he had run out of mussels he walked a hundred yards down river to a little sandy patch where there was also an edge of some noisy rapids, and he was digging in the mud with his toes, concentrating on his search for the big river mussels, when he saw Ted Jackson, the butcher and fireman, and Andy Frith who delivered the milk, standing on the shore. He realised that he had been careless. The stony crackle and bubble of the shallow rapids had drowned their noisy approach so that he had lost his first line of defence – his ears.

'Come on out, Spit,' Andy shouted at him. 'It's time to go home.'

Spit didn't say anything. He looked for a way out. The rest of the big river was too wide and fast to get right across, but he knew that if he dived in he could catch the downstream flow and make some sort of an escape. He ran along the sand bank, over the rapids, and dived in. As he swam with the fast current downstream he could hear Ted Jackson calling out to someone that he was in the river, going hell-for-leather downstream.

Spit kept his eye on the banks as he was carried downstream, but he was surprised when he was swept around a bend to see Ron Jackson, one of the best swimmers in the town and one of the fastest runners as well, waiting on the bank and taking off his shoes and trousers and shirt ready to dive in.

Spit knew that he could not outswim Ron Jackson, but he headed across the river anyway, trying to escape him. He was barely halfway across in the current, already carried fast downstream, when he felt Ron Jackson's arm around his neck.

'Come on, kiddo,' Ron said to him as he tightened his grip around Spit's neck. 'The game's up.' Ron was a film addict and his language had to fit the situation. But he was young and friendly to Spit and he was one of the adults whom Spit would call by his first name instead of Mister.

'Let me go, Ron,' Spit said to him as they struggled together in the water. 'You're choking me.'

But water and swimming and struggling were not good for an argument, and it was only when Ron had pulled him up on the bank two hundred yards downstream that he said to Spit as they both caught their breath, 'You can't run away in this town, Spit, so it's no use trying.'

He kept a firm hold on Spit, and by now six of the other hunters had arrived, including Sergeant Collins, Jack Tree and Frank Arbuckle. Spit expected at least one of them to cuff him, but Sergeant Collins said, 'You're as slippery as Ned Kelly, Spit. But you got careless, like all bushrangers.'

'I'm not a bushranger,' Spit said. 'I haven't stolen a damned thing.'

The others laughed and Jack Tree said to him, 'We don't want to hunt you down, young feller, but we can't have an eleven-year-old running around alone in the bush. It's for your own good.'

Spit knew they were trying to do something for him and he knew all these men: Sam Allenby the greengrocer, Billy Andrews from the power house, Peter Macrae who was the shunter, and all the others. But he also knew at a glance that the only real swimmer among them was Ron Jackson, and Ron had gone back to get his trousers and shirt and shoes, two hundred yards upstream where he had left them.

Sitting on the bank getting his breath back Spit watched Ron Jackson through the trees, and at the moment when Ron was putting on his trousers Spit stood up slowly and before the others realised what he was doing he had jumped into the river again, and this time he was determined to get across to New South Wales where there was thicker timber and he could outrun Ron if he got enough start.

But unluckily this was one of the places where the river was widest and fastest, and it was another mile to the junction of the little river. So Spit knew that he was going to be carried downstream more than across. His real problem was to use the stream in his favour before the rivers joined; but above all to get as far ahead of Ron Jackson as he could.

He heard Sergeant Collins shout, 'Ron, he's back in the river. Get down here quick or we'll lose him.'

It was then that Sergeant Collins told Jack Tree and Frank Arbuckle to hurry back to the little river, get the boat, and row across the big river to cut off Spit's escape into New South Wales.

12

When Sadie saw her father and Frank Arbuckle launch the boat on the other side of the little river, she had been sitting on the steps waiting for someone to appear with news of Spit. When she called out to her father, he told her what had happened and as he began to pull the boat downstream to the junction of the big river, he called out to her, 'You go off back home, Sadie. You're not to hang around waiting for me to come back. Go on ...' he called out as he disappeared around the bend.

But Sadie was not hanging around waiting for her father to come back. She was telling herself unhappily that she was waiting to see if they caught Spit, and she was going to defy her father and sit on the mud steps to see what was going to happen now. She was running up the slope to the house to get her father's field glasses when she saw her mother crossing the railway line on her way back from the funeral. Sadie continued on up the slope to tell her what had happened.

'He could drown in the big river, couldn't he?' she said to her mother as they both hurried back to the boiler steps.

'He could,' Grace said, 'but he's a strong swimmer and if he doesn't exhaust himself he'll be all right.'

'I hope they never catch him,' Sadie said as they reached the steps to wait again for someone to reappear with news of Spit.

'The only trouble is,' her mother said, 'he can't stay out there forever, Sadie. Although I wish they could have done it some other way.'

'What'll happen to him when they bring him back?' Sadie asked.

'I don't know, I really don't know. But if they try to send him back to Betty Arbuckle he'll only run away again. So I don't know what is to become of him.'

'Maybe Sergeant Collins will have to lock him up?' Sadie said.

'I wouldn't put it past any of them,' Mrs Tree said unhappily. 'Even though they all think they're doing their best for the boy.'

'It's unfair,' Sadie said.

'Yes, it is,' her mother replied, and she sat down near her daughter to wait.

Half an hour later they saw the rowing boat coming heavily upstream, and in it were Jack Tree, Frank Arbuckle, Ron Jackson and Spit.

'Oh, they got him,' Sadie said bitterly, standing up.

As Sadie and her mother watched the boat approaching, the rest of the hunters and seekers emerged from the clump of gums on the island to wait to be picked up.

'Where did you catch him?' Sergeant Collins called out to the boat.

'Ron caught up with him,' Frank Arbuckle replied. 'And just in time. He was almost done for.'

When the row boat reached the steps Ron Jackson jumped into the water and stayed there because he was in his underpants. Jack Tree manoeuvred the boat so that Frank Arbuckle could get Spit up the steps, and seeing his wife and Sadie he said angrily, 'I told you to go home, Sadie. Now get. And quick. We had to take Spit's pants off him so he wouldn't run off again, so turn your back and run straight up to the house.'

Sadie had seen Spit huddled in embarrassment in the back of the boat without realising why. Bursting into tears she ran up the slope to the house. When

Frank Arbuckle tried to get Spit out of the boat he resisted violently, and now Mrs Tree saw that he too was in tears, not, she knew, for his defeat but for his naked humiliation.

'It's all right Spit, I won't look,' she said to him, turning her back. Then she added angrily to her husband, 'Jack. Give him back his trousers.'

'Not on your life,' Jack Tree said. 'He'll be off like a shot.'

'No he won't. Do as I say, Jack. I'm telling you,' she said so firmly and angrily that Jack Tree hesitated only a moment before telling Frank Arbuckle, 'Give him back his pants, Frank, but keep a good grip on him.'

Mrs Tree waited until they had landed Spit then she turned around to face her husband and Frank Arbuckle.

'Spit, come here,' she said to him.

Spit, weakened by his humiliation, did as he was told. Mrs Tree didn't touch or comfort him or look at him in his humiliation, even with his pants on. She was looking straight at her husband.

'Where do you think you are taking him now?' she asked him.

Startled by her temper, her posture and her sudden defiance, Jack Tree said, 'I don't know, Grace. We'll let Joe Collins decide that.'

'No, you won't,' Grace said. 'He's not moving from here. I'm going to take him up to the house, and he's going to stay there until we've sorted this all out.'

'Don't be such a fool,' Jack Tree said to her. 'He'll run off again the first chance he gets.'

Grace Tree looked at Spit now and said, 'Will you run off again Spit if I promise not to let them take you back to Mrs Arbuckle's or send you away?'

Spit was also surprised by Mrs Tree's anger and temper; and because he was beginning to recover himself he knew he had an ally, for the time being at least.

'All right,' he said. 'I won't run off. But just so long as it isn't a trick.'

'It isn't a trick,' Grace said.

But Frank Arbuckle resisted. 'He's fooling you, Grace. He'll duck off again the moment your back is turned. You don't know him.' Frank was hurt by Grace's remarks about his wife, and he also had to face Betty empty-handed.

'You might not trust him, Frank,' she said, 'but I'm willing to, and you're not going to take him away simply because you don't believe him. He's staying with me, and I'll take full responsibility for him until something sensible is decided about him. Come on, Spit,' she said firmly and, walking ahead, she didn't bother to turn around to make sure that Spit was following her.

But he followed, and as they went up the slope Spit heard Ron Jackson calling out to Sergeant Collins, 'Did you bring my pants and shoes, Joe?' And Joe Collins reply, 'No, we clean forgot.'

Ron swore and said, 'What a pack of bloody fools ...'

Spit thought that pretty good, and though he liked Ron Jackson, he was glad in view of that first grip around his neck that Ron had to go back for his trousers, although he was also grateful to him for having reached him in midstream, because Spit knew that he was almost done for when he felt that sudden, tight forearm around his neck for the second time.

13

Whatever Spit learned later about the next few days and weeks in his life, he knew little about them at the time. He was aware that something was being fought out over him, so that eventually the whole town seemed to be taking sides. He was aware too that he had caused serious trouble between Mr and Mrs Tree, so much so that Sadie was unhappy about the continuing though often hidden dispute going on between her mother and father.

'I wish they wouldn't quarrel,' Sadie had confided in him after a week of it and when Spit was doing what Jack Tree had told him to do – cut kindling wood for the fire.

'What are they arguing about anyway?' Spit asked her.

'I don't know. They've never argued like this before.'

But Sadie knew, and Spit guessed that he was the cause of it. He didn't know what he could do about it himself except to run away again, but he had promised Mrs Tree so he could not do that. And there was no need to do it yet anyway. What made both Sadie and Spit particularly aware of the trouble was Grace Tree's stubborn resistance to her husband's usual habit of making decisions and then assuming that they would be automatically obeyed.

It had now become a simple issue of what to do with Spit. Grace Tree had first of all consulted Sergeant Collins and asked him what he intended to do about the boy, now that he had no home.

'He'll have to go off to that Boys Home in Bendigo, Grace,' Sergeant Collins told her. 'I don't see any other way. But in fact it isn't my decision. You'll have to go up to the Shire Office and ask them what they are going to do with him. It's more their responsibility than mine. And you'll also have to cope with Betty Arbuckle, if you're thinking of anything else. She already wants me to go and get the boy and bring him back to her place.'

'Don't you dare,' Grace Tree said in her quiet way. 'He's not leaving my house.'

'All right. All right,' Sergeant Collins said. 'I'm fed up with the whole business; always have been. You settle it with the Shire Office and I'll do whatever they tell me.'

Grace Tree went to the Shire Office and spoke to the only man she knew there, Pat Stillman – the dark and affable Pat Stillman who told her that there was no way locally that Spit could be looked after. There was no place and no organisation that could take care of him. So the logical place, no matter which way you looked at it, was the Boys Home in Bendigo.

'That's awful, Pat. There ought to be something else.'

'Unless you want to take him over yourself,' Pat said and laughed. 'In that case you'll have to look into the legal side of it before we could agree to anything. But that I'd love to see,' Pat said and he laughed again, because he was a determined laugher at everything, including himself. 'I'm a round peg in a square hole,' he loved to say to anyone admiring his untidy and crowded office, walled-in with square pigeon holes stuffed with files and documents.

It was when she was walking home from the Shire Office that Grace Tree made up her mind. She could not, physically, have any more children of her own, but even if she were able to have them it would not have altered her resolve. It was a startling decision, almost frightening, but she knew what she must do. She would adopt Spit. That was the simplest and cleanest solution and she knew it was right. That is, if they (whoever 'they' were) would let her adopt him.

14

Grace's first obstacle was her husband, and when Spit and Sadie had gone to bed that night she said to Jack, 'I'm going to try and adopt him, Jack. He's a good boy and Sadie likes him, and I trust him because he has always been very honest. So I'm going up to the Shire Office tomorrow to see how to go about it.'

'You'll do no such thing,' Jack Tree said incredulously. 'You must be out of your mind to think of it. I forbid it.'

'I'm not out of my mind at all, and I'm going to do it.'

Jack Tree was seated at his roll-top desk making out his complicated reports on herd testing, a task that his wife would not normally have dared interrupt. But Grace stood at the side of his desk looking so close-mouthed and determined that Jack Tree was nonplussed.

'I'll tell you this,' he said, taking off his spectacles with a snap. 'Even if you want to adopt him, you haven't a ghost of a chance because Spit is a Protestant and you're a Catholic. They'll never let you do it.'

Grace had already considered this most obvious of problems in a country as divided and as passionate as Australia was by sect and prejudice, but she had not come to that problem yet so she had pushed it out of her mind.

'I'll face that when I come to it,' she said, 'but I wish you would think about it,' she told him, appealing to him now as if she would be quite willing to return to her docility if he would only agree. 'He's still so young, and whatever you think is wrong with him now, you can do something with him. I like him, Jack, and I don't want him to end up in an orphanage. It would be so wrong, and you know it yourself. Think of Sadie, if something happened to us.'

'If you start thinking that way you'll end up with all the lame ducks in the town at your doorstep. I'm not going to turn this place into a charity.'

'I'm not asking you to. I'm simply asking you to let me adopt him and bring him up properly.'

'It wouldn't work.'

'I'll make it work.'

'You would spoil him. He's already twisting you around his little finger, though how on earth he does it I don't know. Or even why.'

'That's not true, and you know it. I'm thinking of the boy.'

'All right, then. I have a suggestion.' Jack pointed his spectacles at her which was usually intended to intimidate her. 'Will you do what I tell you?'

Grace hesitated and said for the first time in their married life, 'I'm not sure, Jack. But what are you saying?'

'Will you go and talk to Betty Arbuckle and see if you can persuade her to adopt Spit instead of sending him off to that home in Bendigo?'

'I'll do no such thing,' Grace said angrily. 'Betty Arbuckle is a very kind woman. She means well. But Spit is not for her. He would simply turn against her and become a criminal or run away or do something terrible.'

'And what makes you think you could do any better with him?'

'Because if I were a child I would sooner be our Sadie than Ben or Joannie Arbuckle.'

'Well I can tell you this, Grace. Betty Arbuckle is

not going to stand aside and let you adopt a Protestant boy like Spit MacPhee. She'll fight you tooth and nail.'

'Then I'll fight her tooth and nail. I've made up my mind, Jack, and I only wish you would too.'

'I have. And I say No.'

'I think you are wrong, and if I can adopt him I know that you'll change your mind.'

'Have you considered for a moment what his influence would be on Sadie?'

'Sadie is a very quiet girl. She doesn't make friends easily because she is too quiet. But she likes Spit and I know he would always look after her, so I'm not worried about that. I didn't tell you before but he taught her to swim, which I thought was a good thing, living so near the river.'

'He what?'

'He taught her to swim.'

'Why, for God's sake, didn't you tell me?' Jack said angrily and yet helplessly.

'Because you would have stopped her.'

'I give up,' Jack Tree said in exasperation. 'Do what you like, but don't expect any help from me.'

Grace Tree stood quietly for a moment, troubled that she should be so determined about something which affected her husband as profoundly as it was affecting her, perhaps more so. If he wanted a son, which he couldn't have from her, he obviously didn't want Spit as a substitute. Yet she was sure he would change his mind if she succeeded in adopting Spit. And, falling back on her old habit of silence, she left him to his work, although this time her silence was not an admission but rather a denial of his authority, which surprised and troubled her as much as it did her husband.

15

Grace was not sure how to go about it, but she put on a print frock and a straw hat and went back to Pat Stillman at the Shire Office. She had no way of going about it except the simplest and the most direct.

'Pat,' she said. 'I want to adopt Spit MacPhee, so how do I go about it?'

Pat tried not to interfere in anybody's life, even his wife's, but because of his round-peg-in-a-square-hole joke about himself he had the reputation of being a soft and helpless man. In fact he knew and liked his job and did it well.

'Hang on a bit, Grace,' he said. 'I wasn't serious yesterday when I said you might take him on yourself.'

'That's all right,' Grace Tree said. 'But I'm serious now so how is it done?'

Pat became thoughtful; and here in his small dark office behind the Shire Hall he was less inclined to laugh at everything because he was safe here.

'Well, I'm not too sure, but I'll look it up for you and find out all I can. But are you really sure about it?'

'Yes.'

'What does Jack say?'

'He said I could do what I liked, although he wouldn't help me.' She knew that was not quite the whole truth but she was not going to open up any little doors to her private life for Pat Stillman or anyone else.

'Hmmmm … Hmmm … But did you stop to think that you are a Catholic and Spit's a Protestant, and you know what it's like in this town. The Protestants won't like it.' Pat was a Catholic himself so he was talking within the family.

'They may not like it but all they want to do is send him off to a home in Bendigo and that's wrong. Anyway I don't think they all want to get rid of Spit like that. I know Dorothy Evans wouldn't think like that, and plenty of other Protestants. But I'll face that when I have to. What happens first?'

Pat laughed. 'Good on you, Grace,' he said. 'I'll do what I can. But I'll bet that first of all there'll be a lot of forms. You can bet your life on that. But I'll look into it and let you know.'

'Thanks, Pat,' Grace said and stood up because she knew there was nothing else she could do here.

'One thing,' Pat said as she waited for a moment. 'If I were you I wouldn't tell anyone what you are doing. Not until you have to, because the further along you are before they start getting worried, the better.'

'I have no intention of telling anyone at all,' Grace said.

'Not even Spit himself,' Pat told her.

'I wasn't going to do that either. I'm not going to build up his hopes.'

'You're full of surprises,' Pat said slyly as she left. 'But watch out for the dingoes, Grace,' he called after her. 'They're always looking for lost strays like young Spit MacPhee.'

She wasn't sure what he meant by that, but she guessed that he was warning her to trust nobody but her fellow Roman Catholics. But what she first had to contend with, as she waited out the weeks for her intentions to reach some sort of shape, was Spit himself. She discovered that Spit was not a girl, and though it was an obvious realisation, nonetheless it was the one she had to deal with first. She and Sadie had always been very close, and without having to think about it she could pull things on and off Sadie, walk in and out of her room at any time, put her in a bath, push her into bed, plait her hair, touch her and tell her or discuss with her what she ought to do, or ought not to do.

But she discovered that she was shy with Spit, which surprised her. Why should an eleven-year-old boy make her self-conscious? She did her best not to let it show. But trying to fit a ready-made Spit into a ready-made household that was quite unprepared for him was more difficult than she had thought, particularly when there was nothing sure about his future. If it had been certain that she was going to be allowed to adopt him she could have started from scratch. But because there was still a shadow on him, still a likelihood that it wouldn't be possible and that he might be taken away from her, she felt unsure and limited in what she ought to start, or even what she could do for him at all.

All this too in the face of Jack's resistance and some from the town. When her idea of adopting Spit became known in the town she felt rather than heard the opposition of those who thought it wrong for a Protestant boy to be adopted by a Catholic family when there was a perfectly good Protestant home waiting for him elsewhere, even if it was an orphanage. And, to add conviction to this sort of opposition, she knew, as every Australian knew, that there had always been certain rules to the sometimes savage game which both sides played with their religion.

But she refused to think of Spit's adoption as a religious battle. A Catholic orphanage to Grace was no better than a Protestant one; it could even be worse. This was true also of her opposition to Betty Arbuckle. It was not because Betty was a Protestant, but rather her ideas on restraint and abnegation, and her passionate method of conciliating her God by de-naturing herself and all those around her. To Grace it was simply wrong, particularly for Spit.

So whichever way she looked at it, Catholic or Protestant, Grace knew that none of it would benefit Spit if it became an issue of religion. What surprised her, as her intention became known in the town, was not the obvious degree of hostility to it but the support she got from women whom she hardly knew, including Protestants among them. When she met women in the street like Mrs Finch, the Stock and Station Agent's wife, who was a good Methodist but who had never spoken to Grace before and Mrs Finch said, 'I hope you can save young Spit MacPhee from that awful Bendigo home. It would be terrible if he had to end up there,' Grace felt that her isolation was not as serious as she thought it was. When other women, and even men like Mr Williams the draper said the same thing to her, she had a quiet woman's satisfaction in listening to them. But she had to be worried and unhappy about Jack because he refused to understand, and she knew he was even less likely to understand when he saw the long form that Pat Stillman had unearthed for her to fill in – the form that outlined the statutory and legal requirements which were going to make Spit's adoption far more complicated than she had imagined.

What finally disturbed her was a visit from Betty Arbuckle as she was cleaning a cod which Spit had caught that day. Grace had never curtailed Spit's life on the river, nor his fishing, nor even Sadie's companionship. But Jack had forbidden Sadie to go too near the water now that it was high, and he had ordered Spit in a soldier's voice not to take her any further up river than the boiler, so that when Betty Arbuckle came, unannounced, dressed in a long, dark, heavy frock and buckled shoes, Grace felt as if she was something of a libertine for allowing Spit and Sadie to be together on the river bank enjoying themselves. And she had to pay the price for Betty's radiance – for Betty's light and passionate eyes and for her almost ethereal beauty. Being a plain woman, Grace Tree couldn't help but admire and envy the face that God had given Betty Arbuckle, even though she disagreed with the spirit that went with it.

16

'Why didn't you come and tell me you were going to take the boy away from me?' Betty Arbuckle said in a hurt voice. 'You know you had no right to do that, Grace.'

Grace Tree felt defensive, but she told herself that she would have to do her best. She must somehow match this curious woman's childlike conviction which had always seemed impenetrable and inviolable. Grace remembered her as a girl at school, and she had been the same then as she was now, almost unchanged except in fulsomeness. 'I didn't take him away from you, Betty,' she said. 'Spit ran away on his own account.'

'But Frank told me that when they rescued him

from the river, you told him he was not to come back to me. You forbade him.'

'I did no such thing,' Grace Tree said, dropping the fish and the knife she was using, and standing up. She had been bent over the little table near the outside tap where she often peeled potatoes or cleaned fish. 'I did say he was not going back to your place and that he was not leaving here; but that's what I told those men who were dragging him naked by the scruff of the neck. All I told Spit was that he could do what he liked. And he chose to stay here. So please don't come here accusing me, Betty. You are wrong.'

'I'm not accusing you,' Betty said. 'But you know that I have always been worried about the boy, and for years I have been trying to help him. It was only his grandfather who made it difficult. Now we have a home for him in Bendigo, and I think you are wrong to interfere. You mustn't try to keep him. It is best for him if he is properly looked after in a proper place, instead of running around like a poor, unfortunate, barefoot, African heathen.'

'That is what I think too,' Grace Tree said. 'But I don't want him to go to a Boys Home in Bendigo. I don't think that's the best thing for him and I won't let you send him there.'

'But everybody knows that your husband doesn't

want him,' Betty insisted. 'So he won't be happy here. He would only turn bad. He needs all the things that will help with his own salvation.'

'Don't worry about that,' Grace Tree said. 'Jack will change his mind.'

'But Spit's one of us, Grace. He's not one of yours.'

'I don't think Spit is one of anybody's at the moment.'

'But you'll try to convert him, you always do.'

Grace was still determined not to get Spit mixed up in a religious quarrel and she said, 'Does it matter what religion he is, Betty, as long as he has a good home?'

'But that's what a good home is. There's a terrible difference between us. The Lord Jesus is not ...'

'Stop,' Grace said. 'Stop it, Betty.'

Betty Arbuckle and Grace Tree had been standing face to face in the sun, and for Grace it was a disturbing experience. Like most people in the town she had always, since childhood, considered Betty a bit of a crank, if only because Betty herself made such a point of elaborating her evangelism into a punishing oddity. But standing close to Betty, watching her face as it advertised her feelings, and looking into her crystal clear eyes, Grace knew that Betty was a naturally innocent woman who longed for the rest of the world to be innocent with her. Or, failing that, to be made innocent through salvation. And, in her passion for Spit's future, Betty was also sure that what she wanted for Spit was his real welfare and his real salvation, so that without knowing why, Grace said to herself in a puzzled, incredulous way: 'What a terrible pity. She would have made such a marvellous nun.' But, dealing here with the subject of a barefoot boy, Grace knew that Betty's innocence and passion and conviction were very down-to-earth, and she would probably be unbeatable if she went ahead with her plans for Spit to end up in a Boys Home in Bendigo.

'I can't let you do it, Grace,' Betty was saying to her, and Betty was now at her most obdurate. 'I can't let you interfere.' And after a brief search into each other's souls over a Murray cod, Grace knew now for sure that she was facing a real opponent who would fight her to the end.

Picking up the half-gutted fish she said, 'You think I am wrong, Betty, and I think that you are wrong. But I have to do what I think is right. I know that Spit is better off with me, and I am not going to let him go to any home in Bendigo. That would be cruel.'

'Then I'll have to make you give him up,' Betty said in her soft voice. 'You're a good woman, Grace, but your faith is in your priests and your Pope. Our faith is in salvation, and I'm surprised that you don't understand the difference. A boy saved for us becomes a vessel of the Lord, and Spit can only be saved if he is taken to the right place and taught the right lessons and given a chance to save himself.'

Betty Arbuckle turned to leave, but Grace followed her to the gate, feeling rather like a disciple in the steps of the Master. 'I don't think it is salvation that Spit needs,' she said to Betty, 'but a decent home, which is what I thought of giving him.'

'I'm sorry,' Betty said, upset now by Grace Tree's unusual stubbornness, 'but you have no right to do this to the boy. I shall pray for you to give him up, because I am sure that right is on my side. And I am sure that the law is on my side too.'

As she watched Betty walk away like a heavenly body up the slope, Grace was not so much afraid of her influence with the Lord as she was of Betty's secular determination to use even the law if necessary. She knew that Betty would go to almost any lengths to do what she thought was right for Spit, and that meant the Boys Home in Bendigo rather than a Catholic family in St Helen.

'We'll just have to see,' Grace said to herself and went back to cleaning the fish which was one of Spit's silent offerings to the house he now lived in.

17

Filling out the form that Pat Stillman had given her
Grace did her best with the obvious questions about
her and Jack's age, family, financial condition, social
background, and religion (both their own and Spit's).
They were the sort of questions she hated answering,
and she knew that Jack would hate them too. Yet she
was sure that when the time came she would get Jack's
signature on the form. In fact she had to get it because
the adoption application had to come from Jack as
head of the family, rather than from Grace as the wife.

What made difficulties for her were the questions that needed permission of the natural parents,
because the form assumed that adoption was mostly

concerned with unwanted babies, rather than eleven-year-old orphans. Or, if the parents were both dead, she needed a signed release from the nearest relatives. Without that the form was invalid, which meant that her only recourse to the information she needed in order to write 'no surviving relatives' would have to be Spit himself. She could remember the fuss about Spit being left alone with his grandfather when his mother had come and gone so quickly and tragically, but it was only a hazy memory of casual rumours. She remembered Dorothy Evans telling her that there were no other relatives left. So Spit himself would have to be asked.

The trouble was that she didn't know how she could do it. Spit was still a problem, and she didn't want to open up his silent wounds. He had kept his word not to run away again, but she knew that he was being cautious with her, although she understood why. Even in her house he was in a sort of limbo. Sleeping on the verandah he was not quite in the house and at the same time not quite out of it. In studying him so that she could know how best to deal with him she had slowly unravelled some of his private rules for himself, which made Grace almost as cautious with him as he was with her.

Her first duty had been to clothe him, because he

187

had come to her with nothing more than a pair of torn trousers and a shirt. She had discovered that he usually slept in an old shirt, so she had cut down one of Jack's rejects for him. She had been a little nervous about giving it to him as a first offering, but Spit had taken if off-handedly without any fuss. She had then bought some cotton lengths and run him up two new shirts on her Singer, which he had also accepted with his own sort of pride, but without demur. Her trial attempts at making up trousers with an old sheet had defeated her, so she had bought him one pair of khaki shorts and also a grey woollen pair because school was about to start. She had taken him to Williams the draper, and bought him socks, sandals and a school cap which, on his thick, fair hair was a lost cause.

Grace's only way of coping with his impersonal acceptance of her practical gesture was to repeat to herself a simple sentence that covered everything that Spit did: 'He's a strange boy.' But she also knew that his years of self-sufficiency and his loud and childish equality with his tortured grandfather had made him more than just a tough little boy who should be treated as one. Whenever he did any service about the house it was not in gratitude to her, nor even a favour, but was an unthinking contribution to what had to be done. He chopped the wood for her, which saved Jack a daily chore. She had watched him swinging an axe which seemed to miss his bare feet by inches, but though she had winced and turned away at the prospect of a miss, nonetheless she knew that he wouldn't miss and that she must let him do it. When he helped Sadie with the dishes, his tendency to clatter and treat the cups and saucers roughly bothered her, but she said nothing. He watered the garden for her, but unlike Jack, who was economical with water, Spit lavished it on everything in sight. He would walk – never run – up the slope to the shops if she wanted thread or an extra pint of milk or bread, and in this too he was neither willing nor unwilling. He simply did it, and when Sadie went with him it gave her a deep sense of satisfaction to see them go up the slope together without any thought now of being anything but a natural brother and sister. That was when she felt most deeply Jack's reluctance. Why couldn't Jack see it as she saw it?

Finally, she had discovered that, apart from the thick grime-ingrained soles of his bare feet (his sandals would be only for school), he was a very clean boy, although she had to persuade him to use the inside bathroom rather than the outside tap.

'Where did you wash when you were living in the boiler?' she had asked him.

'Outside,' he had told her.

Summer or winter (she discovered) Spit and his grandfather had used a basin of river water on a table outside, and Spit's idea of washing himself was to stand naked to the waist over a basin and, having soaped his face and neck, simply douse himself with a mug full of water. He wouldn't tell her how he did it below the waist, but she suspected something similar, and because there had been no chip-fed hot water heater in the boiler house, it had always been a cold douche. She let him go on doing it in his own way outside; but she persuaded him to finish his lower parts in the bathroom, although he insisted on locking the door.

What surprised her, although she knew she shouldn't have been surprised, was her discovery that he had no naughtiness in him. It was not because he was good. In his certainties he seemed incapable of being silly or childish, even in his childish behaviour, which was another aspect of his self-sufficiency. But he had his faults, and the one that she knew she would have endless trouble with at home was his loud voice and his often aggressive answers of one harsh word in reply to a simple question. She knew that it was the way he and his grandfather had always spoken to each other, but she was a quiet person herself and it bothered her. She tried to correct it by speaking to him in a softer voice than her normal soft voice. She hoped that this would persuade him to speak quietly. It didn't.

But these were annoyances rather than serious faults. What she had to deal with was a brand of wickedness which genuinely surprised her. One morning when he was chopping the wood and a hard lump of mallee root had split off and hit his shins, his instinctive response had been a long line of such bad language that it shocked her. It was not the casual and childish kind of schoolboy curse, but an adult and shameful list of the worst. She didn't say anything to him, but she asked Sadie as she sat on her bed that night, 'Have you ever heard Spit swearing?'

'Never,' Sadie said, shocked that her mother asked her such a question. 'He never swears.'

But Jack had also heard him swearing at the Evans' dog, and he had told Grace that he would have to teach Spit a severe lesson – which meant giving him a good hiding.

But Grace said, 'You're not going to touch him, Jack. It won't teach him anything. On the contrary, it would only make it worse.'

'That's a lot of tommy rot,' Jack Tree said. 'If you don't stop him now pretty soon he'll be using the same language in this house and I won't have that. I won't have it, Grace, so don't start protecting him.'

Grace had not told her husband that she too had heard Spit in full flow, and she knew that she would have to do something about it. 'I'll talk to him,' she said.

They were waiting for Sadie and Spit to come in for lunch. Sadie had been to her piano lesson, and Spit had been trying to sell what was probably the last catch of the season to the houses along the railway line.

'You can't treat Spit the way you treat Sadie,' her husband said. 'He's a tough little beggar and he's not going to listen to kind words and a soft voice.'

'I'll talk to him anyway. And afterwards, if you do hear him swearing, you can beat him as much as you like. But you're not to touch him until I've told him not to do it.'

'How will you know whether he's swearing or not? You weren't there when he was telling off Tim Evans' kelpie in language a bullockie wouldn't use.'

'I'll take his word for it,' Grace said. 'And you'll have to sooner or later. You can't always mistrust him.'

'By God,' Jack Tree said angrily. 'I wish I'd been given some of this treatment when I was a kid.'

Grace smiled at her husband. 'Never mind,' she said. 'Because now you have a chance to give it to somebody else.'

'Well I'm damned if I'm going to let you joke about

it,' Jack said. 'You're dead wrong, Grace, and that's all there is about it.'

Grace knew very well that she could be wrong, and what weakened her resolve was Jack's blank wall facing Spit's blank wall. As they ate their lunch of chops and potatoes and peas, she watched them both to see if she could detect even a glimmer of communication between them. Jack ignored Spit, and for his part Spit kept quiet throughout lunch, answering her questions or Sadie's unusual chatter with loud monosyllables. Grace knew he wasn't going to give anything back to Jack, neither a friendly word nor a whole sentence that Jack might use against him. Listening to his stiff, childish, serious voice in its bold disguise (the only way Spit knew how to talk), Grace knew how difficult it was going to be to break him down – with Jack or without Jack.

'He's still expecting to be tricked in some way,' Grace decided, and after lunch when she organised Sadie to hunt for all the empty jam jars so that they could make some mixed pickles, she took Spit into the garden to help her pick the last of the green tomatoes on the dried up plants, and she asked him why he didn't like Jack.

'He's all right,' Spit said in his untouchable way. 'I like him all right.'

193

'Why don't you talk to him?' she asked.

'He doesn't talk to me much,' Spit said, busy with the tomatoes, deeply involved in what he was doing as he always seemed to be in anything he did.

'Well, try and talk to him, Spit, because we're going to need his help soon.'

Spit didn't ask her why they would need Jack's help, and again she was aware of his suspicion and his childish caution. But she still had to settle the problem of his swearing. 'Why do you swear, Spit?' she said to him.

Spit looked up in surprise. 'What makes you think I swear?' he said.

'I heard you swearing like a trooper the other day when you were chopping wood.'

Spit didn't like that. 'I only swear to myself,' he said. 'I don't go around swearing.'

'Do you know what the words mean?' she asked him.

'They don't mean anything.'

'Oh, but they do mean something. And it's better that you don't know what they mean. So please, Spit, don't swear any more. Even when you think nobody is listening. Jack heard you, and the more you do it the more careless you'll be with it, and I don't want Sadie to hear that kind of language.'

'I don't swear in front of Sadie. She didn't say so, did she?'

'No, she said you didn't. But don't swear at all. That's what I want you to promise. And you'll have to keep your promise because we're going to have a lot of trouble if you don't.'

'All right,' Spit said, concentrating on the tomatoes. 'I'll stop swearing.'

'That means you don't swear at all, even when you're alone. No swearing. Not the way you swear.'

Spit could be obliging and he said, 'Don't worry. I'm not going to hurt anybody.'

Grace was not quite sure what that meant but she accepted it as a promise. Encouraged now by this strange companionship she always felt for him, she asked him if he had any relatives left.

'Anyone anywhere?' she added. 'Did your grandfather ever mention any?'

'I had an uncle once,' he said, 'but he didn't last long. He got killed a long time ago.'

'Was that the only relation you had?'

'Except for my mother and my grandfather.'

'Do you remember your mother?' Grace asked him, on her knees in the tomato patch but more interested in Spit than in the green tomatoes.

Spit was watching her now. 'My mother got burnt in a fire,' he told her.

'Yes, I know. That was so sad.' Grace hesitated, still not sure what to say to him. But then she made up her mind.

'You know, Spit, that I'm trying to adopt you?'

'Yes. I know,' he said.

'You know? How did you know?'

'Mrs Evans told me, and a lot of other people asked me. A lot of people. Jack Ellison asked me yesterday.'

'Then why on earth didn't you come and ask me if it was true or not?'

'I don't know,' Spit said. 'I thought it might be another trick.'

'I wouldn't trick you. Don't you know that?'

'I didn't mean you. I meant them.'

'Who?'

'I don't know. I don't know … It's no good asking me … It's Mrs Arbuckle and all the others. They'll trick me again if they get a chance.'

'I don't think they want to trick you,' Grace said to him. 'They want to do what they think is best for you, and that's why I'm trying to adopt you. I wasn't going to tell you because I didn't want you to think I had worked it all out. I haven't. I have to get Jack's signature on the paper, then I have to take it to the

Shire Office. But I can't do anything at all without Jack, which is why I wanted you to get on with him a bit better.'

Spit was silent. She did not expect any gratitude from him because she knew where his attitude came from; she knew that years ago he had been forced to acquire a childish skin of stoicism so that he could cope with his grandfather, and at the same time help him to survive as a boy. But she suspected that he was secretly frightened now, aware that he was a wisp of nothing, and that his only defence against everybody else's plans for him was to keep himself to himself. There was nothing else he could do.

'Jack doesn't like me much,' he said dispassion-ately.

'It's not that,' she said unhappily. 'Jack's a kind man, Spit, but he's a bit rigid, and he doesn't like things to disturb his life. Sadie and I learned that a long time ago. But when he sees something is right he'll stick by it. And sooner or later he'll see that we are right, don't worry.'

'All right,' Spit said, and once again Grace knew that he had gone as far as he could.

But that night when Grace sat down at the kitchen table, just before sunset, and carefully opened up the adoption form to write into it that Spit had no living relatives, she knew she was about to change the light and shadow of her own life, and she half-wished that when she handed in the form tomorrow that nothing would come of it. She was frightened of what she was undertaking. Until now she had never felt lonely or separated from Jack. On the contrary, she had always been satisfied with his set of rules for Sadie and herself. She had thought of them as no more than the ministry of a rather stiff man who was trying to order life decently, knowing that he was married to a very quiet woman who had no rules of her own except a desire to live from day to day without harshness or conflict. She had always been satisfied with the kind of protection and care that Jack gave her with his certainty that he knew best.

But now, for Spit's sake, she was undoing the pattern of it.

'I hope to God I'm doing the right thing,' she said because she now had to get Jack's signature on the adoption form, and how was she going to manage that?

Grace had no guile, she was incapable of scheming, particularly against her husband, so that when she decided to use Sadie she was not thinking up a quiet little plot of her own. She was trying to influence Jack, she told herself, the only way she knew how. As she waited for Sadie and Spit to come back from the railway station with the two boxes of laboratory test phials that Jack had sent them for, she looked around at her home and knew how valuable it was, and how safe and secure it had always been. Even the mustardy smell of it at the moment made the point.

18

Grace had spent the afternoon preparing and boiling the marrow, cauliflower, cucumber, tomatoes and onions for the mixed pickles she made every year for Jack. Sadie had helped to wash and cut and salt the vegetables, and Spit had fed the fire and scattered the peel and skins to the hens, and then stirred the mixture of mustard and vinegar as she poured the vegetables into the big copper kettle. Now the sideboard was packed with twelve jars of mustardy pickles, and the kitchen was still heavy with the air of pickling which Jack always liked. When he came in after six o'clock and said, 'I could smell those pickles halfway to Nooah,' she was pleased, because they needed that reminder of their old peace and security, even in the smell of cauliflower and tomatoes and onions and mustard and sugar and spiced vinegar.

But the evening meal was not familiar, nor was it relaxed, and she was glad when it was over, when Sadie and Spit were helping her with the dishes and Jack was at his roll-top desk. It was quiet and dark outside, and it was only a matter of waiting now for the right moment to send Sadie in to her father. Grace was on the point of doing it when the Evans' dog began to bark, and because she knew how that dog annoyed Jack she decided to wait. It was a persistent and worried dog, and the barking went on long enough for Spit to say, 'What does he think he's barking at?'

'It's not you this time,' Sadie said.

'Maybe he knows I'm in your kitchen,' Spit said.

'He's not that good,' Sadie told him, and they heard someone at the back door calling out in a loud whisper, 'Spit, are you there? Spit, can you hear me?'

'Who on earth is that?' Grace said.

'I don't know,' Spit said and went around the table to the back door, with Sadie and Grace at his elbow. When they looked into the darkness all they could see was a small figure with a cart.

'It's me, Ben Arbuckle.'

Ben's defiant whisper suggested a father and mother ready and waiting in the shadows to catch him. 'I brought your things back, Spit. I've got them in the cart.'

Spit had been missing his cart and the small store of family possessions he had left under the Arbuckles' house. He had thought once or twice of going back in the middle of the night to get them, but he had decided against it because Mrs Arbuckle might be waiting to catch him, using the cart and his grandfather's things as bait.

'Come in, Ben,' Grace said to him. 'Don't stand out there in the dark.'

'Well … I don't know, Mrs Tree,' Ben said.

But Grace insisted. 'Come on in,' she said, and went down the steps to take Ben by the arm and bring him into the kitchen.

The usually neat Ben was in a mess. He had no boots on, his smock and trousers were dirty, and his legs and arms and face were smeared with the mallee dust the town was built on. Spit knew why he was dirty. Ben had obviously crawled under the house in the dark to get the bits and pieces of his grandfather's things.

'You haven't got your boots on,' Sadie told him, pointing to his bare feet.

202

'No,' Ben said. 'I threw them in the river.'

Spit laughed, but it was Grace who noticed that Ben's dirty face was smeared and streaked as if he had been crying, and she asked him if his mother knew that he was here.

'No, and I'm not going to tell her,' Ben said.

'Do you want a piece of cake?' Grace asked him.

'I'm not allowed,' Ben said, but then changed his mind. 'All right,' he said, and he turned to Spit and told him that he had borrowed his cart a couple of times. 'But I've got some wheels of my own.'

'Where did you get them from?' Spit asked him.

'From Billy Cotsman. I've hidden them under the house.'

'What about an axle?' Spit said as Ben bit into the cake Grace had given him. 'They're not going to be any good without an axle.'

'Billy didn't have one, but I'll get one somewhere.'

'All you have to do is get the fruit box and the axle,' Spit said. 'But if you want me to help you build it you'll have to get the stuff down to the old boiler yourself. I'm not going up to your place.'

'All right,' Ben said, and with his mouth full of cake he backed out as if his defiance was rapidly running out. Grace saw what was happening to him and hurried after him, catching him by the arm before

203

he could run off. 'Are you sure your mother doesn't know you came down here?' she said to him. 'Is that why you've been crying?'

'She doesn't know anything,' Ben said. 'I got into trouble for throwing my boots in the river.'

'What did you do that for?' Grace said.

'Well ...' But Ben's defiance was now exhausted. And shouting, 'S'long Spit,' he was off on his bare feet, not to the gate but to the nearest part of the fence which he scrambled over as a last gesture of resistance to good order.

'Poor old Ben,' Spit said.

'What do you think he's up to?' Sadie asked. 'Why would he throw his boots away?'

'I don't know,' Spit said. 'But it's not his fault. He can't help it.'

'That's why Tim Evans' dog barked,' Sadie said as they went inside.

'What do you mean?'

'He thought it was you with the cart.'

Spit was delighted. 'Well I fooled him that time, didn't I?' he said.

Grace listened, and when they were in the kitchen she sent Spit to check the front gate in case Ben had left it open when he brought the cart in. 'Otherwise the dogs will get in,' she said.

Alone in the kitchen with Sadie she gave her the adoption form and said, 'This is what I had to fill in so that we can adopt Spit, so take it in to your father and ask him to sign it.'

Sadie knew about the adoption. She knew about the tension it had caused between her mother and father, but mother and daughter were so close that they both knew what had to be done, so she took the form in to her father.

When Spit came back Grace, who was tense now and nervous, sat him down at the kitchen table and asked him if he had a birth certificate somewhere. 'Because,' she said, 'I think I'll need that too.'

Spit shook his head. 'I never saw one,' he told her.

'Do you know where you were born?'

'In White Hills near Bendigo,' Spit said.

'Then I suppose I'll have to get your certificate from Bendigo,' Grace said, not quite sure that what she was saying really mattered. She was simply talking in order to talk while she waited for Sadie to return.

Sadie, standing behind her father at his desk, had hesitated to interrupt him. He disliked being interrupted when he was filling in the long yellow form of stock lists, or the weigh bills of the summer's wool clip shipped out of the town. But Jack looked up at his quiet daughter and felt for a moment the affection that always touched him when he was aware, as now, of Sadie's natural and delicate shyness. He took off his spectacles.

'All right,' he said. 'It must be something you want badly, so what's up?'

Sadie was about to say that her mother wanted him to sign the form, but she changed her mind and said, 'I just wanted you to sign this form about Spit. That's all.'

'What form?'

'So that we can adopt him.'

'Did your mother put you up to this?'

Sadie shook her head. 'No, it's me. I want us to adopt Spit so he can stay with us. It's my own idea as much as Mum's.'

'It's an idea I don't think much of, Sadie, and your mother knows it.'

'But it won't hurt you,' Sadie said.

'Do you know what it means if we adopt Spit?' he asked her.

'Yes. He'll have to live here with us all the time. I know that,' she said.

'That's not even the half of it,' Jack said. 'We'll have to bring him up like a son. We'll have to be responsible for him, no matter what he does ...'

'He won't do anything wrong, Dad. Not if he can help it.'

'Even if he doesn't, your mother will have to look after him all the time. Did you think of that?'

Sadie could keep very still and she was very still now. 'She won't mind. She likes him.'

'And you'll have to live with him every day. If you up and decide one day you don't like him any more you won't be able to send him packing off to Bendigo. Once I sign that paper Spit becomes as important to me as you are. Do you want that, Sadie?'

Sadie, like her mother, knew that she had to stand her ground. 'Yes,' she said. 'If you don't mind, I don't.'

'You want me to treat him like a son?'

Sadie compressed her lips, but this time all she could manage was a vigorous nod.

'Well I'm damned if I know any more,' Jack said in despair. 'I don't know what you see in him.'

Sadie, finding her courage again, said, 'Spit has never hurt anybody, and he never will.'

Jack was trying not to be impatient with Sadie but he laughed his dry, impatient, military laugh. 'I'll bet he's had more fights in your school than any other boy his age,' he said.

'Spit only fights when they say something about his grandfather. Everybody likes him. And he knows how to do everything.'

Jack's response was a surprise even to himself. He

207

did not snatch the form from her hand and tear it up, which is what he wanted to do. Angry with Sadie's resistance and angry with Grace, he wanted to make a punishing remark to his daughter, one that he knew would get a submissive reply. 'So what do you think you're going to do young lady,' he said, 'if I refuse to sign that form? What will you do then?'

Sadie, facing defeat, was silent for a moment. 'Nothing,' she said. 'I couldn't do anything, could I?'

Jack knew that he had won his private little contest but, looking at his daughter's calm face which was trying to give nothing away, he knew that her eyes (uncontrollably wet), and her lips grimly (for her) compressed were an argument and a conviction that he could not face up to any more. It was too much.

'All right. All right,' he said. 'Give me the form.'

Taking it from her he turned it over, found the place where he had to sign, dipped the pen, scrawled his signature and gave it back to her.

'Give it to your mother,' he said.

Sadie was so surprised that she simply took the form. Uneducated in gestures and untaught in affection she said, 'Thanks, Dad,' and feeling very sorry for her father she took the signed form in to her mother in the kitchen.

19

Grace was not sure what should happen next but she
was surprised when she gave the form to Pat Stillman
at the Shire Office only to have him hand it back
to her.

'You'll have to take it to the county court office,'
he told her.

'What on earth for?' she asked him.

'Because it's the court that will decide if you are a
fit and proper person to adopt and care for that poor
little orphan, Master Spit MacPhee.'

Grace wished Pat wouldn't joke about it because
suddenly it was irritating. 'Why didn't you tell me that
before?' she said to him.

'Because I didn't know. We've never had a legal adoption in this town before, and it was only when I wondered myself what happened next that I found out. I got that form from Henry Fennel at the county court, he's the clerk of the court, and even he didn't know. But then he found out, and so I found out, and now you've found out, and pretty soon everybody else will find out.'

'You mean it will have to be some sort of court case?'

Pat shrugged. 'All I know is that you've got to go before a county court judge, and he will take everything into consideration,' he said in a sepulchral voice. 'That's what Henry says.'

In love with his stuffed office, lovingly in command of his square pigeon holes that told him how much water was used in the town, how much the roads and footpaths cost to repair and what were the regulations about drains and fires, Pat was smiling at Grace because he couldn't help it, even though he was sorry for what he was about to report to her. 'There's now another little fly in your ointment, Grace. Betty Arbuckle is doing exactly what you're doing.'

'What do you mean?'

'She wants to adopt Spit herself. She was here yesterday asking for one of these forms, and she wanted to know if you had already made an application.'

Grace had always known that Betty Arbuckle would do something drastic, but she had not expected Betty to put in a rival claim for adoption. It shocked her. It was all right for Betty to think of Spit as an orphan in need of the care and protection of her evangelical Boys Home, but Grace thought it cruelly personal and wrong for Betty to want to adopt Spit herself.

'Why would she want such a thing?' Grace said. 'She knows that Spit ran away from her, and I'm sure she doesn't really want him.'

'She wants to save his soul,' Pat said with a laugh.

'Don't laugh, Pat. It's serious. Spit would hate living with Betty in that house. He would only run away again if she tried to make him stay with her. He'd never stay.'

'Are you sure that your little switch-ditcher would stick it out with you, Grace? He's a wild kid.'

'He's not wild, Pat. He's had to look after himself, and it's made him a strange little boy, but he's certainly not wild. I know that much about him.'

'Well, he certainly seems to have dug himself under your thin skin, and now that he's getting himself between Betty Arbuckle's teeth God help the both of you.'

'Spit's all right,' Grace insisted firmly, 'and I don't

know now what I'd do if they took him away from me, Pat. That's how I feel about it.' Grace was surprised that she could say such a thing to Pat Stillman who was no more than an old acquaintance from school. But she needed to talk to someone about it.

'What do you think I should do now?' she said, appealing for help even though she knew that he couldn't give it.

'Take that form to Henry Fennel down at the court house and he'll tell you what to do with it.'

'Henry's a Protestant, isn't he?'

'Yes, but he's pretty dinkum, old Henry.'

'But that means Betty will have the advantage, won't she?'

'I don't know, Grace. Anyway it won't be Henry Fennel who decides it. It'll be Judge Laker.' Pat still had the form in his hand, and he turned it over and glanced at Jack's signature. 'You didn't forge it did you?' he said teasingly.

'Of course not.'

Pat laughed. 'Then you must have hit him on the head with a sledge hammer,' he said. 'Knowing Jack ...' he added.

'I didn't think it was going to be so complicated,' Grace said, taking the form.

'That's because you think life's a bowl of cherries,'

Pat said, 'whereas it's really a whacking big basket of unbreakable monkey nuts.'

'Thanks anyway,' Grace said and left him in his square pigeon holes, escaping the smell of his carbon paper and cigarettes and the mallee dust and the onions that Pat seemed to eat raw, even for breakfast.

She knew Henry Fennel by sight and she couldn't imagine him giving her much help. He was a short, tight, springy man with eyes that told you not to treat him in any way but seriously. Gingery, with a small moustache and rimmed pince-nez spectacles, he seemed to Grace to be a friendless sort of man. She remembered him as a boy, several classes ahead of her at school, who didn't seem to want friends and didn't have a nickname, so that when she knocked at the door of his little office and he shouted, 'Come in,' she was already sure that he would dismiss her in some way if he could.

'Hello Henry,' she said nervously.

Henry Fennel's serious eyes behind his spectacles flashed their serious warning. 'Hello, Grace,' he said.

Grace looked around her and knew that Henry, as the clerk of the court, was a very square peg in a very square hole. Everything here was in order: rows of curious files tied with blue tape, a neat desk with neat papers on it, a bookshelf with large green books that seemed fitted to size. She decided that she must not waste this man's time; or rather she must not give him the impression that she was wasting his time. She came straight to the point.

'I've come to give you this form,' she said. 'Pat Stillman told me this was the place.'

He took it without comment, spread it carefully on his desk after moving aside the papers he had been working on and, with a sharp pencil in his hand, he checked one by one the questions and answers. When he came to Jack's signature he looked up.

'You should have printed your husband's names under his signature,' he said.

'Oh, I'm sorry.'

'Does Jack have a middle name?'

'Yes. Edward.'

'All right,' Henry said. 'I'll print it in for you.' And with a clipped almost bouncy action he took pen to paper and printed Jack's full name under his signature. 'You want it dated today?' he asked.

'I suppose so,' Grace said.

He added the date and looked up. Grace waited, but he said nothing more.

'Is that all I have to do?' she asked.

'You'll have to be present when the application is considered by the county court. But we'll call on you when we know the date and time.'

214

Grace hesitated. 'I know that Betty Arbuckle has made an application …' she began.

'I can't say anything about that,' Henry interrupted in his clipped voice.

'I don't want you to,' Grace went on quickly. 'All I want to know is if they'll stop me adopting Spit because of my religion.'

Henry looked at her without saying anything, and Grace knew then that in the cold blood of his honesty he would give her a fair chance.

'I know you're a Protestant …' Grace began.

'That's got nothing to do with it,' Henry said sharply.

'I know that, Henry. But you know that I'm a Catholic and Spit is a Protestant, so can't you tell me if that's going to make it impossible?'

Again Henry hesitated. 'I don't know. But religion does count. It always counts. And in a case like this it could be decisive. So if I were you, Grace, I'd get some legal help.'

'How?' Grace asked. 'What sort of legal help?'

'You'll need someone to argue your case if you hope to have even half a chance,' Henry said slowly. 'So I would advise you to get a barrister – a lawyer – to appear for you.'

'A lawyer? But that would cost money, wouldn't it?'

'Certainly.'

'How much money?'

'That depends on the man, and the sort of arguments he'll have to prepare.'

'I see ...' Grace said. 'But who on earth can I go to?'

Henry's cold eyes had never left her face, and Grace had stared back at him as if in their different shades of honesty they had found a direct route between them.

'That's not for me to say. It's not my business to advise you. But ... if I were you I would go and ask Edward Quayle if he would help you.'

'Mr Quayle? But he's a Protestant.'

'Nonetheless, if you want your case argued, and argued in your favour, he's the man I would go to in a situation like this.'

'But surely he hates Catholics. You know all about him and Lockie MacGibbon.'

'Never mind that. He's the one who might give you a chance. And I would get to him quick before someone else does.'

Grace looked back at those threatening eyes as if, in all these years, she had missed the value of the boy and the man behind them.

'All right, Henry,' she said. 'I'll do as you say.'

He returned the form. 'He'll need this,' he said,

and as she left he called after her, 'Whatever you do don't tell him I sent you.'

Wondering now if she should wait and consult Jack before she took another step, another plunge into what was becoming a multifarious mess, she walked slowly down the main street until she reached the little sign that said, *Edward Quayle. Barrister and Solicitor.*

She stopped for a moment but walked on past it, quarrelling with herself about the expense, about Jack, about the deepening complications she was getting into. It was the possible expense of it that she must decide on first. She was determined not to ask Jack for money, which meant that the fifty pounds which had been left her by her Aunt Cissie, which she kept in the Commonwealth Savings Bank, would have to pay for the lawyer. She wondered if that would be enough. And, as well, would she have to pay something to the court or the State for adopting Spit? Turning back, she went into Mr Quayle's office, having decided that if she began to question anything now she would probably give up the whole idea of adopting Spit.

In the first little office it was Tom Quayle, Edward Quayle's younger son, she saw. He was sitting at a tiny desk writing vigorously. Even in his penmanship Tom looked like an athletic boy who should be anywhere at all except in an office when the sun was shining outside.

'Hello Tom,' she said. 'I've come to see your father. Is he in?'

'Yes, he's in, Mrs Tree,' Tom said. 'But I think he's working on something. What's it about?'

'Well ...'

'It's all right. I work with my father,' Tom said.

Grace liked Tom, but he looked so young and out of place that she was reluctant to explain anything to him.

'All right,' he said, 'I'll see if my father is busy. You wait here.'

Grace waited while Tom went into another little room, and though she could hear voices she couldn't understand what they were saying until Tom put his head around the door and said, 'Come on in, Mrs Tree. Come in.'

What Grace found was another modest room, neatly but hopelessly over-stacked with files and books and papers so that there was little room left, even on the floor. She knew then that Edward Quayle – represented here by his office – was a man who cared little for anything extra to the law and order of his profession, so that he would not expect anything more than the bare information needed to get his work done.

'Good morning, Mrs Tree,' Edward Quayle said in his English voice, flinging his spectacles on his desk. 'Please sit down.' He pointed to a hard chair near his desk, and he swivelled his around to face her. 'Tom,' he said, 'if Mr Jackson comes in, tell him I shan't be a minute. Now,' he went on. 'What's on your mind, Mrs Tree?'

She handed him the adoption form. 'I want to adopt young Spit MacPhee,' she said, 'and here's the form I had to fill in. I've been told that it had to come up before a county court, and I think I'll need some help with it.'

'Why? Isn't it straightforward?'

'I don't know, Mr Quayle,' Grace said.

She waited while Mr Quayle looked at the application. He turned it over. 'It seems all right,' he said. 'Why would you need my help?'

'You see,' she said, realising now why Henry Fennel had sent her here: Edward Quayle was the same kind of man as Henry himself, except that he wasn't gingery. But he was red-faced. 'Somebody else is making an application to adopt him.'

'Ahhh ...'

'It's Mrs Betty Arbuckle.'

'I see.' Mr Quayle seemed to be making a quick summation of the problem. 'That does make it a little more complicated,' he said.

219

'Yes, and there's one other thing,' she went on.

'Yes?'

'I'm a Catholic and the boy is a Protestant. And Mrs Arbuckle is a Protestant too. That will make it difficult for me, won't it?'

Edward Quayle sighed, and later he would say to Grace that according to the Greeks a man usually sighed when he didn't want to feel the inevitability of pain. But obviously he understood. 'It will certainly make some difference,' he said, and before she could say anything further he held up his hand. 'In fact this may not be able to come to judgement at all. There may be some stipulation about it in the legislation on adoption – religion being what it is in this country. Particularly with a child. It's most likely, therefore, that a mutual religion will be a requirement for court consent, whatever else is concerned.'

'Even though it would be wrong for the boy to go to someone who happens to be a Protestant?'

'Right or wrong may not have anything to do with it, Mrs Tree. It's possibly a negative requirement you will have to face. That is, the boy simply may not go to you because you're Roman Catholic. But this doesn't mean that he will go automatically to someone else.'

'In other words he could even end up in the Boys Home in Bendigo.'

'Wait ... wait ...' Edward Quayle said. 'I don't know yet what the law says about adoption, I am only warning you before you go any further that you could be disqualified from the outset.'

'That wouldn't be fair,' Grace said.

'It may not even be the case,' Edward Quayle told her, 'but you asked me about the possibility of religion being important, and I am simply warning you in answer that it may be decisive. I cannot say what it is in law until I've looked into it. And if you want me to look into it I'll do what I can. Although I am rather busy at the moment.'

'I'm worried that Betty Arbuckle will get her application in before mine, and that she will ...'

'Don't worry. If it can be argued before the court I'll see that your application is there. But I'll have to look into it, and if I need any more information from you I'll send Tom down to get it.'

Grace stood up. She half closed her eyes and said what she had to say. 'Will it cost a lot of money, Mr Quayle?'

'Money? Well, it depends on what I have to do.'

'I've got fifty pounds of my own money.'

'It won't be that, Mrs Tree. It will never be that. Just let me look into it, and I'll tell you what your chances are, and what you have to do. But don't worry. It won't cost you a fortune.'

Relieved, Grace thanked him and went out through Tom's office, sorry now that she had not opened up more to Tom, who could at least have listened.

'It's about Spit MacPhee,' she said now to Tom as she stood by his desk for a moment. 'I want to adopt him.'

'I guessed it was that,' Tom said. 'And what does old Spit have to say about it, Mrs Tree?'

'Nothing much,' Grace said. 'I think he's as confused as I am.'

As she left Tom and walked out into the street she realised that she had forgotten that Edward Quayle was a Protestant, which seemed to prove Henry Fennel right. In any case she felt relieved that it was now in the hands of an expert, even though he was considered to be a bigoted sort of man, not always liked by many people in the town.

20

When the school year finally started, Spit felt like a
stranger to himself as he put on Grace's home-made
shirt, new grey trousers, grey socks and sandals.

'I'm sorry about the sandals, Spit,' Grace said to
him that first morning, 'but you'll have to wear shoes
and socks sooner or later, and you're too old now to
go to school barefoot. I think they'd send you home if
you turned up with no shoes on.'

'It's all right,' Spit said, looking down at his feet.
'I don't care about the sandals.'

What he *had* cared about was Grace Tree's
efforts to get the soles of his feet clean. She had made
him sit on a chair near the outside tap, and she had

scrubbed the soles of his feet with a hard brush. Spit had submitted to it in silence. But he wasn't used to anyone washing him or fussing over him, and though Mrs Tree didn't fuss he had almost enjoyed the experience of sitting there with his feet in her aproned lap, and that bothered him.

But it was only when he was on his way to school that he knew his old carefree life was coming to an end. It was the clothes and the shoes and the new school bag and the house he now lived in, and Sadie chattering at his side. Pressed, housed, fed and looked after – the Spit MacPhee who accepted Mrs Tree's care and attention was not the Spit MacPhee who was expecting to disappear again at any moment. And something else frightened him. On Sunday, at nine o'clock, Mrs Betty Arbuckle, with Ben at her side, knocked at the kitchen door and said to Grace, 'I've come to take Spit to church.'

Spit, who normally spent most Sunday mornings scouring the town for anything he could find to help him rebuild his workshop in the boiler (which he had been working on now for weeks), was not at that moment wandering around the town. He was making a kite out of old newspapers on the kitchen table, so that when he heard Betty Arbuckle he dropped the scissors he was using and said to Sadie, who was mixing a flour paste, 'I'm off ...'

'No, Spit,' Sadie said. 'Wait.'

'What for?' Spit said. 'She's after me again.'

'Don't worry,' Sadie whispered. 'My mother won't let her get near you.'

'She won't be able to stop her,' Spit said.

In fact Grace was trying to cope with her own surprise, opening the door and suddenly seeing Betty there. It always confused Grace, because Betty's beauty was forever a shock when it arrived on you like that, and Grace was speechless for a moment.

'Why on earth should you come here to take him to church?' Grace said when she had recovered.

'Because I want to be sure that you don't take him to Catholic mass.'

'What a thing to say,' Grace told her.

'Then he must come with me, Grace.'

'Why?'

'Because you haven't been sending him to church or to Sunday school, have you? And you know that is wrong.'

Grace as always felt at a disadvantage with Betty Arbuckle, and the best she could manage was an excuse. 'But Spit doesn't go to any church at all. He's never been to any church.'

'Then how can you expect him to grow up a good Christian if he doesn't go to church. It's wicked.'

Grace knew that Betty Arbuckle was right, and it was a dilemma she had been trying not to face. Sadie went to mass, not every Sunday, but often enough to justify her upbringing as a good Catholic. Grace herself and Jack were not very regular churchgoers, in fact Jack almost never went to church at all. They were, to that extent, pale Catholics but they were loyal ones nonetheless. In fact she had found it difficult even to encourage Spit to go to a Protestant church. It went against her Catholic grain, but here was Betty Arbuckle making a necessity of it. Grace needed a quick ally so she called Spit.

'What for?' Spit said to her.

'Just come here a moment,' Grace said. 'I want to ask you something.'

Spit, beside her, looked over the threshold of his safety at Betty Arbuckle who said to him, 'Spit, dear, I've come to take you to church.'

Spit was ready to take off but Grace stopped him.

'Did your grandfather ever send you to church, Spit?' she asked him before Betty could say anything more to him.

'No. Not me.'

'You have never been to any church, have you?'

Spit looked from Grace Tree to Betty Arbuckle and wondered what made them both so determined to

226

get him. 'I went to the Presbyterian church a couple of times,' he said slowly, 'when the Minister came down to get me, and when my grandfather didn't know what he was doing. But my grandfather didn't send me to church, and that's all I'm saying.'

'What your grandfather did wasn't your fault,' Betty Arbuckle told him. 'But now you are on your own and you'll grow up a heathen ignorant of the Lord if you don't go to church.'

'I'm not a heathen,' Spit said. 'I'm a Presbyterian.'

'Yes,' Grace said quickly, 'He's a Presbyterian. He doesn't belong to your church.'

'Then I'll take him to the Presbyterian Church,' Betty Arbuckle said. 'But he must go to church.'

'Not with you, Betty,' Grace said firmly.

Betty looked at Spit's Sunday bare feet. She neatened her small, black, straw hat which would have been an ugly mistake on anybody else, but surrounding Betty's face it became a perfect frame for her immaculate beauty. 'Spit,' she said firmly, 'you now have sandals to wear, I've seen you with them, so please go and put them on and I'll take you to church.'

They had all been so concentrated on each other that none of them had noticed Jack's presence. Joining them on the step he said to Betty, 'What do you think you're doing, Betty?'

'I've come to take Spit to church,' Betty said.

'You've come all the way down here knocking at our back door for that?' Jack said.

'Yes.'

'Listen, Bet,' Jack said grimly. 'You may think you can come down here and tell us what to do but you're way off the mark.'

'I'm not telling you what to do, Jack. I'm telling the boy. It's a sin …'

'The boy lives here, and if anybody is going to tell him what to do we'll do it ourselves. It's nothing to do with you.'

'But you'll never tell him to go to his own church. You know you won't.'

'Whether we send him to church or not it's got nothing to do with you.'

'I've brought Ben with me,' Betty said. 'He can go with Spit.'

Ben, booted and smocked, was now in the same arena as Spit. Why were they all so keen to get hold of Spit MacPhee? It was more than Spit's bare feet. He glanced at Sadie. She smiled at him. Spit smiled at nobody. He was out of it. He would do what he wanted to do, and Ben showed his admiration by saying boldly, 'What were you and Sadie making?'

Spit still had the scissors in his hand, Sadie's

pinafore was dusted with flour, and nothing could have given Ben such a feeling of hopeless envy and longing as much as scissors and flour on a Sunday morning.

'We were making a kite,' Spit said, 'but we haven't finished yet.'

'You shouldn't do that on the Lord's day,' Grace said to him.

Jack gave Spit and Sadie a little push and said to Grace, 'Go inside, all of you. I'll deal with this.' When they were inside they heard him say, 'Now don't waste your time, Betty. Go and preach the gospel somewhere else. But don't come here telling us how to be good Christians. You don't even know what Christianity is.'

Betty's 'Oh' was audible in the kitchen, and they heard her retreating down the steps and disappearing up the path.

Jack joined them in the kitchen and he stood still for a moment and looked at Grace as if she was little better than the children with her. 'I told you she would be after you,' he said, 'and you didn't listen.'

'I think she was just trying it on, Jack.'

'Well she's going to try a lot more on,' Jack told her. 'In fact she's asked J.C. Strapp to present her own application for adoption to the county court.'

'Who told you that?' Grace said, hardly believing it.

229

'Never mind,' he said. 'You've got Edward Quayle, and she's got J.C. Strapp. So you can guess who's going to win that battle.'

Edward Quayle was known in the town as the poor man's lawyer, and J.C. Strapp was considered a rich man's advocate.

'But how can she afford it?' Grace said miserably.

'How can you afford it?' Jack said.

'I told you, I'll pay for it out of Aunt Cissie's money.' When, yesterday, she had told Jack that she was asking Edward Quayle to help her, he had groaned in exasperation and complained of the expense, but she had told him then that she would pay for it out of her own money.

'All right, all right,' Jack said, returning to his work. 'It's your problem so you'll have to deal with it in your own way.'

'Yes, I know,' Grace said slowly, and catching sight of Sadie and Spit who had their eyes on her, trapped as she was in this undesired confrontation, she said to them, 'Get on with your kite, you two, and please clean up your mess when you've finished.'

21

Now that she knew about J.C. Strapp, Grace was worried about Mr Quayle. In the weeks of waiting and now, only five days before the court hearing which she had been ordered to attend, he seemed to have done nothing except send his son Tom to talk to Spit and then take him down to the ashes of the boiler house. She had asked Spit afterwards what they had been doing there, and Spit had said, 'He was looking for any kind of papers my grandfather left, a tin box or something like that, only we couldn't find anything. He found one of my grandfather's badges, that's all.'

'What sort of badge?'

'Tom said it was a soldier's badge, but I don't know. I never saw it before. It was all green.'

'Is that all he did?'

'He asked me a lot of questions.'

'What sort of questions?'

'He wanted to know where my grandfather came from, and if he had any bank books, and all sorts of things like that.'

'Is that all?' Grace said.

Spit seemed reluctant. 'Well, he kept asking me questions, and then he said he was going up to the hospital to see Doctor Stevens.'

Grace knew that Spit disliked being questioned about himself or his grandfather, and she had not persisted. But she was disappointed that Tom Quayle had not returned to question her, although she wasn't sure what sort of help she could have given him anyway.

But finally, on the day before the court hearing, Edward Quayle did telephone her and asked her to come to his office. 'As soon as you can,' he said.

Grace put on her print frock and hurried up the slope into town. When she walked into Mr Quayle's office Tom was not in the little ante-room, but Mr Quayle called out, 'Is that you, Mrs Tree?'

'Yes,' she said.

'Then come in,' Mr Quayle said, and without

looking up from the papers he was reading he half stood up in a polite gesture and pointed to the hard chair near his desk. 'Sit down please,' he said, and then he looked at her and said, 'I suppose you have received notification of the hearing tomorrow.'

'Yes, I got it last week.'

For a moment Edward Quayle seemed to hold his breath, and then he went on, 'Mr Strapp, who will represent Mrs Arbuckle, has approached the court and suggested that the hearing be held not in a court room but in the chamber where sometimes the court sits for hearings in camera. The point is that it does away with any atmosphere of a court or of a legal dispute. Do you object to that?'

'I don't know, Mr Quayle. What do you think?'

'I think it's a good idea, so if you have no objection I will agree.'

'All right,' Grace said.

'Unfortunately there's one thing I must make clear,' Mr Quayle said, holding up a blue covered document. 'This is the 1928 Adoption of Children Act of the State of Victoria. It's a new Act. Only a few years old. It is the first this State has ever had governing the conditions of adoption, and I'm sorry to say that under this Act, and what seems already to be the interpretation of it, you don't have very much hope of adopting the boy.'

Grace told herself that she had always expected this. She had always known that everything would be against her if it had to be judged by a court of law or by someone else.

'But why?' she said angrily. 'What makes you so sure, Mr Quayle?'

'I'm never one hundred per cent sure of anything in law,' Mr Quayle told her. 'But as far as the interpretation of this Act is concerned, and its application so far, the problem of what they call *matching* makes your application almost dead before it is alive. I half warned you about that. Remember?'

'What do you mean – matching?' Grace asked.

'In all previous cases, without exception, and in the wider interpretation of this law, the religion of the child has had to match the religion of the adoptive parents, regardless of any circumstances that might favour adoption. In other words, it doesn't matter how good your case is, religion is a decisive factor. I told you I thought this might be the case and now I am sure of it in law.'

'I don't care what the law says,' Grace told him. 'It's not right.'

'Nonetheless, I did warn you that the law is the law,' Mr Quayle said.

'Yes, I know you did. But I thought you were going to do something about it.'

'I have been looking into it, Mrs Tree, and all I can say is that all precedents and judgements are against you. The point is that if I know the position in law so will Judge Laker who will decide this case. And I doubt very much if he will want to set a contrary precedent in your case, knowing that it would cause a lot of religious controversy and would probably be overturned by a higher court anyway.'

'You are not just saying all this, Mr Quayle, because you don't want to take it up.'

Grace saw Edward Quayle's brick red face turn a deeper rouge, and he slapped his hand so fiercely on the table that she jumped. 'Mrs Tree ...' he said. 'Mrs Tree, I shall forgive you that uncalled-for remark,' and she felt the anger and contempt in what he was saying, 'because you are obviously under some strain about this boy. On the other hand if you don't want me to go on with your application we can end it now.'

'No. No. I'm sorry, Mr Quayle, I just meant that you're a Protestant, and perhaps you don't want to represent a Catholic if that's what is causing all the trouble.'

'Religion is the issue of your application, Mrs Tree,' Edward Quayle said coldly. 'It is not an issue in my professional support for your application. If I am to represent you, then I represent you regardless. Is that understood?'

'Of course.'

'Then you wish me to go on?'

'Yes, Mr Quayle. I'm so confused.'

'I appreciate that.'

'But what can you do if the law says I can't adopt him anyway?'

'We can always argue, Mrs Tree. Or we can give it up. It's a simple enough choice.'

'But there's not much hope is there?'

'No. I have to tell you that. Even your own case is far from perfect. For instance you don't have the support of your husband in this, do you?'

'How do you know that?'

'I spoke to him, Mrs Tree. He is the formal applicant, not you, so I had to know his feelings about it.'

'What did he say to you, Mr Quayle?'

'That it was all your idea and yours alone, and that he only agreed to sign the form because your daughter asked him to.'

Grace was now able to discipline herself, and she said grimly, 'I suppose that will count against me too, won't it?'

'Naturally, if the other side makes a point of it.'

'So it seems to be quite hopeless. Everything ...'

Edward Quayle sat back in his chair and rubbed his greying chin with his short square fingers. 'The only strength you have for your case, Mrs Tree, is your conviction and faith in the boy. You, and I gather your daughter, really want to keep him, don't you?'

'I don't know what I would do if they took him away now,' Grace said, 'and my daughter Sadie would be heartbroken.'

'You want to have the boy under any circumstances? Is that right?'

'Of course. Just so long as they don't take him away.'

'Do you trust me in this, Mrs Tree? Have you recovered yourself?'

'Of course I trust you, Mr Quayle.'

'I must be absolutely sure that I have your full confidence so that you will understand that what I am doing is best, even when you may not like it or understand it.'

Grace was already ashamed of her doubts about this man, and she didn't hesitate now to say, 'Yes I'm sure you'll do your best, Mr Quayle. It's all right.'

'Even more than that, Mrs Tree, I want you to understand that what I can do is probably all that can be done. Will you accept that and leave it to me?'

'Yes, if you say so.'

'Very well. Make sure that the boy is properly dressed when you come to court. And with his shoes on.'

'Don't worry.'

'Are you willing to let your daughter Sadie speak up for the boy?'

'If that will help.'

'Then that's all, Mrs Tree. Be at the court chamber at ten o'clock on Wednesday. On time please because this judge doesn't like anyone to be late. And make sure a note has gone to the school explaining the boy's absence in case the judge asks about that.'

'Of course.'

'Then good day, Mrs Tree.' Edward Quayle stood up and sat down again.

'Goodbye, Mr Quayle,' Grace said, and emerging into the street she realised that Edward Quayle's persuasiveness seemed to be so strange that she wondered what he really meant when he said, 'Leave it to me.'

22

At five to ten Tom Quayle was waiting at the door of
the court chamber and Grace found herself in a little
room that was almost bare, with three tables shaped
into a U at one end and a long solid bench at the
other. At one of the tables Betty Arbuckle, her husband
Frank, Mr J.C. Strapp and another man (Strapp's assis-
tant, Jock Stone) were already seated.

'You'll have to sit here, you two,' Tom said to
Spit and Sadie. And leaving them on the bench where
Ben Arbuckle was already in place, he took Grace
to the table on the other side of the U facing Betty
Arbuckle.

'I thought it would be just a lot of questions,'

Grace whispered to him. 'I mean – not in front of Betty Arbuckle.'

'The whole thing is a bit odd, Mrs Tree. But don't worry.'

'Where is your father?' she asked him.

'He'll be along. Don't worry,' Tom said.

But when Judge Laker came into the chamber from a back door, with Henry Fennel at his elbow, and they sat down at the head of the U near Mrs Price the stenographer, Grace was worried, particularly when Judge Laker said, 'Where is Mr Quayle?'

'He'll be along in a minute, your honour,' Tom said.

'But he's late,' Grace whispered, remembering how Edward Quayle had told her that this judge didn't like anyone to be late.

'If my father's late,' Tom whispered back, 'then he's deliberately late. Anyway, here he is.'

As Edward Quayle walked on his short legs into the chamber to join them at the table he was saying, 'I'm sorry for my tardiness, your honour, but there were some difficulties.'

'All right, Mr Quayle,' the judge said, 'at least you are here, for which we must be thankful.' He picked up what looked to Grace like her application. 'You are representing Mr John Edward Tree, are you not?'

'That is correct, your honour.'

'I don't see him, so where is he?'

'That was one of my problems, your honour. Mr Tree is our local pastoral and livestock inspector, and very urgent work keeps him away for the moment. But I hope to have him present later on. In the meantime Mrs Tree is here beside me and she will be able to answer any questions the court wants to put to her.'

'You haven't made a very good start, have you, Mr Quayle?'

'No, sir. I haven't, I'm afraid.'

'Very well, let us begin. You, Mr Strapp, are representing ...' he picked up the other application form, 'Mr and Mrs Frank Arbuckle.'

'Yes your honour, they are both here.'

'Then there is nothing more to delay us. But before we begin I must make some serious observations for all those present here.' He looked around him like a schoolmaster addressing a wayward class. 'This is not a trial,' he said, 'it is a court hearing. But because of a unique situation in which we have two applicants applying to adopt the same boy, I have decided that they will both be present to hear the other's case. I have never heard of a situation quite like this. There is no precedent, and because I need to put their qualifications to the test, I think the mutual presence of both applicants here will help that. Are you listening, Mr Quayle?'

Grace had been watching Mr Quayle sorting out his documents as the judge spoke, and he looked up now and said, 'Of course, your honour. I ask your pardon, but I am still trying to organise myself.'

'Then I suggest that you stop organising yourself for a moment and pay attention to what I am saying, because this will have some bearing on your applicant, if you are interested in hearing it.'

'Of course I am, your honour.'

'Very well. What I am saying is that in this case we have a boy who is not represented here in his own right. So it seems to me that what we have is a situation in which both sides will need a better qualification than their own claims to be the chosen one. That is why I have brought you all face to face so to speak. But I warn everybody present that this is a court, even though I have not had it formally constituted as a court. There will be no comment of any kind from anyone unless it is asked for by me or Mr Strapp or Mr Quayle. Any departure from this ruling or any attempt to comment without being asked will be dealt with by expulsion from the court. Have counsel warned their ... their candidates of this?'

'Yes, your honour,' Mr Strapp said. 'It has been done.'

'Well, Mr Quayle?'

'In fact I didn't do so,' Edward Quayle said to the judge, 'because I thought it would be far more effective coming from you.'

'Thank you, Mr Quayle,' the judge said drily. 'Now this hearing will be informal. Statements can be asked for and the procedure will be relaxed. If I feel that someone has to be heard under oath, then I shall call for the oath to be administered. In other words if I don't believe you I shall have you swear to what you are saying.'

Taking a stub of pencil out of his waistcoat pocket Judge Laker pointed it first at Mr Quayle and then at Mr Strapp. 'Now, gentlemen, I know your capacity for rivalry as adversaries, nevertheless I am sure you will not treat this as a gladiatorial combat but as a means to giving this unfortunate orphan a decent home and a decent future.'

Grace, watching the judge, didn't like his way of showing them that he had absolute power over the life and limb of everybody in the chamber. In fact it seemed to Grace that he was relishing the idea of a struggle between Mr Strapp and Mr Quayle. 'A unique case,' he was saying again, and Grace was sure now that he had deliberately arranged it to be an adversarial contest.

'Your honour,' Edward Quayle said the moment the judge had finished his remarks. 'May I suggest, in view of the unhappy problems I have had in my preparation, that you hear the application of my honoured friend first ...'

'Oh no ...' Strapp didn't wait for Edward Quayle to finish. 'I think, your honour, that first or last in this case should be decided by some other reasoning. If I am to open the proceedings it will put me in the role of prosecutor, with Mr Quayle the defender, which is not the role I want in this.'

'If the court pleases,' Edward Quayle said. 'This is not a court for offenders, nor even a court for non-offenders. So my honourable friend seems unnecessarily worried about who goes first.'

'If you put me in first,' Strapp persisted, 'it will give Mr Quayle all the information he wants about our intentions – our case, so to speak. And it will also give him the last word.'

'I hadn't thought of that,' Mr Quayle said. 'So what does my friend suggest?'

'I don't know. Why not toss a coin ...'

Judge Laker rapped his pencil on the table. 'There will be no decision by coin-tossing in my court,' he said. 'Mr Quayle's reasons seem sound enough to me, Mr Strapp, even though he cannot be given high marks for preparation. So perhaps you have the advantage anyway, Mr Strapp, and you may as well go ahead with it. In any case, I shall make sure that neither of you has the last word. I shall have it.'

But Grace, aware now of every turn and twist in what was happening, knew why Edward Quayle had been late and apparently disorganised. He obviously wanted Strapp to begin, and she was sure that he had done it deliberately.

'Well …' Mr Strapp began carefully. 'It is a strange case, your honour, and it has a strange history. Everybody in St Helen knows the boy concerned. He is a familiar figure in our streets, always barefoot, poorly dressed, always pulling a cart or carrying a little bag on his shoulder, always selling fish or crayfish. And he is well known too for his wild haunts along the river. In other words, from an early age, say six or seven, he has been something of a little vagabond around the town.'

Edward Quayle tapped the table with a squat finger and said, 'I really must protest, your honour, at this definition of the boy. To begin with …'

'To begin with,' Judge Laker said sharply, 'you are out of order. As Mr Strapp said, he is not the prosecutor and you are not the defender. If anyone has to defend the boy, I shall. And though certain court rules apply here, I am not going to allow interruptions or formal objections. You'll have your say later, Mr Quayle. Be content with that.'

'As you say, your honour. I accept your ruling.'

'You have no choice, Mr Quayle, so go ahead Mr Strapp.'

'The point I am making, your honour, is not derogatory of the boy. We are not blaming him for his abandoned condition. We are blaming the circumstances of his life which made a little beggar of him. And it is our contention, from the outset, that the only person in this town who, from the beginning, took an outside interest in the boy's welfare, and tried to do something about him, was Mrs Betty Arbuckle.'

'How old is the boy now?' Judge Laker said, and to answer his own question he looked at the application. 'Eleven. And when did Mrs Arbuckle begin to take an interest in him, Mr Strapp?'

'He must have been about six or seven, your honour. In any case it was almost from the first day he arrived in town with his grandfather and then lived with him in an old boiler down by the river.'

'A boiler?'

'Yes, your honour. That's where the two of them lived. The old man himself was already something of a gypsy around the town, a half-mad watchmaker who lived from hand to mouth by getting work from time to time. But he was well known to everyone in the town for his crazy shouting, his insulting behaviour, his midnight wanderings which sometimes frightened people in the town, and of course for the strong influence he had from the outset on his six-year-old grandson who learned early to copy his ways. Not only the old man's peculiarities – his shouting and his habit of wandering around the town – but all the rest of his primitive way of life in his fantastically painted boiler house, which looked more like something out of Dante's *Inferno* than a decent home for the child to be brought up in.'

'Is the boiler still there?' Judge Laker asked.

'No, your honour. I shall come to that later. It was burned down, probably when you were attending one of the other courts of the circuit. But almost from the first day that this five- or six-year-old joined his grandfather, Mrs Betty Arbuckle was down there trying to find out exactly what conditions the boy was living in, and trying publicly and vigorously to bring the boy's condition to the notice of the town, even to the police.'

'Did she succeed?' Judge Laker asked.

'I'll come to that too, in time. The point is that she was always met there with abuse and insults, and sometimes with physical violence from both the old man and the boy, who was usually egged on by the old man. There was a brief interregnum when, apparently from nowhere, the boy's mother joined them in the boiler house, a tragic figure who had been badly burned in a fire near Bendigo, in which her husband was killed – the father of the boy. Here too Mrs Arbuckle tried to help. She visited the boiler several times when the mother was there, offering her help, but the old man wouldn't let Mrs Arbuckle even talk to his daughter-in-law. Then, when the mother died, the boy's situation obviously worsened, because he became entirely dependent on the care of the old man whose approach to life had become a bitter hostility to everything around him. Every time Mrs Arbuckle went down there on her regular attempts to help the boy, the old man became more and more violent, and the boy too.'

'What about the boiler?' Judge Laker said as if Strapp's picture of it had caught his imagination.

'We come to that now. In one of his fits of madness the old man set fire to the extension he lived in, so that the whole place burned to the ground.'

'You mean the boiler too?' Judge Laker said.

'No, your honour. The metal shell of it was left, but the contents were burned out. Which, of course,

248

left the boy homeless. And this time the old man was beyond saving. He died in hospital, completely insane. That is when Mrs Betty Arbuckle took the boy home, gave him a place to live, and tried also to give him some instruction in the Christian faith which the boy knew nothing about, because the old man had simply left the boy to his own devices. As a result, sir, our little vagabond has had no moral instruction from any church or Sunday school at all. He has been living the life of an African heathen. He has become a child desperately in need of saving, your honour, which Mr and Mrs Arbuckle took on as a personal responsibility.'

Grace had been watching Spit to see how he was taking this version of his life with his grandfather, but Spit was quite impassive, as if he was now expert in removing himself from anything that seemed likely to punish him or hurt him or disarray him.

'So the boy is now living with Mr and Mrs Arbuckle, is that right?' Judge Laker said.

'No, at the moment he is staying with Mrs Tree. When the old man died in hospital, the boy subsequently ran away. That is, he swam across the river and tried to live wild on Pental Island. But after causing considerable trouble and concern to Sergeant Collins and other volunteers who set off to find him, the boy was brought back to St Helen by Sergeant Collins. It was then that he was taken over by Mrs Tree who kept him in her house and refused to give him up to anybody. Since then he has been kept there, and despite Mrs Arbuckle's attempts to take the boy to her own home, Mrs Tree has refused to let the boy go, which brings us to the crucial issue of this application, your honour, the issue of matching ...'

'Ahh, I was wondering about that,' the Judge said.

'It's always a touchy subject, as you know, your honour, but there is a problem here which only the court can decide. Under the 1928 Adoption of Children Act, the issue of matching faith to faith is paramount, but what we have at the moment with Mrs Tree is a mix-matching, if that is the right word.'

'Mrs Tree is a Roman Catholic and Mrs Arbuckle is a Protestant, and so is the boy, that's what you are saying, Mr Strapp.'

'Yes.'

'Then say it. It will have to be a wide open issue sooner or later, so better to face it honestly rather than try to smother it in caution and hesitation.'

'Of course, your honour.'

'So?'

'The religion is, we consider, vital to the boy's present care. Mr and Mrs Tree are practising

250

Catholics. If the court allows them to adopt the boy, they become the absolute parents and guardians of the boy, and as such will have a legal right to do what they wish with him. As adoptive parents, they will have the same rights as natural parents, and if they so wish it they can make a Roman Catholic of him. As adoptive parents, they would be perfectly within the law to do so. But this, of course, would become a denial of the boy's own rights, because constitutionally, and in law, Spit MacPhee has the right, even the requirement, to be brought up in the faith to which he was born.'

'Mr and Mrs Arbuckle ...' the judge said, consulting the application again, 'are not Presbyterians. Their church is one of the evangelical sects, is it not?'

'Yes. But obviously their church falls clearly and firmly on the Protestant side of the fence, which is all that counts.'

'Do they intend to bring the boy up in their evangelical faith if they become the adoptive parents?'

'Only if the boy wishes. Otherwise they will insist that he take his religious instruction at the Presbyterian church. In any case a Protestant church, not a Catholic one.'

'I see. Is that your case, Mr Strapp?'

'Yes, your honour, except to say again that the boy is in need of care and protection, not simply for the clothes on his back and the food in his belly. He needs the care of someone who will rescue him from the gypsy life he was unfortunate enough to learn from his grandfather. He needs adoptive parents who are respectable and well liked, and well known in this town for their honesty and stability. And he needs the care of a family who have always been interested in the boy and his welfare. Above all, he needs the under-standing and the help and protection of someone who will give him a Christian upbringing in the Protestant faith of his father and his forefathers, a profound and unshakable historical reality, sir, which this court dare not ignore.'

The judge threw up his hands in a mild gesture of protest as he said to Mr Strapp, 'When advocates tell the court that we dare not ignore something, Mr Strapp, I always have the feeling that, sitting in judgement, I am being blackmailed. Are you trying to blackmail me, sir?'

'There was no such intent, your honour.'

'Then in future do not tell the court what it dare or dare not do. The judgement of this court will be qualified only by the law, and by what is best for the boy. So Mr Quayle, we can now hear your proposition, and I hope that you will not stick pins into me in order to warn me that I am supposed to have blood in my veins as well as vinegar.'

'Nothing would be further from my mind, your honour,' Edward Quayle said, and he waited a full minute, as if he wanted all previous influences to disperse before he began. And Grace Tree, having listened closely and almost breathlessly to everything that Mr Strapp had said, wondered how Edward Quayle would be able to contest what seemed to her to be a perfect case. In a way everything Mr Strapp had said was true, even though she thought it was wrong.

'Spit MacPhee,' Mr Quayle began, looking up from his papers at Spit, sitting on the bench. 'Stand up will you, Spit MacPhee, so that Judge Laker can take a good look at you close up.'

Spit stood up promptly, boldly, defiantly, ready this time to shout at a moment's notice, 'You're not going to get me.'

'There he is, your honour, the boy we are arguing about, and if we want a model for the Australian boy, in perfecto, I can't imagine a better example than Spit MacPhee. A true native of the wide open spaces. A boy born and brought up to look after himself when necessity forgot him. A very bright lad who, in the deepest and best traditions of this new and pioneering country, has shown many adults in this town how best to utilise the country he was born in, how to enjoy it and make friends with it and, at the same time, merge into it like an autumn leaf. A vagabond? A gypsy? A wild thing? Absolute stuff and nonsense, your honour. Take a good look at him and make up your own mind.' As Judge Laker raised his stub of pencil ready to interrupt, Edward Quayle said sharply, 'Sit down, Spit MacPhee.'

But Spit hesitated a moment before he sat down and, sensing Spit's continuing resistance to all this turmoil over his head and around his ears, Edward Quayle said, 'It's all right, Spit. Nobody is going to harm you here, so sit down, boy. Just sit down.'

Spit obeyed, but he kept his eye on the judge who had been studying him with a rather puzzled expression. 'Mr Quayle,' he was saying. 'Why is he called Spit?'

'That's his nickname, your honour.'

'Does he spit?'

'The story is that in a contest at school, some years ago, he beat every other boy at the sport of spitting at passing bumblebees and flies and such. But though he doesn't spit any more, he is known affectionately, and I might even say respectfully, to everyone in this town as Spit MacPhee. But even if it is not a very salubrious nickname I am sure in the Australian tradition that your honour had one just as picturesque in his own youth.'

Judge Laker was startled for a moment. As a boy he had been called 'Lick' Laker because he always licked his pencil before using it, something he still did. 'I don't believe a word of your story, Mr Quayle,' he said. 'It's a little too good to be true. But never mind.'

'Well, your honour, as Mark Twain said: "If it isn't the gospel truth it's at least a possibility."'

'In the circumstances I should call it flim-flam, Mr Quayle. But I take your point about the boy if you really have to make the point.'

'Oh, I do, your honour, because this is not just "a boy". His grandfather was not, as my learned friend kept calling him, "the old man". He was Fyfe MacPhee, and this boy is Spit MacPhee and that is how we shall refer to them, because they must not be labelled and insulted here as nameless vagabonds and gypsies. They were not.'

'All right, Mr Quayle. You have established your characters, so get on with your plot.'

'Well, sir, the plot is really a simple appeal to the humanity and common sense of this court.'

Judge Laker groaned. 'Not again,' he complained. 'We have already been blackmailed with does and dares, and now you are messing me about with humanity and common sense. This is not Olympus, Mr Quayle, so get on with your story.'

Edward Quayle put his stubby fingers together and said, 'In fact it is really the story of a remarkable old man, who, by extraordinary courage and agonising self-control, was able to take care of a very young boy under very great difficulties when he himself was suffering the excruciating misery of pain and disorientation.'

'Is it important about the grandfather, Mr Quayle? Does it matter now?' the judge said.

'Yes, it does, your honour, because Fyfe MacPhee was not a vagabond. He was an old soldier who fought with an Argyll regiment at Ypres and Lille, and suffered very severe head wounds in 1917. I was lucky enough to be able to trace some of his records from an old cap badge we found in the ashes of the boiler, and as far as I can make out he was invalided to Canada in 1917 and given a silver plate to cover the deep gash in his cranium, a very doubtful operation but the best they could do at the time to protect the exposed parts of his brain.'

Spit could take no more of it and he leapt to his feet and shouted, 'My grandfather wasn't mad, I don't care what you say.'

'Of course he wasn't mad,' Edward Quayle said

sharply. 'Nobody is saying that he was mad, so sit still young man. Sit still, and we will do our best for him.'

As Spit sat down again he was blushing this time. He realised that he had spoken out of turn, and Judge Laker pointed his pencil at him and said, 'Any more out of you, Spit, and you'll leave the court.' The judge turned then to Edward Quayle and said in a wearied voice, 'I still ask you, Mr Quayle, is all this so important?'

'Let me finish, your honour. I assure you it is all relevant. The point is that Fyfe MacPhee had been a watch and clock repairer in Edinburgh before the war, and he at least had a trade when the war ended. Bringing his wife and son to Australia he lived in Melbourne for several years, where his wife died, and where his son also became a watch and clock repairer.'

'We know something of that from Mr Strapp,' Judge Laker said.

'Yes, but what you don't know is that when he walked into this town, fifteen years ago, the pressure of that silver plate on his brain was already so severe that it caused him to behave the way he did. He wasn't mad. He wasn't a vagabond. He was a perfectly sane man trying to discipline a damaged brain. And, as Doctor Stevens will confirm, he was always in frightful pain, which sometimes was so noisy in his head and so heavy on his rationality that only shouting and talking

257

to himself, and even a degree of wild fantasy could help him to survive the noise or blot it out. That was the real reason for his peculiar behaviour. He was an old soldier suffering terribly from his wounds. But plenty of people in this town will confirm that he was the best watch repairer we had, and though the way he lived was an inevitable part of his suffering, he believed like an old soldier that he had to isolate himself to some extent so that he did not soak the rest of us with his unpredictable behaviour and his need for noisy, distorted relief.'

'Are you absolutely sure of all this, Mr Quayle?' the judge said, clearly troubled by the story. Judge Laker was an old soldier himself; and didn't old soldiers always bleed for other old soldiers suffering the agony of their terrible wounds?

'Yes, your honour. And if my learned friend opposite or his clients really had Spit MacPhee's interest at heart, they too would have tried to find out some of the reasons ...'

'Oh for heaven's sake – isn't that going a bit too far, your honour?' Mr Strapp said.

'I agree, Mr Strapp,' the judge said. 'Stick to your own case, Mr Quayle and let Mr Strapp fail in his own way.'

'I'm only concerned with the truth, your honour,

and in this boy's story it seems to be all suffering and tragedy, because his father was killed in a fire in Bendigo and his mother badly burned, and that is when Spit MacPhee first came to St Helen to live with his grandfather. That is when his grandfather built those extensions to the boiler and brought home Spit's mother, veiled as we all know from head to toe because her burns were so bad that she wanted to hide them.'

'Surely that is when she needed the help Mrs Arbuckle offered her,' Judge Laker said.

'No, sir. She did not want anyone to see her or help her. She was a tragic, dying woman, and though Mrs Betty Arbuckle did offer to help her, a kind act, Mrs Arbuckle showed little awareness of what this lady was suffering, and why she needed privacy. Mrs MacPhee simply needed to be left alone for the last few months of her life with her son ...'

Grace, listening to the story as Edward Quayle was telling it felt pained and sickened by her own lack of interest in how horrible it must have been for Spit and his family. She looked across the room at Betty Arbuckle who had taken off her ugly hat and was now in tears. Betty, in distress, looked more beautiful than ever, but Grace didn't feel like tears. She felt angry. When Tom touched her arm gently and said, 'There's your husband,' she looked at the door and saw Jack

259

sitting erect on a bench just inside it, soldierly and cold, as if he wanted to be as far removed from this as possible.

'How long has he been there?' she whispered to Tom.

'Since my father started talking,' Tom said.

'He heard everything?' she said.

'He must have,' Tom said.

There was a jug of water on the table near Edward Quayle and he poured some of it into a glass and took a sip before going on. 'You see, your honour, when young Mrs MacPhee died, Fyfe was already suffering so much from his head wound that, according to Doctor Stevens, he must have survived on sheer will-power in order to look after his grandson. And in living with his grandfather, Spit, who was six then seven and then eight and nine, shared the shouting and the apparent quarrelling and the wandering, and the river at the door. Far from vagabondage, it was an education in self-sufficiency that Spit MacPhee was getting from his grandfather because Fyfe MacPhee was never sure, from day to day, how long he could function with the agony and the pain and the terrible moments of his uncontrollable behaviour. Eventually it came to its end in the tragic affair of the fire. Fyfe MacPhee didn't know what he was doing, and later he

260

tried to drown himself as the only solution left, fearing as he always did that in his moment of total mental loss he would do what he had just done – not harm his grandson but commit some foolish act that might seriously affect his life.'

'Where did he die, Mr Quayle?' the judge asked. 'I have forgotten.'

'In the local hospital, your honour. And I think it is safe to say that he died of exhaustion, trying desperately to keep alive for his grandson's sake.'

'But surely life in that boiler must have been rather hard on the boy?' the judge said.

'Not at all, sir. It was an admirable little house. Spit MacPhee had a room to himself, a comfortable bed, plenty to eat, and a devoted guardian to protect him. In fact Fyfe MacPhee was an orderly man by nature. He kept a fine garden, and though his house was painted in fantastic colours, no doubt as a reflection of his suffering, it was always neat and clean.'

Judge Laker held up his hand like a policeman as if that was the only way to stop Edward Quayle. 'Just a minute, Mr Quayle. Just a minute,' he said. 'Now, calmly, not in passion but in cold blood – can you justify that story of insults and attacks on Mrs Arbuckle? Weren't they true?'

'Yes, your honour. The lady made her approaches

in good heart, but to Spit and his grandfather they were threats to their perfectly decent domestic life. It is well known to everybody in this town that Mrs Arbuckle had her mind set on sending Spit off to a Boys Home in Bendigo, even from the beginning. And that is what inspired such a violent response from both of them.'

'So there were some primitive imperfections in their behaviour after all,' the judge said, 'which, I might say, is putting it mildly.'

'There were many imperfections in that household by the river, just as there are imperfections in any household in this town,' Edward Quayle said angrily. 'But lack of affection and attention and care were not among them. If Fyfe MacPhee was loud and sometimes aggressive and negligent about his responsibilities, then his failure, for instance, to give the boy some Christian instruction was simply a reflection of his own condition rather than a slip in his morals. The proof is that Spit MacPhee is an honest boy. Everybody in this town knows that. He has never been accused of stealing or, in normal life, of insulting or hurting anybody. If he has had fights at school, they were usually to defend his grandfather against other boys who called him mad. And that is the true story of Spit MacPhee, your honour; not that farrago of ridiculous nonsense from Mr Strapp. The difference has to be understood if there is to be a fair judgement in this case.'

'You're at it again, Mr Quayle.'

'I know, your honour. But I mean no disrespect to yourself or the court.'

'All right. You have given us the background, you have told us a moving story of the boy and his grandfather, but you haven't yet made a case for your client, have you?'

'I was about to come to that.'

'Time is not on your side, Mr Quayle.'

'I beg your pardon, your honour, but it is important ...'

'In that case,' Judge Laker interrupted, 'I think we had better adjourn for five minutes so that you can catch your breath. But then we will deal with this matter speedily and objectively. In fact I need to remove myself for a few minutes from the influence of your presumptions, Mr Quayle.'

Judge Laker stood up and walked out, and as Edward Quayle leaned back and rubbed an eye thoughtfully, Grace asked Tom what it meant.

'It means,' Tom said, 'that Judge Laker has gone into the back room to have his morning tot of brandy.'

'That's enough, Tom,' Edward Quayle said sharply. He leaned forward. 'I want you to do something,' he said to his son. 'Go over to the bench at the back and tell Mr Tree that I need him up here for the boy's sake. And don't take No for an answer.'

'Do you want me to do it?' Grace said.

'No, no. He might resist you on principle. Moreover if there is to be any resentment it had better be against me rather than you. We shall need the semblance at least of a united family up here for what I am about to do. So tell him that if he resists and refuses to come up here I shall pack up and leave the court and abandon the case.'

'But he won't come, Mr Quayle,' Grace said quickly.

'I think he will, Mrs Tree. In any case, Tom, you tell him that I mean what I say.'

Grace watched Tom Quayle approach her husband. She saw Tom bend over and talk to him. She noticed the slight stiffening of Jack's back, and his face become set. And though she expected the worst, for some strange reason which she could not fathom Jack stood up and followed Tom.

'What on earth did you do to him, Mr Quayle?' Grace said quietly.

'Nothing,' Edward Quayle said, and added drily, 'Old soldiers, Mrs Tree. They are all old soldiers, and as you know, old soldiers never die.'

23

When Judge Laker returned, Edward Quayle was quick to begin again. 'We now have Mr Tree with us so I shall proceed ...'

'Your honour,' Mr Strapp said. 'It looks as if Mr Quayle is going to go on *ad-infinitum*. Surely there has to be a time limit to this?'

'So far,' Edward Quayle said, 'I have had to waste time correcting the false impression of Fyfe MacPhee and his grandson given in this court by my honourable friend, so I haven't had a chance yet to put our proper case.'

'That's one way of putting it,' the judge said. 'So do get on with it.'

'I shall be brief,' Edward Quayle said, 'even though more amplification would help. But I'll skip the rest and come to the point of our appeal. Mrs Tree is a Roman Catholic and Mrs Arbuckle is an Evangelical Protestant. That is an issue, I admit, but our case is based not on religion but on the difference between Mrs Arbuckle's idea of bringing up a boy and Mrs Tree's. No more nor less than that.'

'No more nor less, Mr Quayle?'

'Well, it seems to me, your honour, that in this case religion should have nothing to do with it. And even if it was crucial I would have to point out that there are Protestants and Protestants, and Catholics and Catholics. In other words, in both sects there is dogma and bigotry. There is hostility and hate. There are differences about what is good and what is evil, what is salvation and what is damnation. But what on earth has religious dogma and bigotry, or even the honest differences in faith got to do with fathering and mothering this boy? I refuse therefore, for the sake of this boy, to get involved in an insoluble historical argument which has been going on for four hundred years and may go on for another four hundred years.'

Judge Laker raised his hand again. 'Thank heaven for that,' he said. 'I was all prepared for you to give us a remarkable defence of the Catholic faith from your well known Berkleyian belief in the Reformation.'

'Sir,' Edward Quayle said, controlling his temper, 'I would gladly do that for you, but I am afraid it would be wasted here. Instead I turn to Mr and Mrs Tree as human beings, not as Catholics or Protestants. They are, like Mr and Mrs Arbuckle, a very respectable family in this town. Mr Tree is the Secretary of the Returned Soldiers' League and is an old soldier himself. The Trees have a ten-year-old daughter, Sadie, who is sitting there next to Spit MacPhee. Stand up Sadie,' Edward Quayle said.

Sadie stood up, head down, eyes down.

'Lift your head up, Sadie,' Edward Quayle said, 'and tell us what you think of your friend Spit MacPhee. It's quite important what you think of him because you are one of the nicest and cleverest girls in St Helen, and are highly thought of, so what do you say about Spit MacPhee?'

Sadie kept her head down. 'He's all right,' she said.

'It would be awful if this court took Spit away from you and your family, wouldn't it?'

Sadie nodded.

'So how would you feel about that, Sadie?'

'I'd be sick,' Sadie said, and lifting her head she said, 'It wouldn't be fair.'

'Oh, for heaven's sake, your honour,' Mr Strapp shouted. 'This is going a bit too far.'

'I quite agree,' Judge Laker said. 'So just make your statement, Mr Quayle, and leave the histrionics till later.'

Edward Quayle shrugged a little, waited a full minute again for the air to change, and then sighed and went on. 'What I was saying before these interruptions is that Spit MacPhee is already well established in the Tree household. He is happy there, and is now treated like a son and a brother. And the difference is this, your honour: Mrs Arbuckle in her faith and passion has already had Spit at her home and he ran away because he was frightened of her and unhappy with her. Why? Because she put heavy boots on his winged feet, confined him to quarters, forbade him the Australian life he knew best – the river – and tried to make a good Christian of him with the apostolic convention that he must above all be saved.'

'Is there anything wrong with that, Mr Quayle?' Betty Arbuckle cried out. 'Considering his condition and his wild behaviour. Is there anything wrong with trying to save him?'

'Nothing wrong with it at all, Mrs Arbuckle,' Edward Quayle said calmly, 'for thee and thine, so to speak. But your methods may not be good for everybody, and they were certainly not good for Spit MacPhee. What he wanted, a boy utterly alone at the age of eleven, was a home that asked nothing of him to begin with except his toleration. What he got in the household of Mrs Tree was not a religious or evangelical instruction in papism, which Mrs Arbuckle is so afraid of, but the understanding of a woman who realised what sort of a boy he is. A free spirit perhaps, but also a natural boy in a natural landscape; a boy living on a marvellous river; a boy with many unique talents; an Australian boy who asked absolutely nothing of anyone because he expected others to ask nothing of him. That was how he had been brought up by his grandfather.'

'But it's wrong, Mr Quayle,' Betty Arbuckle cried out again. 'It's not good for a boy to be like that.'

'Well, dear lady, you may be right. It's not the way I would bring up my own sons,' Edward Quayle said. 'But that is what he was. Not your son and not mine but Spit MacPhee, standing on his own two feet. And that is the boy Mr and Mrs Tree are willing to take up.'

'Oh, this is all nonsense, your honour,' Mr Strapp said angrily, wearily, half standing up and then sitting down again. 'We know for a fact that Mr Jack Tree wanted nothing to do with the adoption of the boy; that he was always reluctant. And far from being the united and happy household Mr Quayle portrays, it became a divided one because of the boy.'

The judge tapped his pencil once or twice on the table, to make sure that Edward Quayle was silenced before he could begin.

'Is that true, Mr Quayle? Is Mr Tree reluctant in this?'

'Why not ask him yourself your honour,' Edward Quayle said. 'He is right here.'

Grace got a grip on Jack's arm as she felt him stiffen with resentment. She knew his responses; she knew what was going to happen.

'Well, Mr Tree? Is what Mr Strapp says true?'

'Yes, sir, I was always reluctant.'

'Oh? Why?'

'I don't know. I thought he was a wild young devil in need of a good home, but not necessarily ours.'

'Didn't you like the boy?'

'I didn't like or dislike him, your honour. He seemed suddenly to come into my family, and I didn't want a stranger in it.'

'Oh, Jack,' Grace Tree said miserably. 'You've spoiled everything now.'

'I have to tell the truth, Grace,' Jack Tree said. 'I don't dislike the boy, your honour. He's got a lot of spunk and gumption. I agree with a lot that

Mr Quayle says about him, and I always felt sorry for him.'

'But not sorry enough to want him. Isn't that right?' Mr Strapp said.

Both Jack Tree and Grace Tree looked at Edward Quayle for help, but he was deliberately, obstinately silent.

'I'll tell you this, your honour,' Jack said. 'I didn't know about old Fyfe until now when I heard Mr Quayle's story. I didn't know he had been a soldier, and that it was his wounds that had made him a bit crazy. I never thought of the old man and the boy in that way. But I can say this, sir. Spit MacPhee is certainly no angel, but my wife and my daughter have become very attached to him. And, if it comes to that, I will have the boy and do my best with him. He will certainly be much better off with us than he would be with Mrs Arbuckle; and a damned sight better off with us than he would be in a Boys Home in Bendigo. If he stays with us he will be given a good home, and he and I will have to learn to get on together, which, sitting here listening to all this, I can guarantee a good try on my part. Allowing for all the usual faults of boys of his age, I'm on his side in this.'

'Thank you, Mr Tree, for that very honest account of your feelings,' Judge Laker said. 'Well, Mr Quayle, you have been rather silent all this time.'

'I simply wanted you to have an honest reply from an honest man, your honour. There was no deception in our case, only honesty. Our case is not perfect. There are many imperfections in the boy to be overcome, and in the family situation. But Mr and Mrs Tree are God-fearing, generous people, not narrow-minded bigots with salvation on their minds.'

'That's quite enough, Mr Quayle.'

'Your honour,' Edward Quayle almost snarled. 'What we need in this courtroom is some human discernment, not religious prejudice. Discernment has to count, sir, because Spit MacPhee's future depends on it – more than religion, and more than a pair of good black boots.'

'Is that the end, Mr Quayle?'

'Yes. I've got nothing more to say on the matter.'

Edward Quayle threw his glasses on the table as if he was finally finished with the whole business, and Judge Laker said to him, almost disappointed, 'Are you sure that is it, Mr Quayle? Nothing more?'

'Yes, your honour. That's it. Except that I suggest you ask Mrs Arbuckle why, after being so intent on sending Spit MacPhee to a Boys Home in Bendigo, she suddenly changed her mind and decided to adopt him instead.'

'Hmmm,' Judge Laker said, licking his pencil and

272

writing something in a little notebook he kept in his waistcoat pocket. 'Well, Mrs Arbuckle? What do you have to say to that?'

'I always wanted him,' Betty said passionately.

'That's not true,' Grace cried out. 'It was only when I wanted to adopt him that Betty made an application herself.'

'Is that right, Mrs Arbuckle?' Judge Laker asked her again.

'Yes, that's right,' Betty said, 'because at first I thought he should be given a home with other boys his own age.'

'What sort of a home would that have been?' Grace said indignantly.

'Steady ... steady,' Edward Quayle told her.

'Yes, Mrs Tree. Do be quiet. What changed your mind, Mrs Arbuckle? Why are you here now asking to adopt him?'

'When he came to live with us I tried to treat him like my own son,' Betty Arbuckle said, her delicate skin already pink and lovely with a faint flush, her eyes glistening and her innocence so obvious that Grace knew why nobody could or should doubt her.

Edward Quayle put his spectacles on again. 'Your honour,' he said drily, 'what really changed her mind was her determination not to let the boy go to a Catholic family. Isn't that so, Mrs Arbuckle?'

'Yes, Mr Quayle,' she said and turned to the judge. 'I thought the best way to help save the boy, in his own faith, would be to adopt him for ourselves.'

'So what are your plans for him, Mrs Arbuckle?' the judge said. 'You want to make him a good, Protestant Christian? Is that right?'

'Yes,' Betty said.

'How?'

'He has to be saved,' Betty said in her quiet, determined way. 'Salvation to us is always a witness to the suffering of Jesus Christ, so that thereafter we can always serve him by word and deed; by day and by night.'

'Yes, yes,' Judge Laker said, 'but how does this apply to the boy?'

'But your honour,' Betty protested, 'you can see for yourself. He is like a little African heathen in need of guidance and help and prayer. That is how we bring up our own son and daughter, and how we would bring up Spit MacPhee. He would be one of us in the eyes of the Lord.'

'Thank you, Mrs Arbuckle,' Judge Laker said. 'You can sit down now.'

In her evocation, Betty had been standing up with

her hands knotted tightly in front of her. She looked around her for a moment like a confused child and then said, 'All right. I'll sit down.'

'And Mrs Tree?' the judge said, 'What do you have to say about the boy's religion?'

'I'm not sure, your honour,' Grace said, troubled by the question. 'I don't know anything about salvation, if that's what you mean.'

'That isn't what I mean at all,' the judge said. 'Although as a Catholic you do believe in salvation, don't you?'

'I suppose I do, but only in the eyes of the church, and in accordance with the sacraments or the intercessions of the Holy Mother. That's all I know about it.'

'You would like the boy to be a Catholic, Mrs Tree?'

Grace looked at Edward Quayle who was leaning back staring at the ceiling as if he were miles away, generations away. 'Yes, your honour,' Grace said slowly. 'I have to admit I would like him to be a Catholic if he is to be my son. But he isn't a Catholic, is he?'

'But if he becomes your son, your son absolute so to speak, to do with him what you like? What then?'

'I would like him to be a Catholic. But if he isn't, then he isn't.'

'Is that possible? Is it possible for you to have a

275

son who is a Protestant? Do you think your Church would tolerate that?'

'I don't know, your honour.'

'But I do,' Mr Strapp interrupted. 'I have already consulted Father O'Connel on that very point. I asked him what the church would expect of Mrs Tree if she adopted the boy, and he told me, unequivocally, that it would be absolutely incumbent on her as a Catholic to bring the boy up in the Catholic faith.'

'Do you accept that, Mrs Tree?' Judge Laker asked. 'Can you give me a simple answer to that question?'

Grace knew that she was now at her weakest, and she was already exhausted. She knew that her faith and her affection for Spit were now in opposition, and an answer now was beyond her. 'I don't know, your honour. I just don't know. But if I could, I would just leave him alone.'

'If you could ...' Mr Strapp repeated menacingly. 'But can you, Mrs Tree? That is the question.'

'I don't know,' Grace said miserably.

The judge looked at Edward Quayle with a quizzical, amused expression. 'What have you to say to all this, Mr Quayle,' he said, 'since the question of religion is very important to the decision I must make.'

'Nothing at all,' Edward Quayle said. 'When it comes to the responsibilities and convictions of

Mrs Tree and her faith I am not going to speak for her, or even advise her. She speaks well enough for herself. What we should count on here, your honour, is the boy himself, who, even in this situation, would be perfectly able to look after himself.'

'All right, let us ask the boy,' Judge Laker said. 'Stand up, Spit MacPhee, and see if you can help us solve some of this.'

'Do I have to stand up?' Spit demanded.

'Yes,' the judge told him.

'Well, all right,' Spit said and stood up.

'Thank you,' the judge said. 'Now: what religion are you?'

'Presbyterian,' Spit said.

'You don't have to shout,' the judge told him. 'Just answer quietly. Do you think if you were adopted by Mrs Tree that you would be willing to become a Roman Catholic?'

'I'm a Presbyterian,' Spit said stubbornly.

'But if, as your mother, she insists. What then?'

'I don't know. I don't know what it's like.'

'May I interrupt, your honour,' Edward Quayle said.

'You usually do, Mr Quayle, but for heaven's sake keep it to the issue in hand. Our time is running out.'

'Let me ask you, Spit,' Edward Quayle said. 'If

277

you were to be adopted by Mrs Betty Arbuckle, what would you do?'

'Run away,' Spit said loudly. 'They're not going to get me.'

'Oh dear,' Judge Laker said. 'This is all becoming a little too emotional, Mr Quayle.' He looked over his glasses at Ben Arbuckle and said, 'Who are you, young man?'

Ben stood up. 'Ben Arbuckle.'

'Well, you seem to be the only one here who hasn't had his say, so it's your turn. Do you want Spit MacPhee to be your brother?'

'Yessir,' Ben said in his new loud voice. 'He's the best friend I've got.'

'Then that's about it,' Judge Laker said and made a point of closing his little notebook. 'All right Mr Quayle, one last word from you, brief and to the point please.'

'I think the situation speaks for itself, your honour. Let me measure it *summum bonum* – by the highest good. We assign to men, or try to, the capacity for mental and physical enjoyment of their lives, and we must in all decency, adjust some of these privileges to our children. In this case there is a boy who has to be given the best we can offer him in an atmosphere of a family and a countryside that will give him what every child in this country needs. It is not a question of religion, it is a matter of common humanity. He is already living with a very fine family where he can be taught the simplest commandments of honesty and respect for others. What more can we ask of Mr and Mrs Tree than that, your honour?'

'Is that all, Mr Quayle?' Judge Laker said, obviously disappointed that he was not going to hear something a little more unreasonable.

'That's all,' Edward Quayle said.

'All right, Mr Strapp. But please keep it as brief as Mr Quayle.'

'Well, your honour, it must come back to the question of religion, no matter which way you look at it. How can we ignore it? Every man and woman in this country is born with a faith which is securely their own – historically as well as in daily life. It is strong, it is real, it is inescapable. The boy is a Protestant and should be brought up as a Protestant, even vigorously so in the evangelical way if necessary. The importance of religious matching is clear in the 1928 Adoption of Children Act. There has never been an exception to it. Any precedent here would create a situation that would go far beyond this courtroom. As for the decency and humanity of Mr and Mrs Arbuckle: here is their own son, a perfectly normal and happy boy who would welcome Spit as a brother. So, given the equal character and fitness of both families, given this equal respectability and decency, the weight of the decision must lie with a religious conjunction. At first it may be difficult for the boy to live with Mr and Mrs Arbuckle, but in the long run he would be as happy and contained and as bright as this boy here, Ben Arbuckle.'

There was a moment's silence. Then Mr Strapp raised his hands to indicate that he had finished, and there was a loud and heavy sigh from Betty Arbuckle. 'That's all, your honour,' Mr Strapp said. 'I have nothing more to say.'

'Gentlemen,' Judge Laker said, putting notebook and pencil into his waistcoat pocket. 'I thank you both for your quite remarkable presentations, and I shall give my decision tomorrow morning at ten o'clock in this chamber. This hearing is over, *casus foederis*, so to speak. But if the parents don't object I would like these two children, Ben Arbuckle and Sadie Tree, to come with me into the other room for a moment. Will you do it, Ben?'

'Yessir,' Ben said firmly.

'And Sadie ... you are not frightened are you? It's for the good of your friend Spit, here. I just want to have a few words with you.'

'All right,' Sadie said, standing up and following the judge.

As Edward Quayle picked up the papers that were on the table before him (his self-made brief which he had not looked at) Grace waited a moment and then said, from what she felt was some far away place, 'What do you think, Mr Quayle? We haven't much hope, have we?'

'Only tomorrow will tell us that, Mrs Tree,' he said crisply and told Tom to come along.

Grace and Jack sat quietly, saying nothing and facing Betty and Frank Arbuckle across the empty room. And somewhere between them Spit MacPhee watched them all, swinging his legs, and waiting for Sadie to come back.

24

When they had returned home Grace told Sadie and Spit that they need not go back to school in the afternoon. 'I suppose if you've lost a morning,' she said to them, 'you wouldn't lose much in an afternoon.'

She was being a generous mother. She knew already that she was accepting defeat, sure now that this would probably be the last day that Spit and Sadie would enjoy together, so let them enjoy it.

She had tried to keep Spit close to her for a moment when they had arrived home by asking him to bring in more wood ('I filled the box this morning'), to put the cart away in the garden ('I did'), to see if there were one or two tomatoes left on the plants ('There weren't any left after the pickles'). It was her best attachment to Spit because she knew he would always do what he had to do: that had always been the closest response she could get out of him so that when she went out to the verandah where he slept to see if there might be something there to regret, she realised that apart from the bed he slept in there was almost nothing here to connect him to her. He owned nothing more than the school clothes he stood up in, an extra pair of trousers, two extra shirts, a toothbrush which she had persuaded him to use, and his school books.

'It's all so wrong,' she said bitterly to herself. 'It's so terribly wrong.' She heard Sadie calling out that they were going down to the river, and she called back in reply, 'Don't either of you go near the edge above the bend, because it crumbles away there now that the river is fast.' She had learned that from Spit himself.

'Don't worry,' Spit shouted.

'Off you go then,' she said, and she knew that she did not have to worry with Spit. He would look after Sadie.

The one thing that she could be grateful for, she decided, though it puzzled her, was Jack's change of heart. He had driven them home in the Dodge, silent and unquestioning, and after a silent lunch he had gone straight to his desk. She knew that he had a genuinely urgent problem with a dairy herd test that was going on, but she guessed that he really wanted to think. As she sat in the kitchen, preparing a batch of scones, he joined her and sat at the table for a moment without saying anything. She looked at his tight, disciplined face and felt sorry for him, and she asked him why he had changed his mind about Spit.

'I didn't change my mind,' he said stiffly. 'I didn't know anything about old Fyfe. I didn't know about the wound in his head. I didn't even know he'd been in the war. In fact I wonder why he never told anybody.'

'Tell who?' Grace said bitterly. 'Everybody thought he was mad.'

'He could have told the Returned Soldiers ...'

'What for? If he was so terribly wounded and in pain, he probably wanted to forget the war, not remember it.'

'We could have helped him,' Jack said. 'He was in a bad way.'

'Why should being a soldier have made any difference? In any case I don't think he wanted your help. I think Mr Quayle was right. The only help he needed was to be left alone with Spit. It was probably the only way he could cope with everything, and with that awful pain. Anyway, the Returned Soldiers might have thought it best, like Betty Arbuckle, to help him by finding a place for Spit in some Boys Home,' she said.

'Why do you say that?' Jack said indignantly.

'Because … oh, it doesn't matter now. I'm sure we've lost him anyway.'

'Well if we have, don't for God's sake blame me for what happened,' Jack said.

'I'm not blaming you, Jack,' Grace said, and she took a good new look at her husband, because Jack defending himself was a new experience for her. Forgiving him was another one.

'You did all you could, and I suppose the only thing we can do now is wait.'

Jack got up to go and it seemed to Grace that he wanted to say something more, but the best he could manage was, 'Maybe you'll be surprised.' Which, she decided, was sufficient reparation for his resistance to Spit. In fact she loved her husband for those few conciliatory words, and she watched him walking up the back path to the Dodge as if she was watching a stranger, because she knew that if, by some miracle, she did get Spit, Jack would do his best for him as he had promised to do.

But it was still her own private problem, and she knew that somewhere along the river bank there were her two children, which was the only way she could think of them now. And, thinking of them, she watched her tears splashing noisily on the kitchen table as if they were the heavy raindrops which one always longed for as the heavenly relief to a hellish drought. It helped her, because she was normally too quiet to weep.

The children she was suffering for were themselves trying to find some method of constructing a small plank boat that would stay upright in the fast currents of the river. There had been heavy rains at the source of the big river, and the Water Board had opened up the weir on the little river to relieve the flow. It was now fast and full, so that Spit's little boats could not survive in it. But Sadie said she had seen in one of her father's magazines a picture of a south sea island catamaran which would survive anything, 'Even huge waves.'

'You build two arms on the boat, like that,' she said, spreading her arms and dropping her hands.

'What's the point?' Spit said.

'It stops the canoe tipping over one way or the other. Can't you do that, instead of trying to put a keel on the bottom? It just turns over anyway if it bumps something.'

Spit spread his own arms. 'It'll be too big,' he said. 'Too wide.'

'It doesn't matter if it's too wide,' Sadie insisted.

They were in the boiler where Spit's limited restorations had given him a place to work. 'All right,' he said. 'I'll give it a go.'

She watched him cutting, sawing, shaping, nailing, binding, and hammering, and she gave him advice until he had made a trimaran two feet long and, with outriggers, two feet wide. As he put the mast in the centre-piece he said, 'Where's the message?'

'I haven't written one,' Sadie said.

'I'll bet you forgot the pencil.'

'No I didn't. I've got an old red crayon.' Sadie had the crayon and a sheet of paper ready and she asked Spit what to write.

'Write …' Spit thought for a moment, 'Write … "*this boat belongs to Spit MacPhee and Sadie Tree. If found, please return to owners.*"'

'Return to owners where? You have to put an address.'

'Your place,' Spit said.

'All right. But you have to give a reason, otherwise people won't care. They'll just throw it away.'

'Say we are trying to find out how far it goes.'

'Do you think that'll work?'

'I don't know,' Spit said. 'But what else can you say?'

Sadie didn't know. The old days of piratical

messages were over, they had grown out of their possibilities. So she wrote the message in red pencil and handed it to Spit.

'Wrap it around tight,' she said, 'and tie it on with string.'

Spit did as he was told, and as they walked up river to put the boat into the stream Spit asked Sadie, 'What did that old judge ask you?'

'All sorts of questions,' Sadie said.

'What about?'

'About you and your grandfather and what you did and things like that. What my father and mother did and what you and I did all the time. All sorts of questions like that.'

'What did he ask Ben?'

'Same thing,' Sadie said. 'Where are you going to put the boat in?' she asked him.

'Just above the bend,' he said.

'My mother said not to go near the edge there, Spit, because it crumbles.'

'She was telling that to you, so you'd better keep right back,' Spit said. 'She knows I won't fall in.'

But as Spit lay on the bank, pushing out the trimaran with a long piece of bamboo so that it could flow out into the fast current, the bank gave way and Spit went into the water with it. When Sadie saw his head emerge he was already being carried out to the middle of the river and downstream.

'Spit,' she screamed.

Spit was already in action, arms and feet working, but he lifted his head and spat out some water and shouted, 'I'm all right. I'll come in around the bend.' But then he disappeared again.

Sadie ran downstream to the bank around the bend, watching for Spit as he struggled to get free of the currents that swept him along in midstream. She knew that he wasn't going to make it, but then he put his head under, lashed out with his feet and arms in an Australian crawl and, as he was swept around the bend and reached a patch of dead water, he was momentarily free of the current. After another forceful plunge of arms and legs he reached the bank.

'Look at you,' Sadie said as he pulled himself up on the dry bank. 'You're sopping wet.' Sadie was not sure whether she was near to tears because of fright, or because she was angry with him for his mistake.

'What do you expect me to be?' Spit said as if he too had to make up his mind about momentary fright or his silly mistake.

'You shouldn't have done it,' she said to him.

'The whole bank must have been rotten,' Spit said

indignantly, squelching in his sandals, shaking his legs to let the water run free from his trousers.

'Come on,' Sadie said. 'You'll have to get out of your clothes. And wait until my mother sees you.'

Spit, rarely shamefaced, had to keep his direct gaze averted when he presented himself at the kitchen door for Grace to see.

'He fell in,' Sadie said as she held open the door.

'You fell in!' Grace said. 'My God, look at your clothes.'

'They're wet,' Spit said firmly.

'How on earth did it happen?'

'I was pushing something in the water and I just fell in.'

'Where?'

'Above the bend,' Spit said loudly.

'I told you not to go near the edge up there,' Grace said angrily, already pulling off his jumper and shirt as he stood outside the door.

'I thought you meant Sadie,' Spit said.

'I meant you too,' she said. 'How on earth am I going to dry your clothes in this weather, and you haven't got another pair of shoes.'

'I don't need shoes,' Spit said.

'Yes you do,' she said, still furious with him. 'I don't know what to do with you, Spit. You should not have gone near the edge up there. Take your shoes and socks off and then go inside the bathroom and take your pants off and dry yourself, and I'll bring you what's left of your old clothes. I don't know how I am going to dry your jumper and trousers. And look at your sandals.'

'You can put them in the oven,' Spit said.

'And ruin them?' Grace said. 'You get yourself dry, and when you're dressed you can stoke up the fire. And Sadie, you should have known better.'

'She told me not to do it,' Spit said.

'Then thank heavens one of you listens to me,' Grace said.

She told Sadie to go and get the clothes horse to put before the fire, and as Spit walked barefoot into the bathroom Grace stood for a moment clutching the wet shirt and jumper and socks.

In the grip of what seemed to her to be the worst day in her life, she knew that in losing her temper with Spit she had broken the curious barrier that had always been there between them. After all, he was no more than a boy and she was an adult, and whatever had been equal in their companionship had suddenly been replaced by the response of a mother reprimanding a son. She felt it so deeply that once again, in her failure to keep him, she knew that she would have to go somewhere and have a quiet weep. But that, she decided, would not rinse and dry his clothes. It would not help Sadie, who was looking at her with a curious, worried expression, as if she too was upset, not by Spit's behaviour but by what was happening to her mother.

'I'm all right,' she said to Sadie. 'Go and get the clothes horse.'

'I'm going,' Sadie said, and Grace wondered how she was going to survive until ten o'clock next morning.

25

As they sat waiting for Judge Laker to appear like a materialising ghost through the door at the back of the chamber, Grace whispered to Tom, 'Do you know how much I'll owe you, Tom? I have the money.'

'You don't have to pay now, Mrs Tree,' Tom said. 'My father will send you a bill.'

'But I have the money.'

'He won't take it here,' Tom said. 'And anyway I don't think he's worked it out yet. It won't be much.'

'All right, but I wanted him to know that no matter what happens, I think he did his best. It won't be his fault if I don't get Spit.'

'I'll tell him,' Tom said, and as Judge Laker

appeared so did Edward Quayle – head a little in the air as if he had everything else on his mind except the problem in hand.

'Good morning Mr and Mrs Tree,' he said in his English voice, and Grace was always a little frightened by that slight reserve. He sat down near her and thereafter ignored her and Jack too.

Like actors now, waiting for curtains to rise, the performers themselves were ready. Judge Laker cleared his throat and looked at each one of them as if they all needed to be closely inspected before being judged. A few appellate words from Laker, S.J., and the comedy would soon be over.

But Judge Laker took out his little notebook and looked at it carefully. Then he made another note before beginning. 'I have been looking at the 1928 Adoption of Children Act very carefully,' he said thoughtfully, 'and within the Act there are two quite different directions that, in judgement, I can take. There are very specific limitations about parental fitness that simply must be accepted. But on the other hand the Act gives me fairly wide discretionary powers. The applicants might not understand all this, but I have to put it on record, in view of my decision.

'Now then,' he went on, and Grace had the feeling that he was trying to be as gentle as he could, although he was not himself a gentle man. But he was trying. 'I have tried,' he said, 'to interpret the Act as a protective cover, both legal and humane, for an eleven-year-old boy in need of proper care and attention, as well as using the law to decide whether an applicant is a fit and proper person. In this case, I must decide which of two families can be judged as the better adoptive parents for a boy whom they both want. At the same time I have to think of the boy, not only as he is now, left quite alone, but his life in the future as he grows into manhood. So my decision here is based on both the immediate as well as the long-term needs of the boy. And, thinking about both applications, I find myself worrying more about the long term than the short term in this.'

Judge Laker bent forward a little as if he had suddenly noticed that both Sadie and Ben were sitting in their places on the bench.

'What are they doing here?' he asked. 'There is no need for them to be here this morning.'

'I thought you might need to question them further, your honour,' Mr Strapp said. 'That is, for our part.'

'I simply forgot to tell them they weren't needed, your honour,' Edward Quayle said. 'I apologise, although I suppose you might have needed them.'

'No. No. I have finished with them. They can go. They're better at school than they are sitting here.'

Spit, who felt that he had swallowed his silence long enough, suddenly stood up. 'I don't want to go to school, your honour. I'm not leaving here now.'

Judge Laker looked a little startled, and then he made a fragmented gesture with his pencil as if to recognise Spit as a factor in the case rather than an object of it. 'What do you want to stay here for, young man?' he said. 'You're not needed, you know. You don't have to stay.'

'What if I don't like what you're going to do to me?' Spit said in his loudest voice.

'Mr Quayle,' the judge said, amused enough to allow himself a slight smile. 'Don't you want to say something?'

'No, your honour. If you'll permit it, the boy is doing rather well for himself.'

'Well, then,' Judge Laker said, leaning forward to look a little closer at Spit. 'What if you don't like what we decide? What will you do about it?'

Spit closed his mouth in a tight, stubborn grip, and it was Sadie who leapt up and said, 'He'll run away again, your honour. He won't do what you can't make him do …'

For a moment there was an almost passionate silence in the room. Everybody in the court looked at the two children; at Sadie who was blushing but who nonetheless had her head well up; and at Spit who was staring into the space he seemed to be aiming at.

'Is that true?' the judge asked Spit.

Spit still kept his mouth grimly shut, but he nodded as if words now meant nothing.

'Don't you trust us, Spit?' the judge said.

It looked as if Spit would persist with his threatening silence but then he burst out, 'Next time, your honour, they'll never catch me. I'll go so far ...'

Edward Quayle raised a hand then and said, 'That's enough, Spit,' and he said to the judge, 'As you can see, your honour, the boy has spirit, and he already has a real if naive sense that his destiny is being decided here. So I suggest that you allow him to stay so that he can understand what we are trying to do for him, whatever the outcome. But I must point out too that he is warning us, sir, and I think the court must take him seriously. We don't want a tragedy ...'

'Oh really, Mr Quayle,' Strapp interrupted. 'That is ridiculous.'

'Now really, Mr Strapp,' the judge said. 'Has this become a private argument between you and Mr Quayle?'

'Well, sir, let us not exaggerate,' Strapp said, his hands in the air.

'Speak for yourself, Mr Strapp,' the judge said.

'Personally I am in no fear of my own exaggerations. And I'm sure Mr Quayle isn't either, since he is a past master at it sometimes.'

Edward Quayle ignored the judge's easy jibe at him and said, 'Can I also suggest that Sadie Tree be allowed to stay if her parents don't object. The boy deserves the moral support he needs from this young lady, who is virtually his surrogate sister.'

'Mr Quayle,' the judge said sharply. 'Don't take advantage of everything that comes your way. Don't press your case all the time.' He turned to Spit and Sadie then, and he said, 'All right. You can both stay. But no more declarations of intent, please, from either of you.'

It was Ben then who stood up and said, 'Can I stay too, your honour?'

The judge looked down at Ben and sighed in despair. 'Oh dear. It's becoming a children's matinée. All right, Ben. If your parents don't object you might as well hear it out too. But sit down and don't wriggle.'

As Ben and Sadie and Spit sat down the judge swallowed in his dry throat as if he longed now for a short brandy to get him through the rest of this.

'Now for heaven's sake let us get on with it,' he said and looked carefully at his little notebook. 'First of all,' he went on, 'I must make an important comment about the boy himself, because it may help both applicants to understand my decision. Spit MacPhee is obviously a very self-sufficient Australian boy, intelligent and, if a little turbulent, at least able to be guided by a firm hand if the firm hand is the right one. At the same time he seems to be very stubborn, and in his determination not to be restrained he could become a potential danger to himself and others, particularly if he is confused by conflicting interests, or resentful of restraint and discipline.'

He turned then to Betty and Frank Arbuckle. 'So let me take your application first, Mr and Mrs Arbuckle. You are obviously fine and respectable people, and I liked your son Ben and the way he spoke up for his friend Spit. He is the best advertisement you could have given me for your claim. I was always impressed too, with Mrs Arbuckle's deep convictions, and her belief in a faith that, in her severe devotion to it, could move mountains. But is Spit MacPhee a mountain? That was the question I had to ask myself, and I decided that he wasn't a mountain. Spit MacPhee is a small, rough, ready-made little boy who would certainly be unable to accept Mrs Arbuckle's faith as a guiding light, or even as a discipline. Not the way he is now. The boy himself is obviously determined not to be guided or disciplined by Mrs Arbuckle's evangelical methods.

And I have to take very seriously his childish threats to abscond if he is forced upon them. I don't really believe he would do anything violent to them, but what his threats really mean is that a powerful resistance is at work which, if he is forced upon the Arbuckles, would almost certainly make a bitter rebel of him. As an adult he would probably become a man who would retain a deep and violent resentment as well as a bad memory of what had been done to him by this court. Inevitably that would lead him into serious trouble.'

Judge Laker took a glass of water and sipped it this time as if it was brandy or whisky – anything but Murray river water.

They waited on his lips, his wiped mouth, his slight sniff.

'So,' he went on, 'with this background to a difficult choice I must unfortunately reject the application of Mr and Mrs Arbuckle, much as I am sorry to do so ...'

'But he would learn our ways, your honour,' Betty Arbuckle cried out. She was standing up, her hands over her breasts and her face on fire. 'And we would love him like a son.'

'I'm sure you would, Mrs Arbuckle,' Judge Laker said, 'but love is not enough. And in your case I don't think the justification of your Protestantism is enough.

In your case it would, I'm afraid, become an impediment to this boy.'

'But please ...' Betty Arbuckle cried out again.

'Sit down, Mrs Arbuckle,' the judge said sternly. 'It's done and you cannot change my decision. Your application is refused so please be quiet. Now ... before giving my decision about Mr and Mrs Tree, I would like to tell both sides that, in order to be fair to both applicants, in order that I am not seen to be favouring one family or the other, or that I am making a simple choice of one against the other, I made it my business to look into the question of my discretionary powers on alternatives, such as adoption agencies and existing homes for boys like Spit MacPhee.'

'But your honour ...' Betty Arbuckle tried again.

'Be quiet, Mrs Arbuckle. Otherwise I shall have to ask you to leave the court. I am already familiar with the two Boys Homes in Bendigo. I have had dealings with them for reasons of probation. So they don't frighten me as they might some people. Nor does the prospect of a boy like Spit MacPhee ending up there seem to me to be necessarily a bad thing, if it becomes necessary. Particularly for a boy like this one whose self-sufficiency would survive very well among a lot of other boys equally endowed. He would easily fit in and make his own way quite well. So I thought I must

301

take that into consideration in all fairness, although I felt from the outset that a family home would be far more desirable than an institution. So I come now to Mr and Mrs Tree.'

Judge Laker pulled in his lips and looked down at Spit MacPhee with an almost puzzled air, as if judgement here was so difficult that he might still change his mind. Spit was wriggling, and as if a small postponement might help his decision, the judge asked Spit what he was wriggling for. 'You usually sit there as still as a statue,' he said.

'I think I'm still wet,' Spit said.

'What does that mean?'

'He fell in the river yesterday and got wet,' Grace said hurriedly. 'But it's his imagination. I dried and ironed his trousers thoroughly, your honour.'

'Then sit still, Spit,' Judge Laker said to him, 'otherwise you're a disturbance.' He then made a curious, resigned sort of gesture towards Edward Quayle, as if he wanted to attract his attention. But Edward Quayle looked so impassive and so still that he was obviously not going to be tempted to be anything else. 'So I come now to your clients, Mr Quayle,' the judge said.

'We are waiting, your honour.'

'You have made a very persuasive and sympathetic case for Mr and Mrs Tree, Mr Quayle. If the Arbuckles had been as flexible as your clients they would have had the boy without question. But Spit obviously prefers Mrs Tree, and I know from their daughter Sadie how well he has fitted in there, even if he has kept his own particular rules for his own particular behaviour. I note, too, that Sadie looks on him already as a brother. Is that right, Sadie?'

'Yessir,' Sadie said.

'So in all fairness,' Judge Laker went on, 'It has to be said that with Mr and Mrs Tree Spit MacPhee seems to have found something near his own environment. Everything sensible and possible, everything desirable, everything I could ask of adoptive parents is there. And yet ... And yet ...'

Judge Laker was so reluctant that Grace felt sick to hear those words.

'... And yet I have had to consider the problem of religion. I am not afraid of making an unusual decision in this. I am not afraid of setting a precedent. But I have to consider this question of legality in parentage; the legal rights of the adoptive parents, automatically, to have the right to do what they wish with a child within the limits of civil law. It is a very difficult obstacle to overcome.

'The 1928 Act makes it clear that in the long run the primary need is to match the faith of the child to the parents. I cannot ignore this. If I did, it would be a limitation on the boy's inalienable right to be what he was born to be. It would become a serious denial of this right if I hand him over to adoptive parents who would have a legal right then to do what they like with him. The right to a faith in our law is not simply a civil right. It is a constitutional and historical one, bound into our lives by hundreds of years of opposing concepts, bitterly fought over, and yet defined constitutionally into a human right. In the case of a child it is a right that has to be protected by the courts if his own protections are lost.

'So I am dealing here with something far more important than the faith of one small boy who could easily be thrown to the winds of fate. I am dealing with a vital heritage that in law I cannot and dare not alienate. It is not my choice. It is the law itself which, quite rightly, insists on safeguarding and protecting a child's right to the faith of his forefathers. So, with real regret ...'

'Just a moment, your honour,' Edward Quayle said brusquely, standing up. It was surprising enough to be startling. 'Your honour ...' he said again as the judge began to protest. 'If you please ...'

'What on earth is it, Mr Quayle?' Judge Laker said. 'What are you interrupting me for?'

'Before you go any further, your honour,' Edward Quayle said in a calm voice, sitting down again, 'I wish to withdraw Mr and Mrs Tree's application for adoption before you pass any judgement on it.'

'You what?' Judge Laker said, astonished.

'I withdraw our application for adoption, your honour.'

'Now? At a minute before midnight? What is this, Mr Quayle? One of your tricks?'

'Certainly not,' Edward Quayle said, still calm. 'I am withdrawing the application for a very good reason.'

'It had better be good, Mr Quayle, and you had better explain yourself.'

Grace, staring at Edward Quayle in amazement, was trying to find in his English face an explanation of what he was doing. She could see nothing but the unshakable man she was used to and did not always understand. 'What on earth does he mean?' she whispered to Jack. 'What's he doing?'

'I don't know,' Jack said. 'I just don't know.'

'He's going to send me away to Bendigo,' Spit whispered to Sadie.

'No, he isn't.' Sadie whispered back. 'It must be something else.'

'Well, Mr Quayle?' the judge was saying. 'I'm waiting.'

305

'As I understand it, your honour, you did find Mr and Mrs Tree desirable applicants on the face of it.'

'Yes, I have said that.'

'And that if it were not for a legal impediment, concerning religion, they would get the boy.'

'Yes. Does it need explanation?'

'Not at all, your honour. I just want to establish that you are concerned here with the civil right as well as what you have called the birthright of Spit MacPhee to remain a Protestant; and that there must be some sort of guarantee to protect his rights.'

'That is correct.'

'You feel that in handing over to adoptive parents a right which they would have in law, to determine his religious faith, you would be handing over a right that you feel is beyond your legal powers to do so.'

'I wouldn't put it that way, Mr Quayle, but if you wish I shall simplify it again for you. A man and his faith is such a serious right that a court cannot hand over the choice of it, in circumstances like this, to another person or persons. It is not correct in law, particularly when there is a defenceless child involved. I cannot do it in law, and that is the truth of it. I cannot give away a constitutional or a statutory right, even though it may never be used. Mrs Tree may never exercise her right to make a Catholic of Spit, but I cannot give her that right. I repeat – it is wrong in law, Mr Quayle, as you well know.'

'Exactly, your honour,' Edward Quayle said. 'And that is why I have another suggestion to make. You were thinking, were you not, of your option to send the boy to a Home in Bendigo?'

'Yes, I was coming to that.'

'But there is another discretion open to you, sir, and I am applying to you now for an order in court, under the Neglected and Criminal Children's Acts of 1871, 1872 and 1884, and under the 1928 Adoption of Children's Act to appoint Mr and Mrs Tree the foster parents of Spit MacPhee ...'

'Foster parents?'

'Yes, foster parents, not adoptive parents.'

'And how in God's name do you think that is going to help, Mr Quayle?'

'As foster parents, your honour, they will have no legal rights over the boy except to his care and attention. They will have no legal rights whatsoever outside the rights defined and even limited by this court. If you, sir, want to make a ruling that they can be judged as fit and proper foster parents only on condition that there will be no attempt to change his religion or to influence him in any way to change his religion, then you may do so. You can put any restraint on them that you like, in law, because in effect though they will be the foster parents in law, Spit MacPhee would remain a ward of the State of Victoria, and the court will be able to withdraw him at any time should it think fit. In every aspect of his upbringing, including the protection of his faith, Mr and Mrs Tree would have to answer to the Attorney General by regular assessments of the boy's condition, attested to by two assessors appointed by yourself ...'

'I can't have this.' Strapp was on his feet. 'I really can't have it, your honour. I have to object in the strongest possible terms.'

'Just a moment, Mr Strapp.'

'But this is nonsense, your honour. Mr Quayle springs something like this on us without warning, without considering ...'

'I said just a moment, Mr Strapp, and I mean it. You can have your say later. In any case this is not a litigation or a prosecution that needs one side or the other to be informed.'

'Even so, your honour. Even so ... It is surely unprincipled.'

'Let us hear Mr Quayle out, Mr Strapp, and I will judge whether it is unprincipled or not.'

Incredulous, and watching these three men at their work, Grace knew that at this moment they each had an almost life-and-death grip on each other. She wasn't sure whether Judge Laker and Mr Quayle were now in mortal combat, or whether they were in some strange accord against Mr Strapp. But none of them seemed concerned now with Spit MacPhee. They had found something in law that was far more important and absorbing to them than the will-o'-the-wisp it was all about.

'What I would like to know, Mr Quayle,' Judge Laker was saying irritably, 'is why you did not make this your original application? Why on earth did you go through all this adoption charade if you were willing to ask for foster parentage in the first place?'

'But I was not willing to ask for foster parentage in the first place,' Edward Quayle said. 'I always preferred adoption. But what I wanted above all else was a fair hearing on the rival qualifications of the two parties, so that if it came to a different kind of choice, your own judgement could be clear. I wanted what you have so generously given to us, your honour – a chance to dispose of all other alternatives.'

'Then you shouldn't have caught me unawares, Mr Quayle.'

'I am sorry, your honour, but there was no other way.'

'So what do you want, Mr Quayle? Are you actually

asking me to make a court order, here and now, on an application for Mr and Mrs Tree to foster the boy?'

'It's perfectly straightforward in law, your honour. The requirements are more or less the same as for adoption, and we could easily complete the technicalities later on. There is a question of a small government grant which Mr and Mrs Tree will probably waive. And the court will have to decide later on what happens to certain monies that Fyfe MacPhee kept on deposit in two banks. But these are not problems we need settle here and now. The point is that, under the various acts, you are empowered if you so wish to make the order, simply on the evidence of fitness you have heard.'

'And what about the assessors to protect the boy, Mr Quayle? Do you have them up your sleeve too?'

'I have them ready and willing, your honour, which is a much better place to have them. I have spoken to Father O'Connel, our local Catholic priest, and the Reverend Duncan Mackenzie of the Presbyterian Church. They have both agreed to act as regular assessors if the court agrees. Together they will cover the two aspects required – the continuing fitness of the foster parents to keep the boy, and the protection of his birthright as a Protestant.'

'You mean they have actually agreed? You have persuaded them?'

'Yes, sir.' Edward Quayle allowed himself a thin, dry smile. 'In law it could be the ideal combination, your honour, and I thought it would appeal to you. On the one hand a protection for the boy's religion from the Reverend Mackenzie. And on the other hand some protection for the foster parents against false accusations from any outside source which I am sure Father O'Connel would see to. For the rest, your honour, I think we can leave it to the two prelates themselves to continue their historical debate, their old and bitter contention, as they walk up the slope from the Trees' household on their way back to their armigerous congregations. In any case they can settle or compact their differences in divine argument, but not with the body and soul of an eleven-year-old boy.'

'It is beyond belief; it is a travesty, your honour,' Mr Strapp shouted. 'If Mr Quayle can make an application on these ... on these flimsy grounds, so can Mr and Mrs Arbuckle. They are equally qualified and I hereby do so ...'

'Your honour,' Edward Quayle interrupted. 'I waited until the very last moment of your summing up to make my application because I wanted to be sure that, given your own preference in judgement, apart from the impediment of religion, your choice would have gone naturally to my clients. Do I understand that to be the case?'

'Mr Quayle is right, Mr Strapp,' the judge said. 'The only impediment to choosing Mr and Mrs Tree was the religious one. Now Mr Quayle seems to have removed that.'

'It's not fair,' Betty Arbuckle cried. 'It's wicked.'

'Oh dear ... Oh dear ...' Judge Laker said wearily. 'Now it is wicked. But what is wicked? What is right? What is wrong? What is humane? Now, for heaven's sake, if I am to be a Solomon in this, then I must be allowed some qualification of my own. Do Mr and Mrs Tree agree to your proposition, Mr Quayle?' he asked.

'Yes, I can speak with certainty of that. Although they may want to say so themselves.'

'Mr and Mrs Tree?'

'Oh yes, your honour. We agree,' Grace said. 'We agree to everything Mr Quayle has said.'

'Then you have my good wishes,' Judge Laker said quickly. 'I can make the order now, appointing you foster parents to Master Spit MacPhee, but with all the various provisos that will be defined later, including the assessors and the method of reporting to the court, as well as the need for regular visits by the assessors as well as the financial arrangements of the grants, if any ...'

'We don't want any money for it,' Grace Tree said.

'According to Mr Quayle there is some money available from funds left by Fyfe MacPhee, but use of that will have to be decided later by a court order. As far as this hearing is concerned, the matter is closed and you may all go home.'

Judge Laker let out his breath, stood up, shook his head a little, raised his eyes in wonder at the ceiling – at God above – and, followed by Miss Price the stenographer and Henry Fennel, he left the victims and the victors and the children to organise themselves into what was now the new shape of their things to come.

Betty Arbuckle was in such large tears that they were pouring down her lovely cheeks. In a moment's passion she rushed at Spit, who was standing up, and embraced him. 'You must be good,' she said. 'You must never give in.'

Spit, astonished, didn't pull away but waited for her breathless grip on him to exhaust itself. Betty squeezed him hard again and then reluctantly let him go. She took Ben by the hand and, with her husband walking invisibly behind her and Strapp in front, she left the chamber almost overcome by her distress.

'Somehow …' Grace said, unable to move but trying to get a grip on herself. 'Somehow I will have to find a way to thank you,' she said to Edward Quayle who had gathered up his papers which he had never bothered to look at. 'But I don't know how I can do it, Mr Quayle. I don't know how I can thank you.'

'Are you satisfied, Mrs Tree?' Edward Quayle said.

'Oh yes,' Grace said. 'Of course I am. I thought that ...'

'And you, Mr Tree?' Edward Quayle interrupted, turning to Jack. 'Will you object to your house and home being inspected from time to time by Father O'Connel and the Reverend MacKenzie? Well, Mr Tree? Is that going to please you?'

'You might have asked us first,' Jack Tree said. 'But as far as I am concerned they can come any time they like.'

'And the boy? How will you treat him?'

'Don't worry. I'll look after him,' Jack said. 'You don't have to worry.'

'But I do have to worry because I am turning the responsibility for him over to you, and I have to be sure that I have done the right thing, because I can still ask the court to recall its decision.'

'I told you,' Jack said. 'I'll do my best with him. He'll be all right.'

'In that case,' Edward said, 'I shall bid you both good-day. You will have further details to settle later on, but you can do that with Tom.'

Edward Quayle left them without a glance or a gesture in Spit's direction. But Tom waited a moment, laughter in his blond, blue eyes. 'But are you really satisfied, Mrs Tree?' he said almost teasingly.

'Of course I am Tom. I can't tell you ... And you have to thank your father again for me. I don't know what we'd have done without him. And never mind what Jack says about telling us. Just thank your father.'

'No good thanking my father,' Tom said. 'He'll say, "It's the law, Mrs Tree, the law." That's the way he sees it. If the law is there he will use it. Anyway, I'm glad for old Spit's sake,' he said, and he laughed again as he followed his father.

Grace and Jack were left with Spit and Sadie, bunched together like flowers in the field. When Grace, still a little bewildered, asked, 'What do we do now, Jack?' Spit said, 'Well, we don't have to go back to school anyway.'

'Oh, yes you do,' Jack said. 'Both of you.'

'But it's almost lunch time,' Sadie pointed out.

'I don't care what time it is. I'll take you up to school in the car,' Jack said. 'The holiday is over, so come on. The both of you.'

When the Dodge stopped outside the school gate – the silent school gate with a silent playground behind it and a low enclosure beyond it with children there,

315

in learning, Grace said to Spit as he waited for Sadie to get out of the car from the other side, 'Do you want to say anything to me, Spit?' She too waited as Jack and Sadie joined them.

'I don't know,' Spit said, embarrassed now. 'Are you and Sadie's father supposed to be my father and mother now? Is that what the judge said?'

Grace hesitated, knowing that she must think carefully before she replied; realising too that she would have to think carefully before she answered many more questions that Spit would have to ask her in order to clarify himself – to find out who he was now and who he would become.

'No, Spit,' she said. 'You can only have one mother and father. We'll be what the judge said – foster parents, which is simply another way of saying that we will be responsible for you.'

Spit had to think about that word 'responsible'. He knew what it meant and what it could mean. 'You won't change anything, will you?' he asked her reluctantly.

Grace simply shook her head.

Jack Tree took a deep breath but said nothing, and Sadie stood carefully aside as if she knew that Spit and her mother had to settle something between them. She knew too how hard both of them were trying.

'What'll you do if I run away again?' Spit asked.

'I don't know, Spit,' Grace said. 'It'll depend on why you do it. If I think you're wrong I'll be very angry. If I think you're right I'll tell you so. But are you going to threaten me like that? Is that fair?'

Spit shook his head. 'But I'm not going to forget my grandfather,' he said aggressively. 'And if anyone laughs at him I'll only get into another fight.'

'I'm not going to stop you,' Grace said. 'Nor will Jack.'

'I'm not going to go to church either,' Spit said.

Grace restrained Jack who was about to say something, and she said, 'I don't know how we'll solve that one, Spit. I simply don't know.'

Grace also knew that Spit was trying to come to terms with her, lasting terms, not with promises but on some agreed possibility of mutual respect. And though she knew that Spit didn't exactly know what he was doing, it was obvious enough to her. It was obvious in the grip he had on the school gate, in his bold eyes which went down and then up again to meet hers – watching, waiting, testing.

'Come on, Spit,' Sadie said then. 'We'd better go.'

But Spit didn't move, as if for a moment he couldn't move; as if he knew that one life was about to come to an end here and another entirely different one was

317

about to begin. In that grip he had on the school gate he was holding on to something for a lost moment, to everything that was about to disappear. The gate was the only thing at hand that he could hold on to, and it was Grace who gently undid his fingers from the gate and said to him with one of her gentle smiles, 'Yes. Go on, Spit. We can't stand here all day.'

'I know,' Spit said. 'I'm still wet though. I can feel it.'

'Nonsense,' Grace said, and she watched the two of them go reluctantly into the quiet school. Then, as Jack got into the car she said, 'I'll walk home, Jack.'

'Why? What for?'

'I don't know. I just want to walk a bit, that's all.'

'You're not going to let this business get the better of you, are you?' Jack said seriously, almost sternly.

'No. I have to think a bit, that's all.'

She left him, and as she heard the Dodge turn around and head into the hinterlands, where Jack did most of his work, she walked through the town wondering what it was that had made her take on this boy; where it was going to take her and what problems she would have to face. Because she knew, as all parents knew, that the topsy-turvy problems of children would always multiply and re-multiply as they grew older. And, with Spit, there was going to be a big multiplication in her life which would need all her patience and care, and she wondered how on earth she was ever going to do it. But the first thing she would have to do would be to cure Spit of those two bad habits – shouting and spitting – which would be a terrible burden on him in later life if she didn't make a point of putting a stop to them right away.

Text Classics

textclassics.com.au